"YOU ARE GOING TO KISS ME," SHE MUR-mured as his mouth came near hers.

"Yes," he said, brushing his thumb back and forth along her bottom lip. It did strange things to her equilibrium. "I need to know the feel of you. The taste of you. I need to know if there is passion buried beneath that ladylike exterior you present to the world." His arms were around her. She was pressed firmly against his body—tall, muscular, unyielding. She had never been this close to a man before. Lawrence raised the silk fan between them and brushed his lips along her bare throat, leaving a trail of scorching kisses behind that did strange and wonderful things to her insides.

"Lawrence, that is my throat!"

"I know that. I am well acquainted with human anatomy. You agreed that I could kiss you. You did not specify *where* I had to kiss you."

Her voice was a rasp. "I thought you meant my mouth."

"You were mistaken." There was something in his voice that caught her attention. "I intend to kiss you, my dear Juliet, in each and every place you would be wearing the Deakin Diamonds if they adorned your body tonight."

Suddenly she forgot to analyze. She forgot to think. She forgot to breathe. She never foresaw what would happen next. Nor did she try to stop it. . . .

DIAMOND IN THE ROUGH

"Polished, naturally. Witty, naturally. Sexy . . . wow! Suzanne Simmon's *Diamond in the Rough* is a gem beyond compare."
—Stella Cameron

"Suzanne Simmons is witty and wonderful—destined for the top in the world of romance. *Diamond in the Rough* positively sparkles. A delicious, fast-paced blend of sensuality, romantic warmth and laughter. I loved it! This is the kind of book the romance audience devours in a single-sitting."
—Amanda Quick

DIAMOND
IN THE
ROUGH

by

Suzanne Simmons

A TOPAZ BOOK

TOPAZ
Published by the Penguin Group
Penguin Books USA Inc., 375 Hudson Street,
New York, New York 10014, U.S.A.
Penguin Books Ltd, 27 Wrights Lane,
London W8 5TZ, England
Penguin Books Australia Ltd, Ringwood,
Victoria, Australia
Penguin Books Canada Ltd, 10 Alcorn Avenue,
Toronto, Ontario, Canada M4V 3B2
Penguin Books (N.Z.) Ltd, 182-190 Wairau Road,
Auckland 10, New Zealand

Penguin Books Ltd, Registered Offices:
Harmondsworth, Middlesex, England

First published by Topaz,
an imprint of New American Library,
a division of Penguin Books USA Inc.

First Printing, January, 1994
10 9 8 7 6 5 4 3 2 1

This one is for my mother,
Mary Noeding Simmons,
with love and gratitude.

1

"EGODS, Lawrence, she's a beauty!"

"The lady or the horse?" he inquired, flashing his straight, white teeth in a sardonic smile.

The handsome man beside him laughed and confessed, "Both. The horse is magnificent, and the lady carries herself like a queen . . . or a duchess."

Lawrence Grenfell Wicke, the eighth Duke of Deakin, brought the big black stallion to a halt at the edge of the Ramble. He leaned forward, patted the great beast's neck, and gazed across the Sheep Meadow. "So, that is why you have dragged me out at this ungodly hour of the morning," he concluded with a meaningful glance toward the young woman and her escort. "We are here to investigate yet another Great American Heiress."

"I was set the task of finding you a rich wife, and by God, I intend to do just that," declared his companion. " *'Mater artium necessitas.'* "

"Necessity may well be the mother of invention," he allowed, "but I still have doubts about this ill-conceived scheme of yours and Bertie's."

"Can't understand why," said his fellow horseman as they urged their mounts into a walk.

Lawrence impatiently tapped his riding crop against the side of his fine leather boot. "Hell and damnation, Miles, it was common knowledge you were both in your cups the entire sailing season at Cowes."

Miles St. Aldford, the fourth Marquess of Cork, lifted his redoubtable chin a notch higher in the cool morning air of Central Park and sniffed indignantly. "It was not an ill-conceived scheme, for all that. H.R.H. and I agreed on its basic wisdom and sheer brilliancy *before* we uncorked the first bottle of champagne aboard the royal yacht."

"Sheer brilliancy?" repeated Lawrence, gripping the reins tightly in his gloved hands. The stallion responded by prancing nervously in a circle and snorting once or twice, its steaming breath hanging on the December air like ominous storm clouds. "Sheer lunacy is more like it. To come to this godforsaken country with the intent of selling myself and my title to some empty-headed, social-climbing piece of feminine frippery. It's sheer lunacy!"

"If you have come up with a better idea that will salvage your bankrupt accounts and run-down family estates, then do let's hear it," challenged the marquess.

A scowl settled on Lawrence's features; his lips thinned. He opened his mouth and immediately shut it again without speaking. There was nothing to say. Miles was right, and they both knew it: he had to marry and *well*.

His lifelong friend was sympathetic. "Sorry old chap, but trust me, this is the only way."

"Are you quite sure?"

"Quite."

Lawrence gave a curt nod. "Then by all means, let us carry on with the business at hand."

Miles cleared his throat and made a discreet gesture toward the couple approaching on horseback. "The lady's name is Miss Juliet Jones."

"And what, pray tell, do we know of Miss Juliet Jones?" he asked with a certain grim amusement. "Besides the fact that she sits well on a horse?"

Miles St. Aldford withdrew a small, black book from the pocket of his riding coat, and murmured to himself as he leafed through its pages: "Barlow. Beckwith. Browning. Cameron. Castle. Chase. Harrisson. Lowell. Damn, I've gone too far now. Ah, here it is. Under 'J.' Jones, Juliet." He looked up with a degree of hopefulness on his face. "First, she is unmarried."

"That is the whole point, is it not?" snapped Lawrence. Then he concentrated on controlling his impatience. It was not an easy task since he was not, by nature, a patient man. Especially when it came to female matters. He had more important business to attend to.

"Lawrence—?"

He finally gave a noncommittal grunt and, with a notable lack of enthusiasm, inquired of his fellow conspirator, "How old is Miss Jones?"

Miles quickly scanned the facts and figures at his disposal. "Twenty-four."

"General appearance?"

"Tall, slender, graceful."

"Hair?"

"Blond."

"Eyes?"

"Blue."

"I've always had a preference for blue eyes," Lawrence remarked in passing.

His friend smiled knowingly. "Yes, I am well aware of that fact."

"Anything else?"

Miles studied his notes for a moment. "Full lips. Exquisite cheekbones. A chin not prone to weakness."

Lawrence snorted. " 'A chin not prone to weakness'? My dear Cork, I do believe you have sunk to editorializing."

"I confess I may have taken certain liberties," the other man said, sounding unconcerned. "Perhaps even employed a bit of poetic license—"

"Never mind," he said, waving aside the digression. "Miss Jones is said to be beautiful, then?"

"Miss Jones is said to be beautiful."

Lawrence studied the still-distant figure of the young woman to see if he could discern either her beauty or her chin. He could not. "My dear mother always said that physical beauty was fleeting, at best. She claimed that true beauty came from within."

"The late duchess was, as we all know, a saint," said Miles with sincerity.

"She was an extraordinary woman," said Lawrence quietly, "and a very beautiful one." He gave himself a shake. This was neither the time nor the place to become maudlin. "Please do go on about our Miss Jones."

"She was educated at home by a long line of excellent tutors, which . . ."

"Which what?"

Ignoring him, Miles St. Aldford murmured under his breath: "How dashedly interesting."

"What is?"

"She chose them herself."

"*She?*"

"*Miss Jones.*"

Lawrence fixed his companion with a reproachful glare. "*Exactly what* did Miss Jones choose herself?"

Miles looked up. "Her tutors."

"I fail to see what is so interesting about that," he said reprovingly.

"Beginning at the age of twelve."

"I say."

"The curriculum included such diverse topics as livestock breeding, farm management, bonds and investments, classical languages, and horticulture."

He narrowed his eyes. "An unusual course of study for a schoolgirl, wouldn't you say?"

"For a schoolgirl, yes. For a Great American Heiress"—the marquess paused—"perhaps not." After a moment, he said: "But to continue, the lady reads Greek and Latin. She has traveled extensively on the continent, and speaks fluent French, passable Italian, and a smattering of German."

"At least this one does not have a great empty space where her brain should be."

A rush of embarrassed color flooded Miles St. Aldford's aristocratic features. "I presume you are speaking now of Miss Beckwith."

"You presume correctly."

An explanation was quickly offered. "Miss Beckwith was very young."

Lawrence threw him a withering glance. "Indeed."

Miles's hands shifted on the reins of the roan thoroughbred; the horse lifted its sleek red head alertly. "I had no way of knowing that the lady in question was a half-wit."

"Quarter-wit was more like it," he shot back. "I must confess we have known young ladies with more intelligence than that possessed by Miss Beckwith."

Lawrence found himself laughing out loud. "We have known *horses* with more intelligence."

There was a devilish glint in the marquess's eyes when he added, "The lady did have very large—"

"Yes—?"

"Accoutrements," finished Miles.

He managed to keep a straight face. "Let us speak no more of the lamentable, brainless Miss Beckwith, or of her oversized . . . accoutrements. What is said of Miss Jones 'below stairs?' "

Miles was suddenly effusive. "According to Bunter's sources the servants adore her."

"What is the reason for this adoration?"

The marquess raised an elegant eyebrow. "Apparently Miss Jones is a kind and thoughtful mistress."

"And?"

"And she pays the best wages in New York."

Lawrence frowned. "She is extravagant."

This time it was Miles who appeared amused. "She can afford to be extravagant."

"What of her relations?"

"Her mother and father were killed in a tragic carriage accident when she was eleven. No brothers or sisters. Until recently her only relative was thought to be a great-aunt." Miles turned to the next page. "A dotty old woman named Euphemia Jones."

"Until recently?"

"Several months ago a heretofore unknown cousin presented himself to Miss Juliet Jones."

"What was her reaction to this long-lost cousin?" he inquired, looking straight before him.

"She welcomed him with open arms and joyously took him to her bosom."

The skin of Lawrence's face seemed to tighten. "Joyously took him to her bosom?"

"Metaphorically speaking, of course."

"Of course."

"Apparently family relationships are very important to Miss Jones." Miles furrowed his forehead in thought. "Perhaps because she has so little family herself."

"Editorializing again, my dear Cork?"

"Merely speculating, my dear Deakin."

"Who is the boy with her now?" Lawrence inquired, his voice wintry cool.

"The young man is the aforementioned cousin: Mister David Thoreau Jones of Concord, Massachusetts. He is two and twenty, and a recent graduate of Harvard University."

Lawrence watched as the handsome youth leaned toward his cousin and said something that was apparently amusing. He could hear the sound of their laughter. Then, muttering under his breath, more to himself than to his compatriot, he said, "I wonder what his game is."

"Whose game?"

"Never mind. What of Miss Jones's inheritance?"

The black book was flipped to another page. "There is a summer cottage at Newport."

"A cottage?"

"With thirty-two rooms."

"I see."

"There is also a mansion on Fifth Avenue, a horse farm in Kentucky, and an apartment in Paris. Miss Jones bought the latter herself only last year."

"How did the Joneses go about making their fortune?" It was a vulgar but necessary question in this part of the world, he reminded himself. Americans always *made* their fortune at something.

Miles read down the list. "Railroads. Steamships. Land speculation. Cattle. Horses. Gold and silver mines." He looked up. "Do you wish me to go on?"

"No."

"From all accounts the lady's father was a very clever man. He was known in financial circles as King Midas."

"King Midas?"

Miles nodded his head. "Anything the man touched turned to gold. He literally began with nothing thirty years ago and ended up with everything."

"*Nouveau riche,*" Lawrence said with a hint of distaste.

Miles sighed. "I'm afraid so."

"I suppose it can't be helped."

"I don't see how."

Lawrence brought his mount up short and regarded the lady in question. She appeared attractive enough, even from this distance. "Suitors?"

"Many."

"Why hasn't she married, then?"

Miles seemed reluctant to answer.

Lawrence insisted. "Do you know?"

He began carefully. "It seems that Miss Jones has certain . . . notions."

"Notions?"

"According to one of the footmen, whom Bunter obliging stood to several rounds at a local pub—" Lord Cork stopped himself and reconsidered. "They don't call them pubs in this country, do they?"

"No. I believe the Americans refer to their

public drinking establishments as barrooms,"
supplied Lawrence.

"Dreadful word, 'barroom,'" murmured
Miles. "Anyway, after a few draughts in one of
the public drinking houses the footman confided to Bunter that Miss Jones has got it into
her head that she will never marry."

Lawrence made a slight, inarticulate sound.
"How the devil did a footman come by such
knowledge?"

"The usual way."

"Household gossip." It was a statement of
fact, rather than a question.

The marquess nodded. "The upstairs maid
told him. They step out together on their afternoon off."

Lawrence gritted his teeth. "And *why* has
Miss Jones got it into her head that she will
never marry?"

The marquess shifted uncomfortably in the
saddle. "Apparently she is convinced that gentlemen take one look at her and see only her
fortune. The lady wants to be loved for herself."

"How quaint."

"Indeed."

Lawrence straightened his already perfectly
straight shoulders and commented in a lofty
tone as they urged their horses forward, "I am
afraid, Cork, that these Americans are a nation
of hopeless romantics."

"So it would seem."

"On the other hand," he observed as they rode
along the bridle path that skirted the lake, "we

English—at least those of us who live in the rugged North Country—are a practical people."

"I have always thought so."

"What has to be done, will be done." Lawrence paused for a moment, and his eyes took on a hard sheen. "That has always been the way of the Wickes."

There was admiration as well as genuine affection written on Miles St. Aldford's slightly dissipated face when he said: "I have always thought it was that attitude that made you so bloody damn effective as a cavalry officer. I was proud to serve under you, Deakin."

"Thank you, Cork."

By unspoken mutual consent, they rode for several minutes in silence.

Miles spoke first. "Does this mean you will woo Miss Jones, in spite of what you now know?"

Lawrence's mouth showed a stubborn and determined line. "I will woo Miss Jones, my friend, precisely because of what I now know."

The words were weighed carefully. "I hesitate to bring up an unpleasant subject."

"Then don't."

"It concerns money."

Lawrence grimaced. As far as he was concerned money was the root of all evil. Or the *lack* of money was, anyway. "If you persist on that particular subject, you will ruin my day, and certainly my morning," he warned Miles.

"I don't think so. I believe it would be wise for you to know the extent of the young lady's income."

"If you say I must."

"I do."

Lawrence composed his face and waited. "Well?"

Lord Cork seemed to be almost enjoying himself. "I have it on the best authority that Miss Jones has something in excess of three hundred thousand."

Despite his reputation for being one of the finest horsemen in the realm, Lawrence nearly toppled off his horse.

Miles added: "Per year."

"Per year?"

"Per year."

Lawrence could scarcely find his breath. He forced the air in and out of his lungs. "Dollars?"

His companion shook his head. "Pounds."

Lawrence brought the stallion up short and said feelingly: "Jesus, Mary, and Joseph!"

"I thought you might be impressed."

"Three hundred thousand pounds per annum?"

Miles smiled smugly. "And compounding every year. Miss Jones has apparently inherited her father's financial wizardry along with his vast fortune."

"The woman is a bloody heiress!" Lawrence exclaimed.

"That was the idea, you will recall."

"Good God, do you realize that that kind of money would solve all of my problems?"

"All of your financial problems," corrected his friend.

"I must be very clever about this business of Miss Juliet Jones," Lawrence purposed, his mind already going to work on how best to court the lady. "She will not be one to suffer fools gladly."

"You are going to have to be more than clever," admonished his countryman. "You are going to have to be sincere."

"Sincere?" he scoffed. "With a woman?"

"With this particular woman, yes. Surely that is not too great a price to pay under the circumstances."

Lawrence put his head back and laughed darkly. "You are a fine one to speak of sincerity when it comes to dealings with the fair sex. You are renowned for your winning ways and your glib tongue."

"I can afford to lie," the well-heeled marquess pointed out. "You cannot."

"True."

It was true. Miles had inherited a substantial bank account along with his titles and lands. He could be married *whenever* he wished, to *whomever* he wished.

"First we must plan how you are to meet the young lady," said the marquess. "Invitations have been pouring in at an astounding rate for luncheons, the opera, dinner parties, balls. We will need to choose wisely." Miles tapped one gloved finger against the bottom lip. "I believe the place to start is Mrs. Astor's ball." He turned, and his eyes leveled on Lawrence. "There is just one hitch."

"And what is that?"

"According to my sources, Miss Jones has not received an invitation."

That took Lawrence by surprise. "The reason?"

"The Joneses are still considered to be *arrivistes*."

Lawrence muttered a soft, explicit oath under his breath. "In other words, Miss Juliet Jones has yet to be accepted by New York society."

"I'm afraid so. Have no fear, however. I will see to the matter," Miles reassured him.

Lawrence gave him a brief smile. "Somehow you always manage to." He blew out an expressive breath. "I don't suppose there is any other way of going about this business of securing a wife."

Lord Cork was adamant. "Not for you."

He frowned and confided to his fellow peer: "It's hellish at times being a duke."

"I dare say." Miles sighed sympathetically. "The pressures of privilege are heavy ones, indeed."

Lawrence's frown deepened. "Everyone looks up to me, depends upon me, willingly—even eagerly—hands over every responsibility to me." Lawrence rambled on, failing to notice that he was alone. He finally glanced back over one shoulder. Miles was at a standstill on the riding path. His gaze was fixed on an object in the distance. His posture was alert. His expression was dumbstruck. "Cork?"

"Egods, Lawrence!"

"What is it now?"

"Look!"

He turned in the saddle. Within the space of a second, perhaps two, certainly no longer, he saw it all. Miss Juliet Jones in a deep blue riding habit that matched the deep blue of her eyes, eyes that were quickly filling with fear. She clutched at the reins, trying to control her mount, but the animal refused to respond. The frenetic horse reared up on its hind legs, pawed the air with flailing hooves and let out a startled cry that made his blood run cold.

"The blasted animal is going to throw her," Miles called to him as they pressed their horses into a gallop.

"Not throw her," amended Lawrence, as the figure of horse and rider streaked across the Meadow. "The damned mare is running away with her."

"I'll go after her," volunteered his companion.

"You see to the boy," shouted Lawrence, as he set the black stallion on an intercept course with the runaway. "I will take care of Miss Jones myself."

2

SOMETHING was dreadfully wrong.

One minute she had been riding along, chatting and laughing with dear Cousin David as he leaned toward her and shared a delicious tidbit of gossip about a certain Miss B—, and the next her horse reared up on its hind legs, let out a spine-chilling cry and took off across the Sheep Meadow.

Thank Heaven she was not an hysterical sort of female, Juliet reminded herself. Otherwise she might be tempted to scream bloody murder, and that would not do at all.

Still, there was no getting around the fact that Hera was running away with her. The frantic mare was racing at breakneck speed across the open plain of Central Park, scattering sheep to the four winds as if the Devil himself were on her tail.

"Hera, easy girl! Easy!"

Juliet tried to be heard above the bleating of the ewes and the thundering of the horse's hooves tearing into the sod, flinging it at random into the chill morning air, spewing forth bits of mud and twig and brown grass into her hat, her hair, her face.

The thoroughbred paid her no heed. It was almost as though the poor animal were running for its very life. Indeed, it seemed that Hera intended to keep running until the heart burst in her breast.

Juliet did not understand. No small rodent or rabbit or furry, fleet-footed creature had startled the normally calm mare. There had been no loud gunshots to set her off. No barking of dogs. No terrified whinnies of other horses. Hera had always behaved like a perfect lady in the past. Juliet simply could not fathom the reason for the mare's sudden crazed behavior.

"Hera! Please stop—"

It was to no avail.

Juliet did the only thing she could under the circumstances: she clutched the reins tightly in her hands and held on for dear life. Glimpses of barren earth, great dark trees, and deep blue sky flew by her. Her heart was pounding in her ears. Cold air was flooding her lungs. She began to feel quite giddy, perhaps even a little lightheaded, as if she had imbibed a trifle more champagne than she should have.

What if she *were* suffering from hysteria?

She had read once in one of her books that it was a commonly held notion that a hysteric woman was suffering from disturbances of the womb. As a consequence of her unexpected and wild ride through the park, particular parts of her anatomy—very possibly her womb among them—were definitely "disturbed." She must be hysterical.

Juliet knew full well that even an expert rider like herself could be thrown from the saddle, her body trampled underfoot and dragged, immodestly—her boot caught in the stirrup, her petticoats flapping in the breeze and, God forbid, her French lace-trimmed drawers showing—the length of the park.

The prospect was mortifying.

Tears suddenly burned in Juliet's eyes. What if something should happen to her? She tried to imagine her great-aunt—sweet Aunt Effie, dear Aunt Effie, kind and lovable but definitely dithery Aunt Effie—reading the headlines concerning the accident, dealing with the resulting horde of reporters, lawyers and bankers, commanding servants and shopkeepers and stable hands.

It boggled the mind.

There was Cousin David, of course. But he was so young and knew so little of the ways of the world. And, truthfully, he and Aunt Effie had not quite taken to each other yet.

Then there was Brambinger and Mrs. Hudson and the small army of faithful retainers who had served her family for nearly thirty years. None of them were getting any younger. Indeed, Brambinger was under a physician's care for his heart condition and Mrs. Hudson for her chronic rheumatism.

Poor Aunt Effie. Poor Cousin David. Poor Brambinger. Poor Mrs. Hudson. How would, how could, any of them manage without her?

The question was purely rhetorical. Juliet already knew the answer. They couldn't manage without her. They needed her. Every last one of them. She was the glue that held it all together. She had been since the death of her parents many years before.

Nothing must happen to her.

Unfortunately Hera raced on across the Sheep Meadow, her chest soaking wet and heaving from the exertion, and headed straight for the wooded Ramble.

The winter wind—it had not seemed so bitterly cold until now—whipped through her and around her, tearing Juliet's riding hat from her head, tossing hairpins helter-skelter in every direction, tugging at the heavy coil of hair at her nape until it came undone and created a golden frenzy that blew in her eyes and blinded her.

For a minute or two Juliet could not see a thing. But she could hear the impending approach of another horse. There was no mistaking the pounding of its hooves on the frozen turf, the heavy snorting of its nostrils sending steamy vapor into the air, the masculine shouts of its rider. Someone was heading straight for her. Someone was coming to the rescue.

She called out in a husky voice: "My hat—"

There was a disbelieving snicker. "Your hat? Blast your hat!"

She tried again. "Please, would you help me, sir?"

"Bloody hell, what do you think I'm trying to do?" came the response in a deep, biting baritone.

"I—I don't want to fall," she admitted at last.

"You're not going to fall. Just hang on until I tell you to do otherwise."

The next thing Juliet knew, a large, powerful, masculine arm encircled her waist. Simultaneously, one large, powerful, and very definitely masculine hand reached out and grabbed her left breast just above the ribcage.

Juliet opened her mouth to vehemently protest the intimacy, but no sound issued forth.

At that very instant her rescuer ordered in a commanding voice that would brook no argument: "I have you now. Let go of the reins!"

She let go.

Without ceremony, or any particular care for her comfort, Juliet was plucked from her horse and flung face-down across the stranger's saddle. Her head bobbed up and down on one side of his great black beast, her feet on the other. In between her figure protruded into the air, providing the man looming above her with an unprecedented view of her backside.

She was mortified.

Perhaps falling off her horse would have been the preferable course of action, after all. For Miss Juliet Jones of 665 Fifth Avenue, of the green, rolling hills of Kentucky, of fashionable Newport in the summer, and of Paris, France, was quite certain she was going to die of embarrassment.

3

MISS JONES had a very nice derriere.

Lawrence was able to discern that much even through the excessive padding of her petticoats and the long skirt of her riding habit.

He could also vouch for the fact that she possessed a fine pair of breasts: they were round and full and fit well in a man's hand. He should know. He'd had his hands on her, however briefly and inadvertently, however buffered by corsets, boned stays and her bodice.

He recalled the poet's musings on the subject of the feminine figure. Indeed, it had been Mister Robert Browning who had penned the immortal words: "The breast's superb abundance where a man might lay his head."

Lawrence had always considered himself something of an expert on the subject of female breasts. First, they came in all shapes and sizes. Some were no more than a slight protrusion with a pinpoint center. Some were truly of gargantuan proportions with huge red nipples. Perfection lay somewhere in between. Perfection might well be the breasts of Miss Juliet Jones.

Would hers be as lovely to look at, as delectable to kiss and caress, as responsive to passion as they appeared to be to fear and to winter's cold tongue?

For a moment Lawrence closed his eyes and pictured the lady in his mind: tall and slender, with long, lovely legs. Flawless skin with the translucence of rare porcelain. High, full breasts, their tips like deep pink rosebuds. And everywhere, soft, golden hair: gracing the arch of her brows, falling in a swath of sun-kissed silk to her waist, forming an enticing, inviting vee between her thighs.

He felt his body's instant response. His groin tightened and began to press uncomfortably against the hard, cold leather of the saddle.

Bloody hell, Lawrence swore silently as he balanced the shapely form of Miss Jones over his knees. He was no eager schoolboy, no green youth, no rutting young buck to be at the mercy of his sexual urges. He was a man, for God's sake; a man of experience and discriminating tastes. He was not at the mercy of anyone or anything, let alone that vulnerable male flesh which he carried around between his legs.

"Easy, Zeus!" He brought the big, black stallion to a halt at the edge of the Ramble and quickly dismounted. Then he reached up, grasped his passenger around the waist, and lifted her down. He set her on the ground.

With a trembling hand, the young woman swept the disheveled hair back from her face, and Lawrence Grenfell Wicke—once a stellar student at university, a highly decorated soldier for Queen and country, a natural-born leader of men, the former Viscount Lindsay, now nearly thirty years old and the latest in a long line of distinguished dukes—stood there, staring at the most beautiful creature he had ever seen.

She took his breath away!

For Miss Juliet Jones *was* tall and slender, although the top of her head scarcely reached his chin. Her skin *was* flawless and translucent. Her breasts *were* high and full. Her hair *was* golden silk cascading around her shoulders and down her back.

But it was her eyes that held Lawrence transfixed. He had never seen eyes that color before.

Blue.

Yet not merely blue.

One minute they reminded him of a spring meadow overgrown with bluebells and lavendar. The next they were the velvet mist that clung to the forest floor where, as a boy, he had spent many happy hours exploring to his heart's content. Then they changed again, their color brightened and they seemed to burst into flames.

Blue fire.

"By the blood of Christ," Lawrence gritted through his teeth as he snapped the riding crop smartly against his thigh. The resulting sting was felt all the way down his leg.

He was becoming fanciful. Addlebrained. Foggy in the crumpet. In fact, if he didn't know better, he would think he was behaving like a besotted fool.

Fortunately the sting of the small whip had quickly brought him to his senses. Miss Juliet Jones was attractive enough, he supposed. Her eyes were an agreeable shade of blue. And she did present a fine figure of a girl. No more. No less.

He was not in New York on a whim. He was here on business; he must never forget that. The well-being, the very lives, of hundreds of people were his responsibility. Not to mention ten thousand acres of farmland, several villages and churches, sundry schools, cottages, and stables, herds of sheep and cows, and a wooded park filled with wild deer, pheasants, partridges, and grouse.

Pro rege, lege, et grege: for the king, the law and the people. The Wicke family motto had literally been chiseled in stone above the fireplace in the Great Hall by one of Lawrence's predecessors when the family seat, Grantley Manor, was built during the late fifteenth century.

His inheritance last year of his father's titles and estates, including Grantley Manor, had turned out to be both a blessing and a curse. Becoming the eighth Duke of Deakin had given a much needed direction to Lawrence's life. Unfortunately, the family holdings had been sadly neglected since the death of his mother, the duchess, some years before. The heart, even the will to live, it seemed, had gone out of his father with the loss of his beloved Clara.

Lawrence's black brows, the same color as his black hair, drew together in a studied frown. Truth was, the damnable fireplace, the Great

Hall, even the Manor itself, were crumbling around him. Consequently, as the elder son, it was his duty to rescue the family estates before they collapsed altogether. Since money—or the regrettable lack of it—was at the root of the problem, it had become his business to acquire a rich wife.

This pretty piece of business with Miss Jones must be strictly that: business, he reminded himself. A wise man never attempted to mix business and pleasure.

He took a good hard look at the disheveled young woman standing in front of him. She was clearly flustered and out of breath.

"Sir, I must insist"—she stopped and gasped for air—"that you unhand me."

"Madam, I already have," he pointed out to her without a trace of humor.

The clear pallor of her cheeks instantly flooded with red. "So—so you have." She waited until her breathing returned to normal, cleared her throat and then proceeded to explain to him, all the while swaying precariously on her feet, "I fear my horse was running away with me."

He reached out to steady her. "It did appear that way."

"I don't believe she intended to throw me."

"Perhaps not."

The lady was obviously still not quite herself. Through the fine leather of her gloves and the material of his coat, Lawrence felt her fingernails digging into his arm.

"I can't imagine what set her off," she said, bewildered.

"Something did," he insisted.

"Yes. You're right, of course," she admitted in a dismayed voice. "It's just that Hera has never behaved in such an irrational manner before. I can't think what she was about."

Neither could he. "This isn't the first time you've ridden the mare?"

"No. Indeed, it isn't," she hastened to inform him. "In fact, I've ridden this particular horse along the identical pathway every morning for the past three weeks."

"In that case, it's unlikely to be inexperience," he said, rubbing his jaw judiciously.

"The mare's?"

"Yours."

"I beg your pardon." Her elegant nose went a notch higher in the cool morning air. "I will have you know, sir, that I am considered an excellent rider."

Lawrence was tempted to ask *who* considered her an excellent rider, but decided to let it pass.

She took a fine linen handkerchief from the pocket of her *princesse* dress and discreetly dabbed at her face. He noticed her hand was trembling.

"Are you certain you're all right?"

"Yes. A bit shaken perhaps."

"Perfectly natural under the circumstances," Lawrence mumbled, wondering what in the hell he was going to say or do next.

Miss Jones brushed at the bits of twig and

mud splattered down the front of her riding habit, embedded in the folds of her skirt, and entangled in her hair. "I must look an awful fright," she said with a slightly self-mocking smile.

He didn't trust himself to contradict her, for there was an utterly charming speck of dirt still clinging to her chin and another, like a beauty mark, poised beside a generous lower lip, drawing attention to her mouth.

Miss Juliet Jones had a very nice mouth.

Lawrence heard himself say the first thing that popped into his mind. "You've lost your hat."

Her hand swept to her bare head. "So I have," she replied as if neither had mentioned her hat before.

"Please allow me to retrieve it for you, madam," he said, bowing ever so slightly in her direction.

"You are too kind, sir," she responded with the same excruciating politeness.

With a click of his heels, Lawrence did an about-face and marched across the partially frozen ground to the spot where the black beaver hat had landed. Unfortunately, it too was splattered with mud. The stylish blue gauze veil wound around the crown had caught on a low branch and was torn in several places.

"I'm afraid it's somewhat the worse for your experience," he said, presenting the trampled riding hat to her.

She accepted it, nonetheless. "Then I will just

have to save my pennies and buy another, won't I?''

Lawrence nearly laughed out loud. No doubt Miss Jones had a dozen such fashionable black beaver whatnots in her wardrobe at this very moment.

"Thank you for rescuing my hat," she said in a surprisingly forthright manner. "And thank you as well for coming to my rescue."

Miss Jones was about to dismiss him. Lawrence could hear it in the formal tone of voice, see it in the features utterly devoid of expression. He should know; he had used the technique often enough, himself. But the Duke of Deakin wasn't accustomed to being dismissed, not by anyone, man or woman—save the Queen, or perhaps H.R.H. And even Bertie took care not to play too much the prince with him.

He had to think quickly. He didn't want Juliet Jones to leave just yet. "What did you say the mare's name was?''

Blue eyes widened slightly. "Hera."

"The stable boy told me the stallion I'm riding is called Zeus."

Her brows came together in a delicate line. "Hera and Zeus of Greek mythology."

"Weren't they husband and wife?" he said in an attempt to keep the conversation going.

A spot of bright color appeared in the center of each porcelain cheek. "I—I believe so."

Miles was right: She *was* bright.

And if he were a betting man, Lawrence mused, he would be gleefully rubbing his hands together and wagering one hundred pounds that the lady knew Hera and Zeus were brother and sister, as well as husband and wife. Such a relationship was unacceptable, unthinkable, shocking by human standards, but not for the gods who had once reigned on Mount Olympus.

He took a deliberately relaxed stance, planting his feet a foot or two apart and folding his arms across his chest. "I seem to recall from my schooldays that Hera was noted for her resistance to her husband's authority."

"Perhaps he was an autocrat," she proposed.

"An autocrat? Zeus?" It didn't seem very likely to him. "Hera was also known to be vindictive and jealous."

"Only because her husband took so many lovers," blurted out Miss Jones in the goddess's defense.

"But wasn't it Zeus's union with Alcmene which produced the legendary . . ."

"Hercules," she supplied.

Lawrence nodded and then added: "We mustn't forget that Hera sided with the Greeks during the Trojan War."

"She had her reasons."

He arched his brow quizzically.

Apparently Miss Jones was more than willing to explain. "Paris chose Aphrodite over Hera as the most beautiful goddess. She couldn't forgive him for the slight."

He shook his head from side to side and clicked his tongue disapprovingly. "Vanity, thy name is woman."

"Actually the line is 'fraility, thy name is woman.' "

"Spenser?"

"Shakespeare."

"Much Ado About Nothing?"

"Hamlet."

Lawrence decided he had better sharpen his wits if he wanted to keep up with Miss Jones.

He tried once more. "I believe it was Homer who called Hera 'ox-eyed.' "

"It was, indeed. But he meant it as praise," came the swift rebuttal.

His opponent seemed very sure of herself for one so young *and* female. "Did he?"

She was emphatic. "Hera had very beautiful and very large, full eyes."

Lawrence allowed his frown to slowly dissolve into a smile. "Madam, I concede the point to you."

The point, perhaps, but certainly not the battle and most assuredly not the war!

Lawrence suddenly realized he was enjoying himself immensely. Their conversation was unconventional, to say the least. Miss Jones was unconventional, but he couldn't remember the last time a woman had interested him on any level but a mundane physical one.

It was damned disconcerting.

"Well, speaking of Hera . . ." he muttered, catching a glimpse of something large, something brown, moving just at the edge of his peripheral vision.

They both turned and watched as the mare wended her way out of the Ramble. She cautiously approached the black stallion who was grazing only a few feet from them. Zeus raised his head and gave a nicker of recognition. Hera returned the greeting.

Miss Jones took a tentative step toward her horse.

"Don't move," he ordered.

She looked down her nose at him, no small feat when he stood nearly a head taller. "And, pray tell, why not?"

"The mare may run off again."

She lowered her voice. "Why would Hera do that?"

Lawrence didn't answer her question. Instead, he inquired, "Are you a female of delicate sensibilities, madam?"

"A female of delicate sensibilities, sir?" she repeated as if he had taken partial leave of his senses.

"When it comes to the sight of blood?"

Miss Jones swallowed. "Whose blood?"

"Your horse's," he said evenly.

She squared her shoulders. "I would have you know that I am not at all an hysterical sort of woman."

"Excellent, because I want you to speak softly to the mare and reassure her. Then I will need for you to hold the reins while I see to the wound on her back."

To her credit, Juliet Jones followed his orders to the letter. "What a fine lady, you are, Hera," she cooed unself-consciously to the thoroughbred, her voice deeper than before, huskier. "I know you didn't mean to run off as you did. I know you wouldn't deliberately hurt anyone. I only wish you could speak. I wonder what frightened you, my brave and beautiful girl."

Lawrence dispensed with his riding crop and gloves, tossing them to the ground without a second glance. Then, as gently as he could, he eased the saddle and the blanket to one side and examined the injury.

"Sonofa—" he bit off sharply.

There was a large, jagged thorn embedded in the horse's hindquarters. Bright red blood slowly oozed from the puncture, but the wound was clean.

From her appointed place at the mare's head, the lady peered at him anxiously. "Have you found something?"

"Yes." A muscle in his jaw started to twitch. "This is going to hurt like hell, so hold the reins steady."

Miss Jones paled slightly but vowed in a firm voice, "I will."

"I wish the devil I had a pair of pliers," Lawrence commented more to himself than to his companion. Then, using his thumb and finger as pincers, he got a good grip on the thorn and pulled.

To his surprise, it popped out.

Hera's head shot up. She snorted once or twice, and danced in nervous circles at the end of her tether until the sound of her mistress's voice finally calmed her. It was several minutes before Miss Jones was free to speak to him. "What was it?"

Lawrence held up the bloodied thorn.

Her mouth formed a small *O*.

"Somehow it became wedged between the saddle and the horse," he told her. "It was the addition of your weight that drove the thorn into her back."

She drew a breath of distress. "But I had ridden Hera for some time before she showed any signs of being disturbed."

An image flashed into Lawrence's mind, an image of a handsome youth bending over to speak to his cousin, and then of the two of them laughing together.

"Where would a three-inch-long thorn come from in the middle of the Sheep Meadow?"

He didn't realize he had spoken aloud until the lady replied, "I don't know."

"Neither do I," he confessed, shaking his head.

Miss Jones held out her embroidered handkerchief. "I hope you haven't hurt yourself."

"I haven't." He stared down at the dainty scrap of lace-edged linen. "What's that for?"

"To wipe the blood from your hand."

"Thank you." He accepted the hanky—it seemed to smell faintly of summer roses—and went on to reassure her that her horse would make a full recovery. "Just make certain the stable boy disinfects the wound properly."

She patted the mare's neck. "I'll see to it myself."

"It must be kept clean."

"I am aware of that."

He added, "Hera shouldn't be saddled for a few days."

The lady flung up a determined chin. "I am

well acquainted with the proper care of horses, my dear sir."

"Can you ride mine?"

That caught her off guard. "Can I ride yours?"

"Do you have the skill or the strength to handle Zeus?" he asked bluntly.

Her eyes shimmered with pride. "I have both the skill *and* the strength."

"Then I offer the black stallion to you, my dear lady," he said, giving her a foot up. "Hera will follow Zeus's lead, your companion will escort you back to the stables and I will ride behind my friend," he said, indicating the approaching pair of horses and riders.

"Thank you," she said from atop her perch.

He gave a slight nod of his head. "It's been my pleasure to be of service."

"You're too kind," she said regally.

"Not at all. It's not every day a gentleman is given the opportunity to rescue a lady."

"Fortunately for we damsels in distress," Lawrence thought he heard Miss Juliet Jones say as she urged the stallion into a canter.

By the time they had returned to their carriage a half hour later, Miles St. Aldford was brimming over with curiosity.

"Well, what do you think?" he demanded to know.

'About what?'

"Our Miss Jones, of course."

"*Our* Miss Jones?"

"*Your* Miss Jones, then. Is she not everything I said she would be and more?"

Lawrence sank back into the corner of the hired carriage and nonchalantly traced the design on the tapestry seat cushions with the tip of his riding crop. "Perhaps."

Miles appeared to take his lack of enthusiasm as a personal affront. "Only *perhaps*?"

"Surely you do not expect me to wax poetic on the lady's supposed virtues." The cloud of disconcert on his best friend's face made him sigh and admit: "Miss Jones is a perfectly presentable young woman."

"P-Presentable?" Miles sputtered in disbelief.

"All right. Miss Jones is beautiful."

"And—?"

"And she is intelligent."

Miles grunted. "At least that is something."

"She is also headstrong and stubborn."

"She is not alone in her possession of those 'virtues,' " muttered his countryman. Then he pointed out: "The lady will be a challenge for you, and she will not be boring."

No. Miss Jones would not be boring. "She is exasperating."

"She is a woman."

"She is outspoken."

"She is an American woman." Miles expounded, "Some men think it is part of their charm."

Lawrence crooked a brow at his friend. "Do they?"

Lord Cork threw up his hands in frustration. "Damn it, Lawrence, there is no perfect woman."

He sighed long-sufferingly. "How well I know that, Miles. How well all men know that."

Miles St. Aldford reached for the small black book in his coat pocket. "Do you wish me to see who is next on our list? I must warn you she will not be as beautiful as Miss Jones. She will not be as intelligent as Miss Jones. And she will not be as rich as Miss Jones."

"No."

"No?"

"Despite her shortcomings, I find myself—"

"Yes?" prompted the other man.

"Intrigued." He turned his head and gazed out the window of their carriage at the bustling streets of New York. "Make certain the lady receives an invitation to Mrs. Astor's ball next week."

"Consider it a fait accompli."

"Miss Jones will do," Lawrence mumbled under his breath. "Miss Jones will do nicely, indeed."

4

"POMPOUS ENGLISHMEN," David grumbled, not very subtly masking his annoyance, while Juliet saw to the wound on the mare's back.

"Did you think so?"

Her cousin nodded his handsome blond head and complained, with a sizable chip on his shoulder, "They didn't even bother to introduce themselves."

"The British almost always wait for a formal introduction," she explained. "It's simply their way. It wasn't meant as a deliberate slight to us."

But David seemed determined to sulk. He kicked willfully at a bale of hay with the toe of his riding boot. "Those two were nothing more than a couple of popinjays."

Juliet bit the corners of her mouth. "They were a trifle overbearing, I agree."

Resentment was thick in the young man's voice. "They thought they were very grand."

"They *were* very grand." She finished dressing Hera's injury, handed the bottle of disinfectant to the stable boy and informed her cousin:

"And it has been my experience that very grand Englishmen do not, as a rule, introduce themselves to anybody."

"The one I rode with was a dandy," David said scornfully, "and the other, who took off after you, looked like the devil himself."

"The gentleman was merely dressed in black."

"All in black, from head to toe. And he rode a huge black beast."

"The stallion's name is Zeus and he was an absolute lamb to ride," she said, taking a handful of grain and offering it to the mare.

David wrinkled up his nose and waved his hand back and forth in front of his face. "It smells in here, cousin. Aren't you about finished?"

She inhaled deeply.

The stable smelled like any stable—of horses and straw and leather saddles. The slightly pungent odor reminded Juliet of her mother and father, and of the happy times they had spent together at their horse farm in Kentucky. That was before the war, of course.

She had been only five when her parents presented her with a pony: a small, white Shetland that she had immediately dubbed The Princess. Her first horse; her first love. For many years they had been inseparable. The Princess had died last summer at the advanced age of nineteen. When the news reached her in Paris Juliet had wept. . . .

She pulled on her gloves, straightened her skirt, and briskly announced: "As a matter of fact, I am finished here. It's time we were on our way home, or we'll be late for luncheon and Aunt Effie will worry."

"Great-Aunt Euphemia always worries," David muttered as he escorted her to their waiting carriage.

"It is a burden for her," she said kindly.

He snorted. "She enjoys it."

"Then we mustn't begrudge Aunt Effie her little pleasures," Juliet said, patting his arm affectionately.

She had grown quite fond of David since he had arrived on her doorstep three months ago with a letter of introduction and legal proof of their family relationship, but he could be somewhat petulant at times. It was excusable, in her mind, due to her cousin's age—he was barely twenty-two—and his circumstances. Undoubtedly it had been very difficult growing up a penniless orphan.

Juliet sighed and uttered a silent prayer of thanks to the anonymous benefactor who had seen to it that David had received an education. Providing a home and a secure future for him were now up to her.

As they approached the carriage, a man in the distinctive blue livery of the Jones' doffed his top hat and inquired, "Where to, miss?"

"Home, please, James," she instructed her coachman, "and not through the park."

"Yes, Miss Juliet."

"Are you going to tell our dear aunt about the runaway horse and the devil Englishman?" David inquired after they were settled in.

"I don't know," she said thoughtfully.

David leaned toward her from his side of the barouche and lowered his voice to a confidential level. "Someone is bound to have seen you, Juliet, and you know what gossip is like in New York."

He was right. Someone had undoubtedly witnessed the entire unfortunate incident. There was no privacy in Society and there were no secrets.

"Please leave it to me, then," she said with a slight edge to her voice. "I will tell Aunt Effie in my own time and in my own way."

"As you wish," David said, conceding to her wishes. Then he flopped back, propped his muddy boot up against the carriage seat opposite and frowned. "I wonder who he is."

"Who *who* is?"

"The devil Englishman."

"I don't know." Juliet dug into the pocket of her riding habit, searching for her handkerchief. Then she remembered: she had given it to her rescuer to wipe Hera's blood from his hand. "I do know that it is extremely unlikely we will ever encounter the gentleman again."

Her cousin shot her a curious glance. "Aren't you interested in finding out his identity?"

"Not in the least," Juliet declared as their carriage left Central Park and turned onto Fifth Avenue.

It wasn't true, of course. She *was* interested in the Englishman, but she was reluctant to admit as much, even to David.

Men were so patronizing.

It didn't seem to matter if it was the elderly rector at her church, the beggar on the street corner, the lawyers and the bankers who hovered about an heiress like vultures, or her own young male cousin. Men invariably took one look at her and assumed she had nothing more important on her mind than the next round of dinner parties and balls, the latest gowns from Worth's, and the new crop of broad-shouldered dancing partners.

It was most annoying.

There was more to life, after all, Juliet reflected, than eating, drinking, and dancing. There was certainly more to her life.

With the untimely death of Stonewall Jackson Jones—"King Midas" to his friends and enemies—the professional moneymen had assumed they would take over the reins of power and run the financial empire bequeathed to Juliet by her flamboyant father.

They were greatly mistaken.

Juliet was first and foremost her father's daughter. She hired herself the best teachers and tutors in the land. She read every book she could find on the subject of money and investments, mining and farming. She traveled extensively at home and abroad. She studied art, music, foreign languages, history, and geography. Indeed, her education was the best that money could buy.

Then she bided her time.

On her twenty-first birthday, Miss Juliet Jones took charge. Of her inheritance. Of her father's vast fortune. Of her life. That had been more than three years ago. New York was still reeling from the shock.

Juliet gazed out the window of her carriage at the busy city streets and allowed herself a small smile of satisfaction. No one—with the exception of Aunt Effie—had thought she could do it. But she had. In fact, as it turned out, she was even better at making money than her famous father. The value of the Jones' estate had doubled since she had assumed control. There was only one subject which she lacked any real knowledge of, she admitted to herself with a blush.

Men.

Well . . . men and women. And the intimacy of the marriage bed.

No one spoke of it.

No one wrote of it . . . except in the most general, florid terms.

No one *did* it, as far as Juliet could determine.

The relationship between a man and a woman was referred to as a "wife's duty," as a "husband's right," and as the "natural course of events," but there were never any details, never any specifics.

It was most frustrating.

Juliet brushed a stray wisp of hair back from her face and reached across the seat for the dark blue chatelaine she had left in the carriage while they were riding this morning. She took out a linen handkerchief—it was always wise to have a second one handy—and dabbed at a speck of dirt by her lower lip. Then she re-

turned to her musings on the subject of that
elusive event that took place between a man and
a woman.

She had read many books in many languages,
of course. It was always the same: they spoke
of love, of grand passion, of urges, and of stirrings. They never said, unfortunately, exactly
what stirred.

Juliet sighed into her handkerchief. Truth
was, in the end, her books had been no help at
all.

Suddenly she thought of the tall, dark, and
handsome stranger who had come to her rescue
in the park. She had felt odd stirrings deep
within her when he'd had his hands on her. But
surely being plucked from the back of one's
horse and thrown across a gentleman's knees
had nothing to do with the intimacy of the marriage bed!

It was most puzzling.

David was right, however. The Englishman
had been dressed all in black from his tailored
coat, trimmed in black Russian sable, to his expensive handmade black boots. He had worn
black gloves and a black expression. His hair
had been thick and luxuriant and black. Black
brows had arched provocatively over cold, intelligent, black eyes.

Would his heart be black as well?

A shiver of excitement ran through her. What
a frightening thought.

What an intriguing thought. . . .

Juliet hastily turned to her companion, who
with his blond hair and blue eyes, was the mir-

ror image of herself and confessed: "I find I am quite famished after our ride, dear cousin. I wonder what we are having for luncheon."

"It was delivered while you were in at luncheon," Brambinger informed his mistress as he held out the gold-plated, calling card receiver.

Juliet picked up the single white card—as was required by protocol the top-right corner had been folded down, signaling that the caller had been paying her respects—and read aloud the name printed on the front: "Mrs. Willam Astor." Her head came up. "There must be some mistake."

"There's no mistake, Miss Juliet."

"I am not acquainted with the lady, Brambinger, as you well know."

"That is, undoubtedly, the reason for her social call," the elderly butler pointed out. "A footman brought the card to the door." He added for good measure, "I saw Mrs. Astor with my own eyes. She was sitting in her carriage."

"They must have stopped at the wrong house," Juliet said, not wishing to seem to attach any importance to the incident.

"That doesn't seem very likely," Brambinger replied, returning the calling-card receiver to its usual place on the Italian marble table. The gold-plated receptacle was named "Hilarity" by its manufacturer and cost a mere ten dollars. There was an identical one in the front hall of every grand house up and down both sides of Fifth Avenue.

She looked the aging retainer square in the face. "You and I both know it is even less likely that the leading hostess of New York society should suddenly decide to call upon me or my aunt after all these years."

Brambinger fell silent, evidently mulling over the possibilities in his mind. Then he ventured: "Perhaps Mrs. Astor has finally seen the error of her ways."

"The error of her ways?" Juliet choked.

The butler nodded his distinguished white head. "Perhaps the lady realized—however belatedly—that no fancy-dress ball or tea party or dinner could truly be deemed a success without Miss Juliet Jones in attendance."

Juliet had never been susceptible to flattery. Nevertheless, she blushed with pleasure at his words. "How very kind of you to say so, Brambinger."

"I only speak the truth, miss. Why, just last week I was remarking to Mrs. Hudson that it was bound to happen sooner or later."

"Bound to happen sooner or later?" she echoed.

He nodded his head again. "A young lady of Miss Juliet's beauty and intelligence and accomplishments couldn't be ignored forever by those damned fool Knickerbockers, I said. Mrs. Hudson agreed, of course."

Juliet coughed discreetly behind her hand. Only Brambinger would conclude that Mrs. Astor, *the* Mrs. Astor, had finally come to her senses and belatedly recognized the Misses Jones as social equals.

She took the man aside and said quietly, "Perhaps we shouldn't put too much stock in Mrs. Astor's call. In fact, it might be best if we didn't mention it to anyone else."

The man arched one hoary eyebrow quizzically. "Not even to Miss Jones?"

"Especially not to Miss Jones."

"But—"

"I don't care for myself, mind you. I never have. But I will not have my great-aunt get her hopes up, only to have them dashed to the ground," Juliet declared dramatically.

His eyes narrowed. "Do you think it's some kind of trick?"

"Possibly."

His eyes darkened. "Maybe a hoax?"

"Very probably."

"Who would do such a thing?" he demanded.

Juliet put her hands together and interlaced her fingers. "I don't know."

"And why?"

"I don't know that, either," she admitted. "I simply think the matter should be kept between the two of us.

The butler raised and lowered his slightly stooped shoulders. "As you wish, Miss Juliet."

"Thank you," she said, greatly relieved. "I knew I could count on you."

Brambinger shook his head from side to side as he shuffled down the long hallway toward the kitchen. "Mark my words," he mumbled, "it was no mistake."

* * *

Juliet had the teapot poised in her hand when a knock came at the library door later that afternoon. Brambinger entered, carrying a small silver salver. There was a single white envelope in the center of the tray.

"This has just arrived, miss."

She continued pouring their tea. "You may put it there on my desk, Brambinger."

The butler did as she requested and then returned to stand beside the tea table. He cleared his throat and elaborated. "It came by special messenger."

"Did it?"

"Yes. I spoke to the deliveryman myself."

"I'm sure you took splendid care of things, Brambinger. You always do," she said with an appreciative smile.

"Thank you, miss. I try."

Juliet handed a cup of tea to her great-aunt and another to her cousin. Then she added milk and sugar to her own, stirred, and took a sip. It was perfect.

"How is your tea, miss?"

"My tea is delicious, Brambinger."

"And the cakes, miss?"

"We were just about to help ourselves to the cakes," she informed him.

"Allow me," he said, reaching around her for the plate.

Seniority had it privileges, of course. Miss Euphemia Jones was offered first choice of the rum cakes. She took two. Rum cake was her favorite, after all.

When the butler came back to her, Juliet

glanced up at him. "You are hovering, Brambinger."

"Yes, miss."

"Is there any particular reason?"

"I live to serve, miss."

With that, she choked on a bite of cake.

Brambinger obliged by pounding her on the back. "Are you all right, miss?"

"Y-yes," she managed a minute later.

"Perhaps if you were to rise and walk about the library . . ." he urged.

Juliet waved aside any further efforts on his part to be of assistance. It was clear to her now that Brambinger was up to something.

"As long as my afternoon tea has been interrupted," she began, standing and strolling across the room to the Louis Quatorze desk, "I suppose I may as well—"

"Open your mail," he suggested.

She picked up the white envelope that had been delivered by special messenger. "It appears to be—"

"An invitation," Brambinger finished for her.

She turned the envelope over and read aloud the names inscribed on the front: "Miss Juliet Jones. Miss Euphemia Jones. Mister David Thoreau Jones."

Euphemia Jones clapped her tiny hands together with delight. "We are all to go!"

David muttered under his breath, "Yes. But go where?"

Their great-aunt's dark blue eyes sparkled with excitement. "Oh, I do love a party. Let me think, what shall I wear? The black velvet? No, too depressing. The coral *damassé* silk? Too cheerful. The gray lace?" Euphemia shook her small, elegant head. "Too matronly. Can't think why I bought it. I know." She perked up immediately. "My new satin and brocade gown from Worth's with the matching satin slippers, and my sapphires, of course."

"You will be overdressed, Great-Aunt Euphemia, if the invitation is for tea," David pointed out.

Juliet felt three pairs of expectant eyes on her as she slit open the envelope and removed the engraved card inside. She read for a moment and then informed her audience, "It is not an invitation for tea."

Euphemia beamed from ear to ear. "I knew it would not be for tea."

"It is doubtless for another interminable charity luncheon to raise money to help feed the poor and destitute," whined David as he helped himself to another rum cake.

Juliet gave her cousin a long, measuring look. "It is not for a charity luncheon or for any kind of luncheon, for that matter." She hesitated. "We have been invited to Mrs. William Astor's annual ball."

There was stunned silence in the library.

"My word," breathed Brambinger, the first to recover his faculties.

"Good Lord, *the* Mrs. Astor?" exclaimed David.

"The satin and brocade will be just the ticket," declared Euphemia Jones.

Juliet looked from one to the other and spoke her mind. "I think we should decline."

"Decline?" came in unison from the disbelieving trio.

"Are you daft, girl?" Brambinger blurted out. Belatedly, his hand flew to his mouth.

Euphemia was confused. "But why?"

"I knew it was too good to be true," mumbled David.

Juliet's mouth formed a soft obstinate line. "I am not daft, and it isn't too good to be true. But I see no reason to give Mrs. Astor or that epicene fop, Ward McAllister, the satisfaction of having the Joneses come running the minute they snap their high society fingers." She stiffened her spine and her resolve. "I have my pride, after all."

Having apparently fully recovered from the shock of his earlier faux pas, Brambinger spoke up from behind the sofa, " 'Pride goeth before a fall.' "

" 'Pride goeth before destruction,' " she corrected in a vexed way, "and a haughty spirit before a fall.' "

"Ecclesiastes?"

"Proverbs."

Euphemia Jones set down her teacup. "I have heard that Caroline Astor's ballroom holds only four hundred people, and that she has a raised red velvet divan from which she watches the dancing. I have always thought it would be glorious, just once, to be asked to sit beside her."

Juliet felt herself weakening.

Dark sapphire-blue eyes gazed up at her innocently. "It would mean invaluable contacts for David as he begins life in the city."

Juliet's resolve was rapidly disappearing.

"And you, my dear, might even meet some tall, dark, and handsome stranger who will sweep you off your feet."

Juliet was tempted to tell her great-aunt that she already had. But it was neither the time nor the place.

"This is possibly the chance of a lifetime for each of us," concluded Euphemia Jones with deceptive docility. "Of course, you must do as you see fit."

Juliet recognized that she had been out-classed, outwitted, and outmaneuvered. There were times when dear, dithery Aunt Effie wasn't, in the least, dithery.

She threw up her hands in surrender. "All right. I give up. I know when I'm outnumbered." She took a fortifying breath. "We're going to Mrs. Astor's ball."

5

"WHERE the devil is she?" Lawrence demanded to know, unable to contain his impatience.

Miles arched a matter-of-fact brow. "I assume you mean Miss Jones."

"Of course, I mean Miss Jones," he said sharply.

"I'm sure she will be arriving momentarily."

Lawrence looked at his friend askance. "Are you certain she received an invitation?"

"I am positive."

"What time is it?"

The marquess took his watch from a waistcoat pocket. "It is precisely five minutes later than it was the last time you asked me that question."

He was in no mood for levity. "I'm warning you, Cork, if I have put up with all of this"—Lawrence spread his arms wide, seeming to encompass the entire Astor mansion and the four hundred socially elite in attendance—"for nothing . . ."

"I promise you, Deakin, it will not be for nothing."

"I have your word?"

"You have my word."

"She will come?"

"She will definitely come."

"Good. Because if I am forced to make small talk with one more fawning matron who smells of perfumed talc and whose ample bosom drips with a king's ransom in diamonds, I will not be responsible for my actions," he said warningly. "And that damned society photographer keeps taking my picture with people to whom I have scarcely been introduced."

"It is the price one pays for being a celebrity," his friend said philosophically.

Lawrence made a disparaging sound. "I don't want to be a celebrity."

"Nevertheless," Miles said with a sideways glance that was disconcertingly shrewd, "you are. It's not every day that a nobleman of your rank and reputation graces the hallowed halls and ballrooms of Knickerbocker society." He cleared his throat and lowered his voice half an octave. "Absolutely everyone is talking about you."

Lawrence furrowed his black brows into a single forbidding line and muttered under his breath, "Bloody hell."

He knew that behind the fluttering fans and skintight kid gloves—which would be worn only once and then discarded—over plates of *paté de foie gras* and glasses of imported French champagne, as they ate and drank and danced the night away, his name was on everyone's lips. Even his hostess for the evening, Mrs. Astor, had confided to him that New York hadn't seen this much excitement since the Prince of Wales had visited some fifteen years before. The Duke of Deakin, it seemed, was all the rage.

And he hated it.

"These Americans will never cease to amaze me," Miles said as they watched the dancing from their vantage point at the far end of the ballroom. "Why, in the past half hour I have heard you are both a devil and an angel."

"I've been called a lot worse," Lawrence reminded his former fellow officer.

"Indeed, a gentleman's reputation, deserved or otherwise, often precedes him." Miles leaned closer and added in a theatrical whisper: "Gossip would have it that you are wicked, dangerous, totally irresistible to women and the greatest lover since Casanova."

"I certainly hope not," he said with a decidedly cynical smile. "Casanova was indiscriminate in his choice of lovers and he was a libertine. He spent the last dozen years of his life impotent, disease ridden and in agonizing pain, forced to give up all pleasures but eating. In the end, he died a horrible death from the pox."

Lord Cork registered surprise. Then he added, "You are in a strange mood tonight, my friend."

"Am I?"

Miles hesitated, then shrugged his shoulders and went on. "Anyway, if I didn't know better, I would think Helena was in attendance and

spreading rumors about your so-called prow-
ess."

Lawrence inclined his head to yet another
middle-aged matron and her marriageable
daughter as they promenaded past him. "Lady
Deerhurst is home in Northumberland with her
husband and children, as well she should be,"
he said between his teeth.

"Only because you refused to bring her
along," pointed out Miles.

"Helena is married to an old acquaintance of
mine and is the mother of his two sons."

"That has never stopped her before."

His voice grew cold. "This woman is rash. She
could unwittingly invite a scandal."

"Even H.R.H. learned *that* lesson the hard
way," Miles said with an enormous sigh.

"I presume you are speaking of the unfortunate affair that took place several years ago in-
volving Bertie and the young Mrs. Mordaunt."

"I am, indeed. I never thought I would see the
day when a Prince of Wales was subpoenaed to
give testimony at a public divorce trial."

Lawrence shook his head. "A messy business."

"Of course, I doubt if divorce is what Helena
has in mind," Miles speculated, always the
pragmatist."Lord Deerhurst and his money
must come in handy for a lady with expensive
tastes. I think she would like to have her cake
and eat it, too."

Lawrence felt a flicker of annoyance and
heard himself state emphatically: "I have no
personal interest in Lady Deerhurst."

Miles lifted his elegant shoulders. "I know that. And you know that. The question is does she?"

His black eyes took on a hard sheen. "I made it clear to Helena years ago that she would never become the next Duchess of Deakin."

"Poor Helena." There was a melodramatic sigh from the man beside him. "You can't say she didn't try."

"She did try," he said testily. "She did *not* succeed."

Miles regarded his gloved hands. "At the time the lady had no money of her own."

He was forced to be blunt. "The lady had no morals, either."

"I'm afraid she never has," agreed his companion.

Lawrence made his position clear once and for all. "I would see my titles and lands and everything that is mine go to my younger brother Jonathan, or to a distant cousin, or even to a complete stranger, rather than to any offspring spawned by that bitch." His mood was growing foul. "That is enough about Helena. I do not with to discuss the woman any further."

The subject was quickly and expertly changed by Lord Cork. "I must tell you, my dear Deakin, that gossip also has it that you are a paragon among men, a likely candidate for sainthood, a first-rate horseman and a damned good sport. Above all else, of course, you are a bloody Englishman with a list of titles as long as your, ahem, arm."

Lawrence laughed out loud at that, and turned to study the painting behind him.

Miles pivoted on his heel and gazed up at the wall of the ballroom. "What are you looking at?"

"A rather good copy of a Turner seascape," was his answer.

"How do you know it's a copy?"

"Because the original is hanging in the Watercolor Room back at Grantley Manor."

"You don't say."

Lawrence stroked his jaw thoughtfully. "My grandfather, the sixth duke, was acquainted with most of the artists of his day, including Turner."

"How very jolly."

"The seascape?"

"No. The dancing," replied Miles. "The next quadrille is being announced."

They watched as a group of young ladies and their partners arranged themselves in the center of the ballroom. From a small alcove at the other end, an orchestra struck up a song and the dancing commenced.

" 'Mrs. Hogg's Three Little Pigs Quadrille.' Rather a silly idea, isn't it?" Lawrence said, referring to the practice of naming the individual dances.

"I was told by our hostess that it was originally performed at a fancy-dress ball given by Mrs. Hogg last month," explained Miles. "It is being repeated tonight especially in your honor."

"It is an honor I would gladly forego," Lawrence muttered under his breath.

Miles did not hear him. He was intent upon watching the ladies present. For Mrs. Astor's Fifth Avenue mansion was filled with classic American beauties: blondes, brunettes, and redheads. Tall ones and short ones. Slender ones, stately ones, and nicely rounded ones.

They were dressed in white cashmere, purple silk gauze, pink crape, magnolia satin with rosy tints, blue cisele velvet, and ivory brocade. Roses, violets, and lilies of the valley were intertwined in elaborate coiffures, cascaded over bare shoulders and trimmed flounced skirts. There were beaded and embroidered bodices, long trains and painted silk fans, satin shoes with buckles of rubies and diamonds, parures of silver and gold, strands of lustrous pearls, and earrings encrusted with priceless gemstones.

It was a sight to behold.

Miles was plainly enchanted. "I say, Lawrence, these American girls are exceptionally pretty and charming."

"Then why not find a suitable wife for yourself?" he put forth.

"A wife? Me?"

"You could marry and take a marchioness back to England with you," he suggested.

"I'm too young to settle into the connubial bliss of the marriage state," Miles claimed.

"You are six months my senior," Lawrence reminded him with a chuckle.

The marquess quickly backtracked. "I am too

old, then." He appeared vastly relieved to announce: "Ah, if I am not mistaken, there is Miss Jones now."

Lawrence's eyes flew to the entrance of the ballroom. It was Juliet.

At long last.

He had not realized until that moment that she stood half a head taller than the average female. The ladies of Society were clucking and clacking around her like so many small, fussy, fancily feathered hens.

Juliet shone like an angel.

She was dressed all in gold from her head to her toes. Her thick golden hair was swept up into a coiled chignon. Her satin ball gown was gold. Her gloves were gold. Her fan was gold. Her matching satin slippers were gold. The sheer silk stockings beneath her skirts were undoubtedly gold as well, mused Lawrence as he felt the first stirrings of arousal.

Yet she wore no jewels. Not a one. The delicate shell of her ear, the long, slender length of her neck, her pale ivory throat, her decolletage, her wrists, her fingers: they were all bare.

She was the jewel.

"Egods, Lawrence!" Miles breathed.

"Egods is right."

"The richest woman in New York, perhaps the richest woman in the New World, and she arrives at Mrs. Astor's ball adorned only in her own beauty. Miss Jones shows them all to disadvantage," Miles extolled, singing her praises. "By God, she is a consort fit for a king!"

Or a duke, Lawrence thought to himself.

Aloud, he inquired: "Who is the older woman with her?"

Miles recovered and answered. "Her great-aunt, Miss Euphemia Jones."

"Why has the boy tagged along?"

"It is always appropriate for a male relation to accompany the ladies."

Lawrence curled his lip in a snarl. "He'd damn well better stay out of my way."

"Mister David Thoreau Jones is young, good-looking and from the wealthiest family in New York. He will be inundated by ample-bosomed matrons and their very marriageable daughters the instant they realize who he is," Miles said dryly. "I guarantee he will not be in your way."

Lawrence plucked an imaginary speck of lint from the lapel of his formal evening coat. "It's time we rejoined our hostess, Cork."

"It is, indeed, Deakin."

"Mrs. Astor will wish to make the proper introductions."

Miles inclined his head and indicated that Lawrence should precede him toward the raised red velvet divan. "I cannot wait to see the delight on Miss Jones's face when she finds out who you are."

Juliet was horrified.

The stranger who had plucked her from the saddle of her runaway horse, who had touched her breast in an intimate fashion, who had been given an unprecedented view of her backside, and who had witnessed the most embarrassing moment of her life was none other than the man all New York was talking about: the Duke of Deakin!

She was quite beside herself.

Yet there was no escape. She could not turn tail and run. The floor of Mrs. Astor's ballroom was not about to open up and swallow her whole—however much she might wish it would. And she could not simply vanish into thin air.

She was stuck.

"The traditional quadrilles are delightful, of course," the duke was saying to their hostess after the formal introductions had been made, "but the waltz is the preferred dance of London society."

"A waltz will be played next, then, Your Grace," declared Mrs. Astor.

The devil Englishman turned to her, as Juliet had feared he would, and suggested smoothly, "Shall we have this waltz, Miss Jones?"

She opened her mouth and closed it again without uttering a sound.

Mrs. Astor took Great-Aunt Effie under her wing—David had been claimed by a pretty young debutante and her *maman*—and issued the most coveted invitation in Society: "Come, Miss Jones. I would like you to sit beside me while the young people dance."

The next thing Juliet knew, she was in the Duke of Deakin's arms and the ballroom was swirling around her in a kaleidoscope of colors and sounds.

Dark eyes engaged hers. "I believe we have met before, Miss Jones."

A faint color rose in her cheeks. "Yes, Your Grace."

"It was last week in Central Park, was it not?"

She stared at his chin. "It was."

"I hope you have suffered no ill effects from your ride," he said with what sounded like genuine concern.

"I am quite well. Thank you for inquiring, Your Grace."

"How is Hera?"

"The mare is fully recovered," she told him, surprised that he had remembered her horse's name.

"Do you still ride in the park every day?"

"Yes, Your Grace."

"Perhaps we will meet again one morning on the Sheep Meadow and ride together."

Juliet did not know what to say except, "Perhaps we will, Your Grace."

They danced around and around Mrs. Astor's ballroom, under the magnificent crystal chandelier and beneath the ornate ceiling that soared a full two stories into the air. Juliet could feel everyone's eyes following them. She reminded herself it was of no consequence. She was used to unwanted attention. She had been the subject of wagging tongues since the day of her birth.

She deliberately raised her chin an inch.

The Duke watched her, gave an approving nod of his head and suggested: "We have a great deal in common, Miss Jones."

"Do we, Your Grace?"

"I would speak plainly."

"I prefer you did."

"You are an heiress," he stated.

It was certainly no secret. "I am."

"You are also a beautiful woman. You must, on occasion, ask yourself if you are sought after for yourself or because you are wealthy and beautiful."

He thought her beautiful. It was most gratifying.

He went on. "Similarly I must ask myself if it is because I am the Duke of Deakin."

She did understand. For a moment, she felt a genuine sense of *simpatico* for the man. "I hadn't thought of it that way, but I do take your meaning, Your Grace."

The Duke of Deakin frowned at her. "I wish you would not call me that."

She seemed to have offended him; she could not imagine how. "Call you what, Your Grace?"

"Your Grace. My name is Lawrence Grenfell Wicke. My friends call me Lawrence or sometimes Deakin."

"Are we friends, sir?" she inquired innocently.

"We are not enemies, madam."

"But we are strangers."

"Not entirely," the Duke reminded her. He continued with no trace of irony in his voice: "I would like you to call me by my first name when we are alone."

Juliet glanced around the ballroom packed with hundreds of society's elite. "We are scarcely alone, Your—"

"Lawrence," he finished for her. "Do you enjoy dancing, Juliet?"

Her cheeks were quite pink by now. "It is pleasant enough."

"But you prefer horseback riding."

"I must confess I do."

"Dancing may be safer, however."

Was he teasing her? Dancing was most certainly *not* safer. Not if he was going to hold her in his arms and gaze at her with those dark, deliberate eyes that seemed to see right through her.

"I suppose it depends upon the dance and one's partner," she stammered.

"Do you not enjoy going out in Society?" the Duke asked, lifting one black eyebrow.

She made an attempt to be diplomatic. "I find it—taxing."

His forehead creased a moment perplexedly. "Taxing?"

She should not have told him the truth, Juliet realized belatedly. She should have lied. She should have given some pretty answer, or remarked upon the paintings adorning the walls of Mrs. Astor's ballroom, or made some innocuous reference to the weather. Now she would have to try to explain, and it was highly unlikely that a gentleman like the Duke of Deakin would understand.

She sighed and said with complete candor, "I am not a schoolgirl, sir."

"No, you are not."

"I am also not a debutante straight out of

Miss Porter's School For the Proper Deportment of Young Ladies."

The Duke appeared to be biting his lower lip. "Thank God for that."

She took a fortifying breath and ploughed ahead. "I am a woman."

He gave her his full attention. "Clearly, you are."

"I have many interests."

"Indeed."

"There is more to life than eating, drinking, and making merry," she declared feelingly.

"I have always thought so."

Juliet was warming to her subject now. "I have a great deal more on my mind than another tiresome social season of afternoon teas, dinner parties, and fancy-dress balls, watching a chukker or two of polo from one's carriage, the latest fashions straight from Paris, and the newest crop of empty-headed broad-shouldered dancing partners." She paused, studied the duke's very broad shoulders for a moment and then added: "Naturally, I did not mean anything personal by that last remark, sir."

"Naturally, I did not take it personally," he assured her, voice and manner dry.

"Just because a gentleman has very broad shoulders, it does not necessarily follow that he is also empty-headed." She seemed to be making matters worse, not better. Moistening her bottom lip, Juliet proceeded. "Anyway, to be frank, most gentlemen seem to find me . . . different."

"Different?"

I may as well make a clean breast of it, she thought. "All right, odd."

The duke held her firmly about the waist and turned her in a graceful circle. "Why is that?"

"I read books."

He put his head back and laughed. "Surely being well-read does not make one an oddity even in America?"

She sighed. "There is more."

"Do go on, madam. I wait with bated breath," he informed her.

"I breed horses."

"As do I," he said with enthusiasm.

Encouraged by his response, Juliet elaborated: "I am a farmer. I raise sheep and cattle. I take a keen interest in stocks and investments. I am fascinated by history, languages, mathematics, classical Greece, politics, gardening, and walking."

There was a flash of beautifully straight white teeth. "My dear lady, politics, gardening, and walking are considered the national pastimes of my country."

"You are most fortunate, then."

"I am, indeed," he murmured, drawing her closer to him and watching her with an intent expression on his face.

It made Juliet nervous.

Suddenly she came to her senses and realized that the music had stopped. Couples were separating and everyone seemed to be milling about the ballroom. "The waltz has ended."

"Then let us have another."

She swallowed hard. "It is highly irregular. People will talk."

"People will always talk." The Duke smiled but there was no humor in his expression. "Do you care?"

"Not for myself."

"For others, then?"

Juliet nodded. "For my great-aunt and my cousin. This is our first time at Mrs. Astor's ball."

The Duke of Deakin slowly lowered his arms and stepped back. "I know."

"You know?" She had an odd, sinking feeling in the pit of her stomach. "How do you know, sir?"

"I inquired."

She was curious. "Why?"

"I wanted to see you again."

She was puzzled. "But you did not know who I was."

"I made it my business to find out."

At first Juliet was flattered by his attentions, but then it dawned on her. "*You* were the reason we were invited here tonight, were you not?"

"It was long overdue."

She stiffened and said, tasting the words as if they were bitter pills, "Thank you, Your Grace, on behalf of my aunt and my cousin."

Black eyes narrowed dangerously. "But not for yourself."

"As I said earlier, Your Grace, there is more to life than balls."

"We agreed there is."

"I have my pride, sir."

"I can see that, madam."

"I do not care to be in any man's debt," she said, and now her voice was brisk.

"You are not in my debt, Miss Jones," he declared. "The invitation was of no consequence."

"Perhaps not to you."

"I did not mean to offend you."

"You have not offended me, Your Grace."

"Then I did not mean to wound your precious pride," he said, impatience creeping into his tone.

"My pride is, indeed, precious to me, sir," Juliet said, a shade haughtily. "And it has now been sorely wounded on two separate occasions."

"But—"

"Our waltz is at an end, and there are fifty eager young ladies of Society waiting for the chance to dance with a real duke. You mustn't disappoint them." To Juliet's dismay, her voice wavered slightly. "Even as we speak, a certain Miss Beckwith is making cow eyes at you. With your permission, Your Grace, I take my leave of you."

She had no intention of waiting for his permission, of course. Miss Juliet Jones spun on her satin heel and, with head held high and back ramrod straight, walked away from the devil Englishman.

He had made a grave tactical error.

He had come unprepared.

He had *not* adequately studied his opponent.

He did *not* know the enemy.

And he had forgotten the first rule of battle: never underestimate a woman!

He was, Lawrence Grenfell Wicke reflected as he stood alone on the dance floor, a disgrace to the uniform. Or, at the very least, a jackass.

The damage could, however, be contained if he acted swiftly and confidently. He must not give the lady time to think. It was clear that Miss Juliet Jones did entirely too much thinking as it was. He must appeal to her on another level altogether. He must appeal to her senses. He must sweep her off her feet, literally and figuratively.

He perused the ballroom. There seemed to be just one hitch. The lady had vanished.

As he went in pursuit of his quarry, Lawrence muttered dryly under his breath: "Wherefore art thou, Juliet?"

6

She had to escape.

She had to get away from the crowds and the stifling heat, the stares and the whispers, and especially the duke.

Juliet swept down the main hallway, her skirts a swirl of golden satin. She wanted to be alone, to be somewhere quiet, somewhere peaceful. She had no interest in joining the other ladies upstairs in the rooms set aside for their convenience: it would be all twitterings and fluttering fans and gossip about the food, the drink, the gentlemen downstairs, who was wearing what gowns and jewels and fripperies.

She wanted none of it.

Juliet approached a room at the end of the hall. There was a servant posted outside the door.

"Is the room occupied?" she inquired, snapping her golden fan shut.

"No, miss," came the reply in a clipped British accent.

"What room is this?"

"The small salon, miss."

"I would like to enter," she said with great dignity.

"Of course." The servant opened the ornately carved door and took a polite step back.

Juliet walked into the small salon, paused and turned. "What is your name, my good man?"

A respectful head was inclined ever so slightly. "Bunter, miss."

"I would prefer not to be disturbed, Bunter," she said to him.

"Your wish is my command," he responded.

"Thank you, Bunter."

"You are most welcome, Miss Jones." The door closed quietly behind him.

Juliet frowned. The man had known her name, but then the servants often did, even if their masters and mistresses did not—or pretended not. She shrugged her bare shoulders and thought no more about it.

The small salon was a pleasant surprise. The furniture was masculine, oversized, and overstuffed. She wondered if this had been the domain of the late Mr. Astor. There was a decided lack of the usual feminine bric-a-brac found in most grand houses. The pictures on the walls were of hunting dogs and sleek brown racing horses and rustic country scenes. The rugs were thick, the windows beveled, the fireplace neatly set. The room was neither too hot nor too cold.

Juliet immediately felt at home.

She sauntered across the salon and stood at the window, and gazed out at the January night. Against the faint light in the courtyard below she could see the soft falling snow. There were stark trees outlined in white and frost-covered ground, but not a single living creature within sight: not a stray dog or cat, not a lamplighter or coachman, not a man or woman hurrying home from the opera. For a moment, she could almost imagine she was all alone in the world.

Indeed, had she not *felt* all alone for most of her life?

Would she always be alone? Juliet wondered. Was that her destiny—to remain husbandless, childless, loveless? Or by some miracle would she someday meet a kindred spirit, the other half of herself, her soul mate?

He would have to be a very special man to see beyond the trappings of her wealth and her physical attributes to the real woman underneath.

Juliet clutched her hand to her chest. Sometimes there was such an ache inside of her, such a desperate need, a desire for something. . . .

She had no name for it. She only knew that it existed. She only recognized that she yearned for it.

She pressed her cheek against the windowpane. Her breath fogged up the square of glass, but the cold felt good against her overheated flesh.

Lately she had been waking in the dead of night in a fever: her bedclothes damp, disheveled, twisted around her legs, her hair wild, her skin covered with a sheen of perspiration, her heart pounding, her lips slightly swollen, her hands trembling, her breasts aching, her body aquiver.

Dreams.

He came to her in dreams. She never saw his face; it was always obscured in shadows. But he was tall, dark, and powerful. And dangerous.

It was the same dream every time: the figure of a mysterious male hovering over her, whispering sweetly erotic words to her, unremembered words later, and then leaning down to kiss her, to touch her, to caress her, to love her.

Juliet sighed, and raised a finger to draw upon the frosted windowpane.

Fairy tales.

A schoolgirl's fantasies.

The "stuff as dreams are made on."

The man in her dreams was merely a figment of her imagination. He was found only in the romantic stories that she allowed herself to read when no one else was about. It was foolish to think that somewhere there was a real man, a special man, meant for her and no one else.

Juliet lowered her hand, stepped away from the window and studied her creation. With the darkness of night as a backdrop, she had drawn what appeared to be a black heart.

Behind her the saloon door opened and closed. She knew who it was without turning around. The small hairs on the back of her neck stood straight on end. Her pulse began to race. The palms of her hands were damp; her legs a bit wobbly. The room was suddenly warm and a trifle stuffy. She spread the gold fan and wafted it back and forth in front of her face.

Still, she did not acknowledge his presence. She did not let him know that she knew he was standing there in the pale light cast by the fire and the single lamp lit in the corner. He was motionless. He was silent. Yet she swore she could hear his heart beating.

Why was she so conscious of this man? What did it mean? She had never been aware of a human being on an intuitive level before. It was almost as if she *felt* his presence.

It was not logical.

It made no sense.

She must be fanciful or overwrought or overexcited by the gala evening. After all, she had spent a grand total of perhaps an hour in Lawrence Grenfell Wicke's company: an embarrassing half hour in Central Park last week, and a few awkward minutes dancing with him earlier tonight.

Nevertheless, a small inner voice warned Juliet that she must watch her step. The duke was dangerous.

"Piffle," she muttered under her breath.

"Ahem—"

Juliet swiveled on her heel and said formally: "We meet again, Your Grace."

He emerged from the shadows and strolled across the room in her direction. "Apparently, Miss Jones, it is our destiny to run into each other at unexpected times and in unexpected places," he said in a deep, resonant baritone.

Polite conversation seemed in order. After all, she could observe the proprieties as well as the next person, Juliet told herself.

"The ballroom was warm," she remarked in a conversational tone, fanning herself.

"Excessively warm," he agreed.

"It was also noisy."

"It was deafening."

"And crowded," she added, after an interval.

The duke halted several feet from the fireplace, stopped and gazed into the glowing embers. "I find that I weary very quickly of crowds."

She paused for a fraction of a second before she admitted, "As do I."

He did not look up. "I especially felt the need to be alone."

"I understand," she said, and made her way toward the salon door.

"Please"—a hand was raised as if to stop her—"don't go."

Juliet hesitated.

He lifted his head and gave her a penetrating look. "I meant alone with you."

All of a sudden the room seemed smaller and more intimate than it had just moments before. "I don't think I should stay," she said, not knowing if her reluctance was the result of cowardice or a sense of propriety.

"I'm asking you to stay." His voice became softer. "Don't leave, Juliet."

Her heart gave a leap. Her brain warned her to flee while she still had the chance. Her feet would not obey. She found herself riveted to the spot where she stood. Even breathing became an effort; it was no longer involuntary. "I suppose I could remain for a few minutes," she said with an attempt at nonchalance.

"Thank you," he said politely.

"You are welcome," she returned in kind.

The duke leaned one arm on the mantelpiece and stared deep into the firelight. He was dressed in traditional formal evening attire: black tails and trousers, waistcoat, white shirt with a high, stiff collar, necktie, and white gloves.

He was quite dashing, Juliet realized. She supposed he would be dashing in whatever clothes he chose to wear since he was measurably tall, very broad through the shoulders and slender around the waist. His features were strong, bold, predominant, yet patrician. There was nothing halfhearted about him, nothing prettified, and certainly nothing with the slightest hint of the effeminate. She could not, for all the world, imagine him costumed as an Eastern pasha, or a foppish-looking Louis XV for a fancy dress ball.

He was definitely a man's man.

"I am not a glib man," he said at last.

Juliet was uncertain of what her response should be to his statement—so she made none.

The Duke's other hand, in the form of a gloved fist, was raised to his mouth. "Conversation, especially conversation with a lady, does not come easily to me. Perhaps because I spent so many years as a soldier."

"How many years?" she inquired.

"Too many," he said dismissively. He impatiently peeled off his gloves and tossed them onto the mantel. His head came round, and they found themselves staring at each other. "The very last thing I meant to do in having Mrs. Astor invite you to her annual ball was upset you."

She let a moment pass. "You had no way of knowing that it would."

"But it did."

She was truthful with him. "Yes."

His mouth turned up at the corners, but it was not a smile. "As you said, you have your pride."

Juliet tilted her head slightly to one side. "Don't we all have our pride?"

"I suppose we do," he said, laughing unexpectedly and uncomfortably.

Juliet found she was no longer angry with him. If, indeed, she ever had been. After all, the gentleman acted out of ignorance, not malice. And the incident in Central Park had been an accident. Nothing more. Nothing less. She was sure he had not intentionally grabbed her breast.

"I was reminded by someone only recently that 'pride goeth before destruction and a haughty spirit before a fall,' " she said with self-deprecation.

He arched a definitive black brow. "Who was quoting the Good Book to you?"

"Brambinger."

"Brambinger?"

She sighed. "My butler."

"Your butler?"

"Well, he began as my parents' butler long before I was born." She sighed again. "He practically raised me. He seems to think it gives him certain rights and privileges."

The duke nodded his head and confided, "Nanny lives upstairs at Grantley Manor. Even at eighty, she doesn't hesitate to order me about as if I were still a child."

Juliet's lips twitched in an effort not to smile.

He squared his jaw. "What is so amusing?"

"I was trying to picture you as a little boy."

"I was adorable." It was impossible to tell whether or not he spoke ironically.

"Were you?" she teased.

"Naturally."

"I would have thought incorrigible was more likely."

"Only on occasion, and I prefer to think of it as imaginative," he claimed, his eyes shimmering like black diamonds.

They fell silent. There was only the crackle of the fire at their backs, the snow against the windowpane, the distant sound of music coming from the ballroom.

He took a step or two closer to her. "As I started to say earlier, I am not a glib man. I didn't mean to wound your pride, or make you feel you are in my debt. I would like to apologize."

Juliet was speechless.

The duke went on. "After our initial encounter in Central Park I wanted to see you again. I did whatever was necessary to accomplish that. Frankly, I did not think beyond my own wishes and desires."

"Few of us do," she said nonjudgmentally. Then she felt it necessary to add: "We all have our faults. Many would say that mine is an excess of pride."

"Brambinger again?"

"At least he speaks out of affection."

"And the others?"

"They are not as likely to be motivated by either affection or kindness."

"They are simply jealous. Your pride is not a false pride. You, madam, are a remarkable woman," the duke declared. His shadow loomed large on the wall behind him.

"Thank you, sir."

"There is no need for you to thank me. It is the truth. When I looked up and saw you in the doorway of Mrs. Astor's ballroom I thought you were an angel." He shook his head in amazement. "A vision in gold."

Juliet held her breath.

"Then I understood."

She wet her lips, and waited.

"It was your way of saying to the world that everything your father had touched in his lifetime *had* turned to gold, including his own daughter."

"How did you guess?" she exclaimed, clapping her hands together.

The duke frowned. "Wasn't your father known in financial circles as King Midas?"

"Yes."

"Wasn't he famous for his flamboyance, his grand gestures?"

"Yes, indeed."

"Are you not your father's daughter?"

"I am."

"Well, then"—he shrugged—"it only made sense."

Juliet was impressed. "I doubt if one other person in the room understood."

"Perhaps not."

"Perhaps not."

She put her head back and laughed with sheer delight. "How wonderful, how splendid, how delicious to have someone to share my little *plaisanterie* with."

"I'm glad you approve," he said, using a tone of voice she had not heard before. He went on talking. "I also noticed that you were wearing no jewelry, not a single piece. I said to myself: no gemstone can compete with eyes that elusive shade of blue, no ruby with her lips, no pearl with her ivory complexion, no priceless diamond with her natural beauty. This is a woman who needs no jewels. This woman *is* the jewel."

The laughter died on Juliet's lips. She gulped. "Sir, you flatter me."

"Madam, I repeat: I speak only the truth." He came closer, stood directly in front of her and stared intently into her eyes. "Will you accept my apology?"

She held her breath. "Your apology?"

"For being a fool."

He was no fool. He was magnificent!

Juliet finally remembered to exhale. "Yes, Your Grace."

"Yes, Lawrence," he prompted.

"Yes, Lawrence." She was flustered. With a flick of her wrist, she opened her fan and began to brandish it vigorously in front of her.

"Are you warm?" he inquired.

"Perhaps a little."

"Shall I douse the fire?"

"That will not be necessary. I'm sure I will be fine in a minute." Juliet snapped her fan shut. "There, I am quite myself already."

Lawrence reached out and plucked the fan from her grasp. "This is lovely."

"Thank you."

He spread it apart and held it up in front of his eyes. "The material is remarkably transparent. Is the fan of French design?"

"Yes."

"From Worth's, no doubt."

She nodded.

"The embroidery along the edge is extraordinary."

"There is a wonderful woman from Marseilles who does the stitchery in pure gold thread. She is very talented. Her name is Colette," she said, rambling. Juliet was suddenly very conscious of the dark room, of the shadows, of the man, the scent of him, the presence of him, the fact that they were alone.

His voice was low and husky. "It never ceases to amaze me what a lady can do with a fan."

"It serves several purposes," she agreed.

He closed the fan with an expert hand. "It could serve several more I imagine you have never thought of, never even dreamt of, my dear Juliet."

"What could they possibly be?"

He drew the finely scalloped border of the fan along her cheek and she shivered. Then he traced the outline of her ear, the sensitive lobe, the delicate cord down the side of her neck, the tiny hollow at the base of her throat.

She shivered again. This time she felt it from the nape of her neck all the way down to her toes.

"Are you cold?" he asked with dark, watchful eyes.

"No, I'm not cold." She confessed, "It tickles."

Lawrence persisted. "Is there anything else?"

"I-I'm covered with gooseflesh."

For some reason that seemed to please him. He continued, tracing an imaginary line along the slender brows above her eyes, down the bridge of her nose, around the curve of her upper lip, framing the shape of her mouth, discovering the slight indentation in her chin.

"Your Grace—" came out in a breathless whisper.

"I do not answer to Your Grace."

"Lawrence—"

"Yes, Juliet?"

"What are you doing?"

"Illustrating the various uses for a lady's fan," he said as if it were a perfectly logical answer to her question.

Juliet knew she should stop whatever it was he was *really* doing. But she wasn't certain why, or how, or even if she wanted to stop him. She had never felt like this before. A whole new world of physical sensations was opening up to her. Her skin was aware of the slightest touch. Her heart was pounding in her ears. Her throat was aching. Her stomach was fluttering with butterflies.

She tried to take a deep breath and found she could not breathe. She tried to speak, but there were no words on her tongue. She tried to think and discovered not a single coherent thought remained in her head.

Juliet had always been in control. Until now.

Then Lawrence slowly dragged the tip of the fan along the swell of her breasts, and she was good and truly lost.

Beneath her corset, her nipples puckered up into two hard buds. There were urges she could not begin to explain or express. There was a melting between her legs that left her feeling dizzy and weak and wanting, and as he came closer she realized that his body was stirring.

Dear God, were these the urges and the stirrings she had wondered about for so very long? Perhaps, at last, she would have her answer.

"Something is stirring," she murmured as they stood together in the darkness.

His nostrils flared and he laughed thickly under his breath. It was a sensual sound that sent shivers spiraling down her spine. "Something?"

She furrowed her brow. "Someone?"

"Yes, someone," he confirmed, smiling down at her. "*I* am stirring. At least certain parts of me are."

She looked up at him and inquired innocently, "Why?"

He lost his smile. "My dear girl, do you really not understand?"

"Understand what?"

"About men and women."

Juliet blushed and informed him: "I have read many books."

"Books?"

"But they never explain in detail."

Lawrence seemed genuinely puzzled. "*What* do they never explain in detail?"

"About men and women," she repeated, embarrassed.

It finally dawned on him exactly what it was she was talking about. "No. I don't suppose they do. At least not the kind of books you would be reading."

Her eyes narrowed. "Are there books that explain?"

He cleared his throat. "They are not appropriate for young ladies."

"I was afraid you would say that."

"Experience is the best teacher, anyway."

She sighed. "Indeed."

"Would you like to know more about—men and women?"

"Of course, I would. I am always eager to learn." She put her chin up." And I have always been a very adept pupil."

"It is one subject, I believe, that is not covered in the schoolroom."

"That is a deficiency of the educational system."

Lawrence appeared at a temporary loss for words. "Have you no guardian, no older woman, no trusted friend to speak to you about these matters?"

She was blunt. "I have no one to speak to me about anything. Anything of consequence, that is."

"Your great-aunt, perhaps?"

"Aunt Effie is a dear, but she is seventy years old and has never been married. She is also a lady of extreme modesty."

He fell silent. Then suggested: "Perhaps a tutor."

"I have had many tutors. They did not teach me a single useful detail about men and women."

Lawrence cleared his throat. "It is usually a young lady's fiance or husband who instructs her in the finer points—"

She looked him square in the eyes. "I am twenty-four-years old. I have no fiance and no husband, and I am not likely to ever have either one."

"You are certain of that."

"I am."

He seemed to make up his mind about something. He reached out and put a hand against her lips. "Have you ever been kissed, Juliet?"

She swallowed hard. "Of course."

"How many gentlemen have you kissed?"

"A lady does not kiss and tell, sir."

She was not about to confess that her experience in that area was limited to a rather obnoxious little count who insisted upon slobbering over her hand last year in Paris, and an occasional buss on her cheek given by her cousin. Lawrence did not need to know these things.

He put the exquisite fan under her chin and lifted her face to his. "You are not a complete innocent, then?"

"No. I am not a complete innocent," she assured him in her best woman-of-the-world voice.

"Then I am going to kiss you."

Juliet went very still.

There was an odd little silence. Then he muttered: "I will probably regret this."

She felt a pang of disappointment. "Lawrence—"

"But I happen to want to kiss you very much."

She was hopeful. "You do?"

"Yes. I need to know."

She frowned thoughtfully. "What?"

His thumb was brushing back and forth along her bottom lip. It did very odd things to her sense of equilibrium. "I need to know the feel of you. The taste of you. I need to know if there is passion buried beneath that ladylike exterior you present to the world."

She could not think why.

"You are going to kiss me," she murmured as his mouth came down on hers.

Her books were no help at all. In fact, nothing she had ever read or done or thought or imagined or dreamed had prepared her for this man's kiss.

Juliet had not thought of herself as a girl for a very long time. But suddenly she was a girl again: shy, uncertain, unsure of herself, overwhelmed, in over her head, flooded from head to toe with unknown sensations.

Lawrence's mouth was both hard and soft, insistent and gently persuasive, demanding and giving. His lips were smooth. His chin was slightly abrasive from the merest hint of beard stubble. He tasted of expensive brandy, the winter wind, and the fire's smoky warmth. She had never tasted anything quite like it, even remotely like it.

There was something very intimate about a man's mouth being on hers that Juliet had not expected. She learned his unique taste. His unique feel. His unique scent. The breadth of his shoulders beneath her fingertips. The soft waves of his black hair as she ran her fingertips through the strands at the back of his neck.

His arms were around her. She was pressed firmly against his body. She had never been this close to a man before. She discovered he was tall and muscular and unyielding.

It was all new.

It was all exciting.

And extremely edifying.

Juliet drew a breath, and Lawrence groaned her name aloud. She became aware of something stirring against her skirts. It was hard. It was large. It seemed to be alive.

Dear God, it was Lawrence. Or, rather, it was that part of him between his legs.

Little wonder no one spoke of it.

Little wonder no one wrote about it.

It defied description. It was beyond words. She could not have explained it in a hundred years, in a thousand years.

Her heart was crashing like thunder during

a storm. Her blood was running hot and heavy in her veins. Her body was tingling in places she didn't know could even tingle. She was more alive than she had ever been in her entire twenty-four years.

Then Lawrence raised the silk fan between them and urged her lips apart. Juliet opened them slightly and the most amazing thing occurred: he thrust his tongue into her mouth. Suddenly she forgot to analyze. She forgot to wonder. She forgot to think. She forgot to breathe.

Passion.

This was passion.

7

THE lady had lied.

Lawrence knew it the instant his lips touched hers: this was her first kiss.

For Juliet Jones was no actress. There was no artifice to her. There were no female wiles, no pretense, no fakery. She was a complete innocent. He was willing to bet the farm on it. And, in his case, the farm was a full ten thousand acres.

Miss Jones was also correct in her self-assessment: she was no schoolgirl. She was no tittering debutante. She was twenty-four-years old. Those who were of a less generous nature might describe her as an old maid, as a spinster, as being a bit "long in the tooth" or "on the shelf."

Nothing could be farther from the truth.

Juliet claimed to be a woman—and Lawrence supposed that in many ways she was—but there was one very important way in which she was not. Indeed, she might as well be an innocent sixteen-year-old.

Come to think of it, he had met sixteen-year-olds with more experience.

That did not keep him from kissing her. Indeed, he could not seem to stop himself. Her
mouth was both sweet and tart, innocent and
alluring. Her lips were unschooled, yet enticing. She was inexperienced, but she was teach-
ing him the meaning of desire.

It was the damnedest thing.

Lawrence was suddenly not at all certain
which of them was the teacher and which the
pupil, who was the seducer and who was being
seduced.

Juliet tasted unlike any woman he had ever
kissed—and he had kissed his share of women
in the past twenty-nine years. There was something exotic, something indefinable, something
a little wild about her. He took another taste.
Then another and another and another. He
found himself wanting more of her, not less.

Juliet smelled unlike any woman he had ever
been close to: faintly of summer roses and
golden sunshine. It was the same scent that had
clung to the linen handkerchief she had given
him that day in the park.

It wasn't fancy perfume, or bottled rose water, or scented soap. It wasn't anything she had
purchased in a store and dabbed on her skin. It
was not strong, or cloying, or overpowering. It
did not hit a man square in the face. It was simply Juliet's natural smell.

He liked it.

It was subtle. It was understated. It would
linger in a gentleman's mind long after the lady,
herself, was gone.

It was also intoxicating.

Lawrence found himself going a little crazy. He wanted to nuzzle her neck, the vulnerable spot beneath her ear, the smooth expanse of her shoulder. He suddenly had an ungovernable urge to take her hair down, to comb his fingers through the golden mass, to bury his face in it. He needed to find out if she would smell of summer roses and golden sunshine everywhere.

In his mind he took it a step farther. He pulled at the bodice of her evening gown until it pooled around her waist, leaving her exposed. He rubbed his nose back and forth from one tender peak to the other, trying to determine if the aroma of roses and sunshine emanated from her breasts. He imagined stripping the clothes from her body and exploring every inch of her to find its secret source.

The feel of her was unlike any woman he had ever touched. Her skin was like silk. Her nape. Her ears. Her throat. Her shoulders. Her arms. Her hands. The inside of her wrists.

And what of that delicate flesh between her thighs? Those musky petals that opened, that blossomed, that dripped with precious dew when they were aroused? Would they be pure silk, as well?

Lawrence groaned silently. He had to stop. He was driving himself insane. He must remember this was supposed to be business, not pleasure.

He slipped the golden fan into his pocket and, not realizing that he spoke his thoughts aloud, complained: "Tell that to your mind and body."

Juliet raised her head and gazed at him with bewilderment. "I beg your pardon, sir."

He recovered admirably, he thought, and tapped the tip of his finger against her lower lip. "Juliet, you have not been honest with me."

Her eyes were glazed over with passion. "Honest with you?"

"About your dealings with men."

Her eyes began to clear. "Are you suggesting, sir, that I lied."

"I'm not suggesting anything of the sort. I'm telling you."

She did not appear in the least repentant. "All right, I lied."

"Why?"

"I thought you would change your mind and refuse to kiss me if you knew." She quickly added: "Several men have tried to take advantage. Naturally, I refused their advances."

"Then why did you allow me to kiss you?"

"It was time."

His lips thinned. "Meaning that *I* happened to be *convenient*, madam?"

"Please don't be angry with me, Lawrence. It was the right time and the right place *and* the right man. There has to be a first time for all of us, doesn't there?"

"I suppose so," he said, somewhat mollified.

She inquired self-consciously: "How did you know it was my first kiss?"

"I simply knew."

"That is no answer."

"A man knows these things."

"That is no answer, either." Juliet put her

head back and looked at him. "My lack of experience manifested itself in some way that you detected."

"I couldn't have put it better myself," he said drolly.

"I did it wrong."

"There is no wrong way to kiss."

"I did it poorly."

"Let us say that you revealed your inexperience through your surprise."

"My surprise?"

He was blunt. "You had obviously never had a man hold you tightly in his arms, kiss you, thrust his tongue into your mouth, and press his arousal against your skirts."

The clear pallor of her face flooded with bright red. "I betrayed myself, didn't I?"

"You did."

She sighed dejectedly. "I'm afraid that I am not much of an actress."

"My dear lady, that is to your credit. Some women play the coquette, the flirt, the world-weary lover, the artful tease to perfection. And some men like it. I am not one of them. I like a woman to be what she is."

"That is all well and good for you to say, sir. You already know how to kiss." Her brow creased. "Although I do not believe for a moment that males are born instinctively knowing how."

"Kissing is a skill that one learns, that one perfects through practice."

She listened attentively and then asked him: "*When* does a man learn to kiss?"

"It is different for each of us."

"That is uninformative."

"Nevertheless, it is true."

"Then perhaps I should rephrase my question. *How* does a man learn to kiss?"

Lawrence did not care for the direction their conversation was taking. "I do not believe it is my place to explain these things to you."

She blinked. "Why not?"

"You are a lady."

"And you are a gentleman." She gave him a quick, penetrating look. "What does that signify?"

"You're an innocent."

"That isn't my fault."

"I wasn't placing the blame on you."

Juliet was visibly disappointed. "But if you do not answer my questions, who will?"

"I seem to have forgotten the question," Lawrence confessed. He hoped she had would drop the subject. There something to be said for a woman *without* an inquiring mind.

"I asked how a man learns to kiss."

"I can only speak from personal experience."

"Naturally."

"It may not be the same for every man."

"That only makes sense."

"There is certainly no universal answer."

Juliet tapped her satin slipper with impatience. "You are stalling."

"You are stubborn."

"We will not leave this room, sir," she boldly announced, "until I have my satisfaction."

Lawrence couldn't help himself. He grinned.

It was not a hint of a grin. It was not a subtle grin. But a wide grin from ear to ear.

Juliet jabbed a finger into his chest. "There! You see. Even a seemingly innocent remark means something to you that I do not understand. Men have this secret language, this private code that they do not wish to share with women. What are you afraid of?"

"It's not that we are afraid, Juliet. It's simply that we are trying to protect you."

"Protect us?" she shot back. "That is the whole problem. Men are always trying to protect women whether they want to be or not. It is belittling. It is patronizing. It is an insult to our intelligence."

He put a stop to her ranting and raving the only way he knew how. He leaned over and covered her mouth with his. She fought him for a second, then sighed and gave into the pure pleasure of their kiss.

It was a kiss that had started with one purpose in mind: to shut Juliet up. It soon had another altogether. It soon became a matter of desire.

He wanted her.

In fact, Lawrence couldn't remember the last time he had wanted a woman as much as he wanted Juliet Jones. He would like to have done far more than thrust his tongue into her mouth. He would like to have buried himself deep inside her body, to ease his hunger by taking her again and again until his appetite had been satisfied.

We will not leave this room, sir, until I have my satisfaction.

He smiled even as he kissed her. She was right. There was a kind of secret language, a private code among men when it came to sex. The dividing line was between women and ladies. A man had sex with one and married the other. Although there were some lucky men, he supposed, who had both with the same lady. Those ladies were few and far between.

Juliet was one of those ladies.

There was passion inside her. He could feel it, taste it, sense it, almost on a subconscious level. With the right man, with the right teacher, she could become a wonderful, responsive lover.

Lawrence kissed her again, and she kissed him back without reservation. She was like the winter night: she was all shadows and smoke, gold and roses, intelligence and sensuality. By the blessed saints, she was a consort fit for a king.

Or a duke.

"Lawrence—"

Reluctantly he lifted his head and dragged his mouth from hers. "Yes, Juliet—"

"I want to know something else."

"What?"

"How did you learn to kiss so beautifully."

"Do you think I kiss beautifully?"

She nodded. "Many women have surely told you so."

He gave a negative grunt. "I don't think anyone has ever told me so before."

She did not believe him. "You jest."

"I do not jest."

She eyed him thoughtfully, and after a brief pause said: "You haven't answered my question."

His mouth twisted into a wry smile. "You are a persistent female."

Her laugh was soft. "You noticed."

Noticed? She was like a pedigree dog with a bone clutched between its teeth. She wasn't about to let her go of her prize. He finally gave in and related an abbreviated version of the story. "I was twelve."

"Twelve-years old?"

He nodded. "Sometimes it seems like a lifetime ago," he murmured.

Juliet appeared intrigued. "Who was she?"

"The daughter of our family cook."

She seemed to be savoring every juicy detail. "How old was the daughter of your family cook?"

"Fifteen."

"Do you remember her name?"

"Elise."

"And what did Elise do?"

"She took me out behind the summer kitchen one afternoon and taught me everything she knew." Which had been a considerable amount, if his memory had not failed him.

"How do you suppose Elise learned to kiss?" Juliet's voice trailed off into nostalgic silence.

"The son of the coachman had taken her behind the dairy shed when she was fourteen. I seem to recall that he had taught her a number of things."

"A number of things?"

The lady didn't miss a trick.

He cleared his throat. "There is more than one way to kiss, to touch, to caress, to make love."

"I see."

He doubted very much if she did.

Juliet planted herself in front of him, closed her eyes and lifted her face. "Teach me."

"Now?"

"Yes. Please, sir."

"I will not kiss you at all if you persist in calling me sir," he grumbled.

"Please, Lawrence."

"You must open your eyes."

Her eyes flew open. "Am I supposed to keep them open?"

"Yes."

"All the while we kiss?"

"All the while we kiss."

"Will yours be open, as well?"

"Naturally. The first rule of kissing is to know exactly *who* you are kissing."

"I assumed that would be apparent."

"Not necessarily. You must go into kissing as you would anything: with your eyes wide open."

"Ah, I see. Kissing, in this case, is a metaphor for life. I did not expect a lecture along with your demonstration," she said dryly.

He took a stern tone with her. Her attitude was entirely too flippant. "You must not lie to yourself, Juliet. This is not make-believe. This is real. I am a real man, and you are a real woman."

"And presumably it will be a real kiss . . . if we ever get around to it."

Lawrence brought his face down to hers. He stopped no more than an inch away. "Can you feel my breath on your lips?"

"Like a gentle breeze. And I can see the smallest hairs on your chin," she said, "where the stubble of your black beard is growing."

"You are not to look at my chin. You are to look into my eyes," he instructed. "I can see a rainbow of color in yours: blue, lavender, yellow, green."

"And there appears to be a speck of something in your left eye. Ah, I see now that it is an eyelash."

"Juliet, this is serious business."

"I apologize, sir."

"Now, try again. Inhale. We can smell each other. We can hear each other breathing. We can sense our bodies are nearly touching. The anticipation builds."

She reached out and placed her hand on his jacket above the spot where his heart was. "Lawrence, I feel the rhythm of your heart. I can count the beats."

"Place your cheek on my chest."

She did as she was told. "I can hear it!" she exclaimed. "Thump. Thump, thump. It is so loud. So strong. So alive."

"Now it is my turn.

He bent over and placed his ear against her bare skin just above the swell of her breasts.

She gasped and held her breath. "I can feel the rhythm of your life. Your heart is racing like a frightened bird because no one has ever done to you what I am. It frightens you and it excites you."

Her eyes turned midnight blue. "You know entirely too much about women."

"There isn't a man alive who knows too much about women," he informed her. "And I will never know enough about you." He was intense. "Now when we kiss, it will be different. We know each other in a way we did not even a minute ago."

He had had enough talk to last him a lifetime, Lawrence realized. He had always been a man of action, not words.

He swooped down and took her lips. He sank his tongue into her sweet mouth. It became entangled with Juliet's and he heard himself groan. Her hands clasped his arms, her fingers dug into his sleeve.

Passion.

This was passion.

It was some time before Juliet drew back from him and said breathlessly, "Lawrence, we must stop. Someone may walk in on us."

"No one will interrupt us."

"How can you be so certain?"

He tightened his grip on her waist. "Bunter is standing guard."

"Bunter?"

"The man outside the door to this room."

"How do you know Bunter?"

"He is my man."

She seemed to consider the implications of that fact. "Then we must stop because no one will walk in on us."

She was right. They were being rash. Foolhardy. Indiscreet. He had gotten carried away with the pleasure of kissing Juliet, and forgotten it was business: pure and simple.

The lady stepped back and tidied herself. Yet there was no mistaking the slightly swollen appearance of her lips: she had been good and truly kissed. There was no disguising the look in her eyes. There was no masking the fact that someone had been making love to her.

Lawrence discovered that he liked the way she looked after his kisses.

He wondered how she would appear after he had truly and completely made love to her, after he had introduced her to all the wonderful things that could take place between a man and a woman. Perhaps business need not be to the total exclusion of pleasure. . . .

Miss Juliet Jones was suddenly all business. "This will not occur again, of course," she stated, picking up her gloves and marching toward the door of the small salon. "This must be the end of it. I wish you good night and goodbye, sir. I rejoin my aunt and my cousin."

"Au revoir, madam," he murmured as she swept from the room.

The end? If his dear Juliet only knew.

This was just the beginning.

8

"I DO NOT normally interfere in your dealings, business or otherwise, my dear, as you know," Euphemia Jones announced in preamble.

Juliet looked up from her desk in the "sun room," as the family and staff referred to the morning room. It was appropriately named since it faced due east toward the rising sun, and was the brightest and cheeriest room in the entire house during the winter months. Her great-aunt was seated at a small eighteenth-century English gaming table, a deck of cards in her hand. Solitaire was, perhaps, Euphemia Jones's single vice.

She let a moment pass. "But—?"

"But do you think it is wise to make a settlement on David"—Euphemia turned over another card and studied it intently for a moment—"when he is so young."

Juliet twisted the fountain pen in her hand. "I am twenty-four. David is twenty-two."

"Chronological age does not always tell the whole story," said Euphemia.

Aunt Effie was right, of course. Juliet knew

that. She was mature beyond her years in many ways, and David was young for his in some.

She put the pen down and rested her hands on her chin. "He is my cousin."

"A very distant cousin."

"He is my only living relation, other than yourself," she pointed out.

"That is true." Sapphire-blue eyes looked up from the cards. "I realize how important family is to you, Juliet. It is important to me, as well."

Juliet smiled at the dear woman who had been with her since she was old enough to remember. "Thank goodness, we have always had each other."

"Yes, thank goodness." Euphemia returned to her game and placed a red queen on a black king. "It is not that I begrudge David the money."

"I know."

"I have enough to last me several lifetimes, thanks to my dear nephew, your father."

Indeed, her great-aunt was wearing ample evidence of his generosity this morning: a pair of emerald earrings, an emerald brooch and a matching emerald and diamond ring. Her father's gifts were among Aunt Effie's favorite pieces of jewelry.

"Papa wanted you to be independent."

"And I am. Financially."

"That is what I want for David," Juliet explained. "I want him to have his own money and the sense of independence that goes with it. I think it is especially important for a gentleman and his manly pride."

Euphemia lifted her head and said, "We both know it is just as important for a lady and her womanly pride."

"That is true."

"I do not mean to be an old busybody. I am aware that you are currently giving David a generous monthly allowance."

"Like my banker and lawyer, you agreed with my decision to do so when we were all satisfied that his credentials were in order."

"I still agree that it is only right and just. A young man, as you have pointed out, must have his own money to spend without having to ask for every penny."

"Especially if that young man has spent his entire life without money," Juliet sighed. "Poor David."

"That is partly why I think you should reconsider making a settlement at this time. Poor David has never had much money to handle. A sum of the magnitude which you will undoubtedly give him may overwhelm the boy."

"Possibly. That is why I have decided upon a trust fund. He may spend the yearly interest as he sees fit, but he may not touch the principal."

Of course, even the interest was a sizable fortune, but Juliet saw no need to mention that fact.

"I should have known you would take care of things properly. You always do. You are so very clever, my dear. I could never be half as clever as you," claimed Euphemia.

"You do not fool me for one minute, Aunt. You are far more clever than you let on," she said, pushing aside the stack of morning news-papers.

Eyes that had diminished only slightly with age peered at her over the lenses of her spectacles. "Me, my dear? Why I am not in the least clever."

Juliet chose not to argue the point. She always lost that particular argument, anyway. She looked at the older woman. "You do not like David, do you, Aunt Effie?"

Euphemia, speaking gently, contradicted her by saying: "It is not exactly that I do not like him."

Juliet sat and waited, her business correspondence spread out in front of her. Business was dealt with at the desk in the "sun room," since it was the "first order of business" after a light breakfast and an early morning ride. Social correspondence was tackled at the Louis XIV desk in the library after tea. Business before pleasure. Juliet had learned that valuable lesson from her father.

"What is it, then?" she probed.

Euphemia Jones laid the deck of cards down on the antique table and gazed out the window into the snow-covered garden beyond. The sun sparkled on the frosted limbs of the trees and bushes, creating a winter wonderland. "I suppose it is because David seems to me like the kind of man who would cheat at solitaire."

Cheat at solitaire? A harmless card game that one played alone? Perhaps this was not one of Aunt Effie's lucid mornings, after all.

"The truth is," Euphemia whispered regretfully, "I do not trust David."

Juliet was astounded. "Has he ever done anything untrustworthy to your knowledge?"

"No."

"Then why do you feel that way?"

"I'm not sure I can explain it. There may not be a logical explanation. It is simply that David reminds me of a young man I once knew. A beau of mine."

"You've never mentioned this to me before."

Euphemia looked at her blankly. "Haven't I?"

Juliet shook her head. "No."

"His name was William," she began. "He was very young and very good-looking. But then I was very young and very pretty at the time. We made quite a handsome couple. Everyone said so." A smile spread across the wrinkled face that echoed still of that prettiness. "Of course, I had no money in those days. Neither did William. It didn't matter to me. Apparently it did to him. I thought we were to be married. . . ."

The breath caught in Juliet's lungs. She had often wondered why Great-Aunt Effie had remained a spinster. "What happened?"

"William married another. A girl with money and buckteeth and a sour disposition. I was terribly hurt. To add insult to injury, he came to see me three months after his wedding and confessed he still loved me. He asked if we could see each other without his wife's knowledge."

The heat rose in Juliet's face. "You mean that William wanted you to be his—"

"Yes. He wanted me to be his mistress." A

bright red dot appeared in the center of each of Euphemia Jones's already pink cheeks. "I couldn't believe my ears. He was not at all the man I had thought he was. He was untrustworthy. He was a cheat and a liar, a bounder and a cad."

"You were well rid of him, Aunt."

"Indeed, I was." Yet the regret on Euphemia's features was still apparent, even after fifty years. "Anyway, David reminds me of William."

Juliet sighed and said diplomatically: "Then your distrust is based on intuition?"

"Yes. Intuition. That is it."

There was not a single fact to support the older woman's feelings. Sometimes Aunt Effie got a bit confused. This seemed to be one of those times. Perhaps, without even realizing it, she was jealous now that she had to share Juliet's affections with another family member. It had been the two of them for so long.

"I promise I will take it into account, Aunt Effie. Will that make you feel better?"

"It will." The woman picked up the cards again and resumed her game. "Is there anything else you believe we should discuss, Juliet?"

She drew a blank. "I don't think so."

Whenever Aunt Effie used a particular tone of voice—and she was using it now—it meant that she already knew, usually from one of the servants or the women she socialized with once a week for tea and gossip, whatever news she was digging for.

Juliet picked up her pen, added up a row of figures and then put her pen down again. Of course, the incident in Central Park. "I have been meaning to tell you, Great-Aunt. It simply slipped my mind."

"Did it?"

"It was not important, truly."

"Was it not?"

"No. The horse was frightened, but I had the situation under control. The Duke of Deakin—although at the time, of course, I didn't realize that he was the Duke of Deakin—took it into his head I needed rescuing."

"Did he?"

"Yes. The man swept me right off the back of my mare. I was frankly aghast. Not to mention embarrassed. I would have told you sooner, but I saw no reason to worry you. The whole affair amounted to nothing in the end."

Euphemia Jones continued to stare at her.

Juliet went on nervously. "No one was hurt. Hera had a minor scratch on her back, but that was seen to immediately. The greatest injury, if you must know, was to my dignity."

"My dear Juliet," Euphemia said finally, "I have no idea what you're talking about."

That gave her pause. "Weren't you referring to the accident in Central Park the week before last?"

"No."

"Oh, I see."

"I was referring to the shortage of rum cakes."

Juliet's lips were numb. "Rum cakes?"

"Yes, we have run out of them the past two days at teatime. I have spoken to the cook, but she insists she is baking the same number that she always has. She claims we are simply eating more of them." A gray brow was arched interestingly. "But since you have brought up the Duke of Deakin, I would much prefer talking about him."

"I would prefer to discuss rum cakes."

"About the duke—"

"There is nothing to say."

"Pah! Everyone noticed you were the first lady he asked to waltz with at Mrs. Astor's ball. Indeed, it was obvious you were the only lady he was interested in waltzing with."

"You are a bit prejudiced."

"I have eyes to see. And I know what I saw. The gentleman is smitten with you."

"Aunt Effie! You must not say such things." Juliet was horrified. "Someone may hear you."

Euphemia chose to ignore her. "Now *that* is what I call a real man."

"What is?"

"The Duke of Deakin, of course. I believe I mentioned at the time we received Mrs. Astor's invitation you might well meet a tall, dark, and handsome stranger who would sweep you off your feet." She chewed her lip and frowned. "Of course, at the time, I had not no idea that he had already done so."

"The duke and I danced once that night."

"Did he ask you to dance a second time?"

"Well—"

Euphemia slapped a beringed hand down on

the table. "I knew it! He did ask you a second time. Why did you refuse him?"

Juliet let out a long sigh. She may as well confess. Aunt Effie always managed to get it out of her way, anyway. "I thought people would talk."

"People will always talk."

"That's what Lawrence said."

"Lawrence?"

Juliet felt her face grow hot. "His Grace."

"Lawrence?" she twittered. "It is going even better than *I* could have hoped for."

Juliet's nose went a notch higher in the air. "I am sure I have no idea what you are talking about."

"You have met the duke on only two occasions and already he is insisting that you call him by his given name. It is most encouraging. It is highly encouraging. On top of that, he left his calling card while you were out fussing at the bank the other afternoon."

"I was not fussing at the bank; I was conducting important business. And the duke's call was purely a formality."

"Was it?"

"Yes."

"He also left a box with your gold fan inside. One wonders, of course, how he came by your gold fan."

"I must have dropped it at Mrs. Astor's ball and he retrieved it for me."

"Out of hundreds of fans at Caroline Astor's that evening, it is amazing—one might even say incredulous—that the Duke of Deakin recognized yours."

"It is nothing short of a miracle," she said blithely, picking up a copy of the *Times*.

Euphemia tapped her fingertips against the jack of diamonds. "My dear Juliet, you do not want to end up an old maid."

"Yes, I do."

"No, you do not. I speak from personal experience."

She shot a sideways glance at her great-aunt. "Has it been that difficult?"

"It has occasionally been awkward and frequently lonely."

Juliet bit her bottom lip. "Aunt Effie—"

"It is all right, my dearest. As fate would have it, you became the granddaughter I never had." Euphemia looked at her, then looked straight through her. "I know what you are afraid of."

There was a count of ten. "What?"

"You're afraid that you will be married for your money."

"It seems like a reasonable fear to me."

"And if not your money, then your beauty. The duke must have similar fears."

She scowled. "That he will be married for his beauty?"

"Do not pretend to be dense. You know what I mean. The gentleman must constantly wonder if he will be married for his title. You'd be surprised what some women are willing to do to become a duchess."

"What?"

"Suffice it to say, anything and everything."

Her emerald ring flashed in the sunlight. "That is why it's so perfect."

"What's so perfect?"

"A match between you and the Duke of Deakin." Euphemia gave a girlish sigh. "He is a handsome devil."

"He is a devil," Juliet muttered under her breath. "That is quite enough about the duke. I want no more matchmaking from you, Aunt. Now I must get these ledgers finished. I'm going shopping after lunch, as you may recall."

The older woman made a face. "If you call *that* shopping. I presume David is going along."

"Yes. He is. I'll go my way while he has an appointment at his tailor's."

"More clothes for the boy? You do spoil him."

"I can afford to spoil him." She picked up another sheet of figures and her pen. "You are welcome to join us, of course."

"Are you going to the Ladies Mile of shops on Broadway?"

"Not this afternoon."

"Then I will forego the pleasure, thank you all the same. I have more important things to do." With that, Euphemia shuffled the deck of cards and began another game of solitaire.

"Miss Jones, what a pleasure to see you again."

Juliet turned on the street outside the art gallery. "Your Grace, what a surprise. I believe you said it is our destiny to run into each other at unexpected times and in unexpected places. Apparently you are correct."

"I attempt to be incorrect as little as possible."

"A worthy goal, I'm sure."

"I called upon you a few days ago to return a certain item you had left in my possession."

She put her nose up a fraction. "Thank you for returning my fan."

"I was sorry you were not at home."

"I was out. I am frequently out. I am a very busy woman."

"Apparently so."

"You seem to have found me at last."

"I stopped to pay your great-aunt a social call this afternoon and one thing led to another and she mentioned that you had gone shopping."

After a moment, Juliet said: "She apparently also mentioned *where* I had gone shopping?"

"She may have." The man didn't even bother to pretend otherwise. Indeed, he stood there and smiled at her on a public street. "Have you been buying yourself some pretty ribbons? A pair of gloves? Perhaps a book? I know how fond you are of reading."

He was quite wicked, reminding her of what she had said to him that night in Mrs. Astor's small salon. Indeed, she blushed to think of it.

"Actually," she said with relish, "I have just purchased a Bronzino."

The Duke's expression was blank. "Is that some new kind of ladies' bonnet?"

Juliet laughed out loud. She couldn't help herself. Public street or not, the gentleman was really too amusing. "It is a painting."

"Ah, *that* Bronzino."

"Yes, *that* Bronzino." Of course, she knew he was totally ignorant of what she was talking about.

Lawrence tilted his head slightly to one side. "Would that be the Italian painter Agnolo Bronzino?"

Juliet's mouth fell open.

He continued. "I believe Bronzino is known for his elegant portraits of sixteenth-century Florentine society, is he not?"

She closed her mouth and nodded.

With a certain savoir faire, Lawrence inquired: "What were you fortunate enough to acquire? Surely not his well-known allegory *Venus, Cupid, Folly and Time*?"

She was stunned. "I have just purchased *Eleanor of Toledo and Her Son*."

"Ah, then you are lucky, indeed. A magnificent example of the High Tuscan mannerist style, wouldn't you agree?"

She could not seem to move her lips.

"I would truly enjoy seeing your painting, Miss Jones. May I have the pleasure of calling upon you soon and finding you at home?"

She was dumbfounded. "Yes."

"When will the painting be delivered?"

"Tomorrow afternoon."

"Where have you decided to display it?"

Juliet was still not in full possession of her composure. "There is a perfect spot above—"

"—the Italian marble table in the front hall."

"How did you guess?"

Lawrence grinned at her. "Because that is precisely where I would have put it."

"Sir, you amaze me."

"Madam, then it is mutual. You have amazed me from the first moment I set eyes on you."

"It is highly inappropriate for us to be discussing art, let alone speaking of personal matters while we are standing on a city street," she said conscientiously.

"You have left me little choice, Juliet."

"You may call on me, Your Grace." He gave her a look of warning. She lowered her voice and said: "You may call on me, Lawrence."

"I trust you will be home this time."

"I will be home."

He gave a polite bow of his dark head. "I look forward to our next meeting. Shall we say tomorrow?"

"Tomorrow will not be convenient. We will be seeing my cousin off on a trip."

"Then the day after tomorrow?"

"That will do."

The duke looked around the icy and snowy street. "Surely, madam, you are not alone."

"Of course, not. Cousin David is directly across the street at his tailor's."

"And your carriage?"

"It is there, as well," she said, indicating where the coachman was waiting.

His gaze began to make her exceedingly uncomfortable. "May I escort you to your carriage? It is slippery after the snow we had last evening."

"Thank you for your offer, but I can manage on my own." She was not interested in touching Lawrence, or in having Lawrence touch her. Not in public. Not in private. "Ah, there is David now," she announced as a familiar blond head emerged from the tailor's shop.

Lawrence tipped his hat. "Until the day after tomorrow, then, Miss Jones."

"Your Grace."

The street and sidewalks were particularly crowded. Juliet looked both ways and was about to step off the curb when a horse and buggy came briskly around the corner. She took a step back to wait until they had passed.

That's when it happened.

She felt the jostle of bodies behind her. They seemed to be pressing closer and closer. It was almost claustrophobic. Then a heavy hand caught her squarely between the shoulders blades and shoved.

Juliet tried to retain her balance. She put out a hand to stop herself from falling, but she grabbed only air. Then she slipped on the ice and went flying directly into the path of the on-coming horse and buggy.

In that split second Juliet Jones realized it had been no accident. Someone had deliberately pushed her. Her blood ran cold. She opened her mouth and was surprised to hear herself call out for help. "Lawrence!"

9

FOREWARNED.

It wasn't the first time it had happened to him. It wasn't the last time it would stand him in good stead.

In that split second before he heard Juliet call out his name, Lawrence experienced a heightened sense of awareness. If was as if he could see more clearly, hear more acutely, feel more quickly, even smell odors he would normally not smell.

There was an odd pricking at the back of his neck, as well, like a bee sting. Only, of course, there were no bees in New York City in the middle of January. Nevertheless, he reached up and rubbed his skin.

Nothing.

Then, above the noise and the hustle and bustle of the busy street, he clearly heard his name. "Lawrence!"

He spun around.

At a glance he took it all in: the fast-approaching horse and buggy, the mass of people, the savage face of a stranger in the crowd, Juliet losing her balance, Juliet trying desperately not to slip on the icy sidewalk and plunge headfirst into the street, and young David Thoreau Jones attempting to come to his cousin's rescue.

It was a bad dream.

It was a nightmare.

Somewhere in the throng, a woman screamed. A man called out a frantic warning. The driver of the buggy shouted to his horse and yanked back on the reins, but Lawrence could see it would be to no avail.

It would be too late.

There was only one thing to do. Although his reflexes were not as sharply honed as they had once been when he had commanded Her Majesty's troops, Lawrence lunged at Juliet, grabbed her about the waist and snatched her from harm's way.

Just in the nick of time.

The horse and buggy came to a dead stop five feet *beyond* where her body would have landed in the snow-covered street.

Chest heaving from the exertion, adrenaline still pumping through his veins like a powerful drug, Lawrence swept Juliet off her feet and held her to him. His arms were locked around her like a vise. His skin was covered with sweat, despite the chill of the winter day. His heart was pounding like a brass drum. His arms and legs were shaking. His breath was coming hard and fast.

He could feel her heart racing even faster than his. Her breath was coming in great gulps, as if her lungs were starved for oxygen. Lawrence knew if he let her go, she would crumple into a heap right there on the sidewalk.

David Jones pushed his way through the crowd toward them. "Get back, all of you. Let me through. Get back, I say."

A policeman appeared and began to disperse the curiosity seekers. "Move along, folks. The excitement's over now. Move along. All but you," he barked, pointing to the driver.

"T'weren't my fault," the man protested. "Anybody here can tell ye that. The lady just ran in front of my buggy. I tried to stop, but there she was before you could say Jack Frost."

Lawrence finally spoke. It was an edict. "The lady did not run in front of your buggy."

All heads turned in his direction.

"Who might you be, sir?" inquired the uniformed policeman.

"He is Lawrence Grenfell Wicke, the Duke of Deakin," came a familiar voice.

All heads turned again at the approach of the exquisitely dressed gentleman. The officer was taken aback, having to deal with so many "swells" at once. It was obviously a new experience for him. "And just who are you, governor?"

"I am Miles St. Aldford," he replied, tapping his gold-tipped walking stick on the snowy pavement. "The Marquess of Cork."

"And I am David Thoreau Jones, the lady's cousin," David announced with a superior air.

"Pray tell, then, what do your lordships know about this situation?"

Lawrence answered for everyone. "The young

lady was jostled by the crowd and deliberately—"

Juliet finally found her voice. "I was accidentally pushed into the path of this man's horse and buggy." She smiled weakly at the nervous driver. "It wasn't your fault. You weren't to blame. It was an accident. I slipped on the ice and I couldn't stop my fall."

"You all right, then, miss?" he inquired, obviously greatly relieved on both of their behalfs.

"I've had quite a fright, but I will be all right as soon as I catch my breath."

"I'll see to it that my cousin is safely escorted home," spoke up David. "Our carriage is waiting directly across the way in front of the tailor's."

"Don't think we should take any chances, sir. It might be better if you were to direct the coachman to bring the carriage around to this side of the street," suggested the policeman.

"I will do my bit by keeping the crowd at bay," volunteered Miles as he took up his post and brandished his walking stick in front of him like a rapier.

Lawrence found himself alone with Juliet for a moment.

She squirmed in his arms. "You may release me now, Your Grace."

He looked at her with a bemused smile and repeated in a mocking tone, "Your Grace?"

"We are in public," she reminded him.

"So we are." Then Lawrence inquired out of genuine concern for her well-being, "Do you think you will be able to stand on your own, Juliet?"

"There is only one way to find out." She glanced up and was aware for the first time of the stragglers from the crowd staring at them. "Lawrence, there are people gaping at us."

"People have been gaping at us, my dear, for the past fifteen minutes."

She buried her face in his coat for a moment and mumbled: "It is like a circus."

"Yes."

"It is undignified."

"Yes."

"It is embarrassing."

"Yes, but it is better than being dead."

She paled. "You saved me again."

"I'm afraid so."

"You put your own life in jeopardy."

"I could scarcely allow you to be crushed beneath the wheels of a buggy."

"But you could have been injured, or maimed for life, or even mortally wounded because of me," she declared with a decided flair for the dramatic. Her eyes darkened to midnight blue. "I am bad luck."

"You do seem a bit accident prone, my dear."

"Please put me down now," she commanded. Then she added, once she was balanced on her own two feet again: "You must stop coming to my rescue. It isn't safe for you."

"I'll take my chances."

"People will talk."

Lawrence suddenly felt like laughing hysterically. In one breath, the lady was worried for his life and in the next she was concerned with gossip. It was insane.

Instead, he shrugged his shoulders and said philosophically, "People will talk, anyway."

"You keep telling me that."

"I do, don't I?"

She nodded her head. "But surely they don't always have to talk about us."

"True."

She heaved a great sigh. "I suppose it will be all over New York by tomorrow."

"It will probably in the newspapers, as well."

Juliet groaned. "Oh, no."

"Oh, yes."

"What shall we do?"

"What people like you and I have always done in the face of adversity: be strong, hold our heads high, and ignore the bloody gossips."

"You're right, of course. You're nearly always right," she admitted, making a quick, seemingly involuntary movement of her hands.

"*Nearly* always?" he teased.

She raised an elegant eyebrow. "You seem to have recovered admirably from your brush with death, sir. I see your conceit has returned."

"And your sharp tongue, madam."

"There is my cousin with our carriage," she said, pausing to regather her strength.

"Before I place you in David's care, answer one question for me," Lawrence said quietly.

"What is it?"

"Why did you lie to the policeman?"

"I beg your pardon—"

"I want to know why you told the officer that it was an accident."

"I-I don't know what you mean."

"Juliet, you and I both know it was no accident. You were deliberately pushed."

All of a sudden tears brimmed in her blue eyes. Her glove flew to a trembling mouth. He thought he detected a muffled sob. "I thought I had somehow imagined it."

He took a solicitous step toward her. "My dear girl—"

"No. Not here. Not now. Please, Lawrence," she pleaded in a voice bruised with pain.

"My God, what is it?"

Her eyes were a little wild. "I thought I was going crazy."

"You're not going crazy, trust me," he stated.

"Cousin David is here with the carriage. We will discuss this matter another time."

Lawrence was forced to revert to the formalities. "May I recommend a glass of medicinal brandy upon your return home, Miss Jones?"

"An excellent suggestion," agreed David.

Juliet was assisted into their carriage. "Thank you again for your assistance, Your Grace."

"It was nothing, madam. I will call upon you the day after tomorrow."

"I will be expecting you."

Just as the door of the carriage was closing Lawrence heard the young Mister Jones growl: "Why is the devil Englishman paying you a social call?"

"The duke has just saved my life, David."

"I was trying to reach you," he whined.

"I know you were. And I do appreciate it." Lawrence heard her add: "Besides, His Grace is an art lover. He is coming to see my Bronzino."

"But I will be away on my trip the day after tomorrow."

"Then unfortunately, dear cousin"—Juliet patted his hand in consolation—"you will have to wait and view the painting upon your return."

As the carriage lurched forward and began to move along the street, Lawrence caught a glimpse of David Thoreau Jones staring at him out the window. The expression on the young man's face was unmistakable.

It was hatred.

And it was directed at Lawrence.

10

"WELL, aren't you the fancy one?" declared the overblown redhead as she slowly circled around him. "Dressed up like a fine gentleman and all."

"I am a fine gentleman," David stated with no attempt at modesty.

She quirked a skeptical brow at him and continued circling. "Are you now?"

"Yes. I am."

He removed his cashmere topcoat and carefully hung it on the one metal hook behind the front door of the shabby flat. There were a row of nails hammered into the wall, as well. They were used for Cora's few pathetic belongings.

"I saw you step out of a hired carriage. Come into a bit o' luck, have you?"

"More than a bit of luck, Cora my girl." David was openly flattering her: Cora had ceased to be a girl before they'd met. She was five years his senior; she looked ten. She had put on weight since he had last seen her, and acquired a few additional lines around the eyes and at the corners of her mouth. Her appearance was hard. Her life was hard. Another ten years and she would be an old woman.

Her brown eyes widened appreciably. "Don't tell me you went and got a job, Davey?"

He hated it when she called him Davey.

"Of course, not. I've told you a hundred times, Cora: a true gentleman does not have a job."

"Humph."

David took a linen handkerchief from his pocket, dusted off the seat of what had once been his favorite chair and sat down. "How about a beer?"

Cora immediately brightened. "Course. I'll get it for you straight away, Davey. You just sit there and put your feet up and relax after your long trip." She was already slipping into her winter coat: a threadbare hand-me-down that had seen better days.

But, then, so had Cora, reflected David.

"You'll need some money," he said, digging into his pocket for a few odd coins.

"Thanks, love." She leaned over and dropped a sloppy kiss on his mouth. "I'll be back in a jiffy."

While Cora hurried along to O'Flannery's barroom—it was just down the street and around the corner—David stretched his legs out and took a good look around him.

The place was a dump.

He had forgotten in the few short months since he had been gone just what a poor house-keeper Cora was. Not that it was entirely her fault. The furniture was secondhand, maybe even thirdhand, and cheap to begin with. The whitewashed walls had faded to a dingy gray years ago. The soot on the windows was thick enough to cut with a knife. There was a rag stuffed into a broken pane. The boardinghouse was located in one of Boston's poorer neighborhoods. Not that there weren't worse.

A lot worse.

He had lived in several of them before he had taken up with Cora last year. She had given him a roof over his head—even if it did leak on occasion. Food. Clothing. And a bed, which she willingly shared with him. In return, he had married her and given her his name.

In a manner of speaking.

Ten minutes later Cora burst in the door of the flat. "Got your beer, Davey."

"That's a good girl," he said, patting her shapely backside with familiarity, and taking a long swallow of the strong, dark brew. "God almighty!" he swore, choking.

Cora's once pretty face fell. "What's wrong?"

David shook his head. It was a half a minute before he was able to tell her, wiping the froth from his mouth: "I'd forgotten how bitter O'Flannery's ale is, that's all."

The woman snorted and rested her work-worn hands on her hips. "S'pose you been drinking nothing but champagne and such."

"As a matter of fact, for the past three months I have had nothing but imported French champagne, the very best food, the softest bed, the finest clothes, and the most luxurious private carriages," he bragged.

Her eyes narrowed with suspicion. "You go and get yourself some fancy, highfalutin lady?"

"You could say that."

"I could, hey?" She punched him. Hard. It was not a love tap.

Cora was strong, but he was stronger. David laughed darkly and with an underlying sense of erotic excitement. He set his beer down on the small wooden table at his elbow. Then he reached out and captured both of her hands in one of his. It left her virtually defenseless. She squirmed like a redgill caught on the end of a fishing hook. "Jealous, my love?"

Her face grew flush until it appeared that her freckles had run together and her complexion matched her carrot-colored hair. "You know I'm terrible jealous; you being so young and handsome and all. But you're my husband, Davey, good and proper and legal, even if we wasn't married in church by a priest." She tried to wiggle free and failed. "It's still a mortal sin for you to poke another woman."

David grabbed her about the waist and yanked her down on his lap. He was already half aroused. "There's no need to fret, my girl. I haven't bedded anyone but you."

She sat unmoving in his arms. "Not in the whole three months you been gone?"

"Not once in the entire three months I was away," he vowed, his blue eyes filled with sincerity.

"Swear it on your beloved mother's grave."

"I swear it on my beloved mother's grave."

Of course, the truth was, he had no idea

whether his mother was dead or alive, or even who she was, for that matter. A beloved and now deceased mother was part of a story he had fabricated for Cora's benefit. He'd had her in tears before it was all said and done.

Nevertheless, it happened to be the truth: he had not bedded a single female since leaving Boston for New York. Opportunities were virtually nonexistent under the watchful eye of Juliet and Euphemia Jones.

He was also convinced that it was necessary for him to live an exemplary lifestyle while establishing himself with his newly found relations. It was a small enough price to pay for the huge rewards he would reap in the end.

And, after all, one way or another, he had found relief for his sexual frustrations.

Cora relaxed in his arms and began to rub up against him with her overripe body. "You're a fine one going off and leaving me to fend for myself."

"You've always managed on your own."

She pouted. "Maybe I have and maybe I haven't." She unbuttoned his collar and removed his necktie. "I missed you, Davey."

His eyes glittered. "How much did you miss me?"

"A little," she teased, stripping off his suit coat and then his shirt. Her nimble fingers went next to the fastenings of his trousers.

His mouth began to water in anticipation of what he knew was inevitably to come. "How much?"

Cora slipped her hand in between his remaining clothing and his bare skin. She raked a sharp nail along the length of his fully erect shaft. David's body twitched. He groaned aloud; he couldn't help himself.

Cora seemed very pleased with herself. "Almost as much as you missed me, I reckon."

Then she released him, and David's hot, heavy flesh sprang free of all constrictions.

"*Almost* as much?" he muttered urgently as he reached under her skirt and petticoats with eager fingers, prying fingers, probing fingers.

There was the sound of ripping cloth. "My drawers, Davy," she protested. "And they were my best ones."

"I'll buy you another pair, a dozen pair, for that matter," he gritted through his teeth as he found what he was seeking. She was already wet and ready. Cora always was. He jabbed a finger roughly inside her and recited part of a childhood nursery rhyme: " 'He put in his thumb, and pulled out a plum.' "

She laughed huskily, then put her head back and moaned like a wild animal baying at the moon.

"And said, 'What a good boy am I,' " David finished as he thrust in another finger alongside the first.

"You are a good boy, Davy. Let's go to bed," she urged breathlessly.

"No."

A look came into her eyes. "You want to do it here?"

"Yes."

David turned her to face him, pushed her

skirt up and positioned her legs on either side of his. He could feel the tip of his manhood poised at the juncture of her thighs. He brushed it back and forth, teasing her mercilessly.

Cora finally cried out in frustration. "Damn you, Davey, do it!"

His grin was wicked. "Do what?"

"Put it inside me," she pleaded, panting.

"What do you say first, Cora, my girl?"

"David—"

"What do you say?"

"Please."

David grasped her by the hips and thrust into her. At the same time he impaled her on his flesh, he repeated in a savage tone: " 'Little Miss Muffet sat on a tuffet, . . .' "

Cora propped her head on her elbows and watched from the rumpled bed as he finished dressing. "You never did tell me how you came by your bit o' luck, Davy."

David straightened his fresh collar and reached for the vest on the chair behind him. "Do you remember the stories I used to tell you about my family?"

The woman ran a hand through her frizzy hair. "Sure. You said you had distant relations on your beloved mother's side who was real rich folks, real society folks—somewhere." She paused for a moment, obviously trying to remember the city. Then she ventured: "Chicago?"

He nodded his head and smiled brightly.

"That's right. Chicago. Well, I found my family at last."

She pushed herself up in the bed, the blanket slipping down around her waist to reveal two freckled, pendulous, bare breasts. "Glory, Davy, that's wonderful."

"Yes, it is."

"Was they nice to you?"

"They were more than nice to me, Cora. They welcomed me with open arms," he said, slipping into his morning coat.

A hand flew to her mouth in astonishment. "Does that mean we're gonna be rich society folks, too?"

David lied beautifully; he always had. He had found it a great asset in life, especially with women. "That is exactly what it means, my dear girl."

Her manner was unusually animated. "Do I get to meet them?"

He gave his lapel several brushes with the back of his hand. "Naturally.'

"When?"

"Soon."

The woman in the bed was suddenly flustered. Huge tears sprang into her eyes. "But I don't have the right kind of clothes to wear."

"Don't fret," David quickly reassured her. "I'll take you shopping for everything you need." He turned his head and smiled down at her rakishly. "Including that dozen pair of new drawers I promised you the first night I was here."

Despite her age and experience, Cora blushed

right down to her roots. "You oughtn't to remind me of that night."

"Why not?"

Her face was ablaze. "Some of the things we
did don't seem proper somehow."

"Don't be a silly goose. You enjoyed every
minute of it as much as I did."

She lowered her eyes and self-consciously fin-
gered the frayed edge of the blanket. "I know."

"You won't go straight to hell and burn there
forever, if that's what has you worried."

Cora's head came up. Her eyes flew wide
open. She quickly crossed herself. "You
shouldn't talk like that. It's sacrilege. It's—it's
blasphemy."

She was suddenly beginning to bore him.

"I have to go out for a while," he informed
her.

"Where you going to, Davy?"

"I have some important business to attend to
in the city," he replied evasively.

"You'll be back in time for supper, won't
you?"

The lies came so easily. Perhaps too easily.
"Of course," he told her.

Cora wrapped the blanket around her and sat
up on the edge of the mattress. "I'll get dressed
and start right away to make your favorite: po-
tato pie."

"That would be nice," he said, dropping a
quick, impersonal kiss on her cheek. She
smelled of onions and stale beer and stale sex.

"I wonder if the woman in the bakery shop
on the next street still has some of them sweet

cakes left. They would be nice for a special celebration," she said, talking to herself.

David was halfway to the bedroom door when he stopped and came back as far as the bureau. He looked into the mirror and said to Cora, "You might need some extra money. I'll leave it here by your hairbrush. Consider it a little gift."

Cora beamed up at him. "You're so good to me, Davy. I'm proud to be your wife." She sighed. "Mrs. David White."

As he walked out of the flat and took a hired carriage to the train station, David Thoreau Jones was once again relieved that he had never told the woman his real name.

11

BRAMBINGER opened the door and announced in his best butler's voice: "His Grace, the Duke of Deakin."

Juliet watched as Lawrence was ushered into the Blue Room, so-called because its predominant color scheme, at Aunt Effie's request, was sapphire-blue. He carried two small, elongated boxes under his arm, each wrapped in a square of silk and secured with a matching ribbon. One was done up all in gold, the other in blue.

He went to the older woman first and, with a degree of familiarity that left Juliet stunned, said: "My dear Euphemia, good afternoon."

"Lawrence, how nice of you to call." She greeted the duke as if he were an old acquaintance.

His smile appeared genuine. "It's a pleasure to see you after our tête-à-tête on Tuesday."

Her great-aunt's eyes were sparkling mischievously. "I enjoyed our game of cards, as well."

"We must do it again soon."

"I would like that immensely," she assured him.

Juliet sat in her chair, mouth agape.

Tête-à-tête?

Cards?

Euphemia?

Lawrence?

When had these two become such close friends that they were on a first-name basis?

Where was the natural reticence of the English gentleman? Not to mention that of an English duke?

It was all highly irregular.

Lawrence began to work his charm on her next. "How kind of you to invite me here this afternoon to view the unveiling of the Bronzino."

Juliet acknowledged him with a formal nod of her head. "Good afternoon, Your Grace."

Euphemia intervened. "Your Grace? Don't be ridiculous, Juliet. You don't have to pretend in front of me. Lawrence has explained everything."

Juliet quirked a distinctly skeptical blond brow at him. "Has he?"

"Yes." Her great-aunt indicated a comfortable chair between the two of them. "Please sit here, Lawrence."

"Thank you, Euphemia." He set the exquisitely wrapped boxes on the table beside the armchair and sat down, making himself at home.

Entirely too much at home, in Juliet's opinion.

He even mused aloud: "This room makes me feel quite at home."

Aunt Effie gave her a particularly pointed

look. "Did you know, my dear Juliet, that there is a Blue Room not dissimilar to this one at Grantley Manor?"

"Grantley Manor?" she echoed blankly.

"Lawrence's home in Northumberland; the ancestral home of the Wickes for the past four hundred years."

"I see."

Euphemia Jones put aside the embroidery she was working on—indeed, she had been working on the same piece for nearly a year now and had made no noticeable progress; Juliet blamed it on her penchant for card games, especially solitaire—and turned to their handsome guest. "We spoke of so many interesting things on Tuesday, my dear man, that I did not think to ask where you are staying during your visit to New York. Are you living in a hotel, or have you rented a house somewhere?"

"Great-Aunt Euphemia—"

Lawrence seemed to take no offence at the personal nature of the question. "As a matter of fact, dear lady, I am doing neither one. We sailed to the shores of your country on the *Alicia Anne*. We live aboard ship."

"I assume 'we' includes that charming gentleman who was with you the first time you called."

"It does, indeed. Miles St. Aldford is my oldest and dearest friend."

"You are living on a boat?" Juliet heard herself blurt out, much to her horror.

"We don't refer to the *Alicia Anne* as a boat,"

Lawrence gently corrected her. "She is 270 feet long and requires a full crew to man her."

"Ship, then?"

"Actually, the *Alicia Anne* is a private yacht."

As long as Aunt Effie was asking questions left and right, she may as well, too, Juliet rationalized. "Whose private yacht?"

"Mine."

"How very nautical of you," Euphemia Jones remarked as she once more picked up her needle and thread.

Lawrence displayed a dogged determination to set the record straight. "Frankly, I am not much of a sailor, myself. I prefer dry land and horses. I suppose it was the reason I went into the cavalry instead of the Her Majesty's navy."

He had Juliet's undivided attention. "Then why in the world do you own a yacht?"

"Well, you see, the sixth duke—that would have been my paternal grandfather—was very keen on water and sailing and boats—"

"Ships," corrected Juliet.

"And ships." She saw his black eyes flicker for an instant. "He commissioned the yacht built and then named it for my grandmother."

"The sixth duchess?"

"Naturally."

"*Alicia Anne*, what a lovely name," interjected Euphemia, her embroidery needle poised in her hand.

"She was a very lovely lady, as well. Her portrait still hangs in what was her personal stateroom."

"I should like to see your grandmother's portrait," Juliet said, without thinking.

"You will, I hope. I would like to invite both you ladies to join us for dinner aboard the *Alicia Anne* one evening next week."

"What a perfectly charming prospect," exclaimed Euphemia. "I shall wear my dark green satin. No. Perhaps my yellow silk would be more appropriate."

"There will be a formal invitation delivered tomorrow," he said looking from one to the other. "But as long as the subject came up this afternoon, I see no reason not to mention it now."

Juliet could hardly argue with his logic. As usual, it was impeccable.

Euphemia pursed her small, pink mouth and said, with an air of utter innocence: "It must be very expensive keeping a private ship the size of the *Alicia Anne*."

Juliet held her breath.

She had been thinking the very same thing, but she would never have dared to voice such an outrageous question. That kind of impertinence was a privilege granted only to those of her great-aunt's "mature" years.

Lawrence looked off into the distance for a moment. Then he finally admitted, "It is. As a matter of fact, I will probably have to sell the yacht upon my return to England."

"What a pity," sympathized Juliet.

He shrugged. "One does what one must." Then he gave them a charming smile. "Ladies, I forget myself. I have brought you each a small token of my esteem." He stood and reached for the boxes on the table beside him. "The sapphire-blue is for you, of course, Euphemia."

She was obviously pleased to put her embroidery down and accept his token. "Oh, I do love gifts. Especially when they are a complete surprise." She gave it a tentative shake and sized up the package the way a child would at Christmas. "I wonder what it is."

His gaze locked with Juliet's as he strode across the room and placed the gold box in her hands. "This one is for you."

She looked up at him meaningfully. "They say, 'Beware of Greeks bearing gifts.'"

"Greeks?" repeated Euphemia Jones, glancing up from the present she was busily unwrapping. There was marked confusion written on her face. "Who is Greek?"

"It is nothing of import, Aunt Effie," Juliet assured her. "Lawrence and I recently had a discussion on the subject of Greek mythology."

"I can't imagine why," she muttered, immediately losing interest in their conversation.

Lawrence lowered his voice and said for her ears alone: "Actually, my dear Juliet, I believe the preferred translation of Virgil's *Aeneid* is: 'Whatever it is, I fear Greeks even *when* they bring gifts.'"

He made an imposing figure, standing over her. It served to remind her just how tall and broad-shouldered and powerful the man really was.

Nevertheless, it made her only that much more determined not to be intimidated by him.

"Am I to take that as a warning, sir?"

"You may take it any way you wish, madam."

She was intensely aware of how close his vibrant body was to hers. " 'Forewarned is forearmed.' "

He shot back: "Cervantes."

"Correct." She paused and added, "This time."

"I believe that is the second time in as many minutes." He smiled, showing white, predatory teeth. "I, too, can be an adept pupil."

"I wonder that there is anything left for you to learn," she said offhandedly.

"I have a great deal left to learn. Perhaps you will consent to teach me."

"Perhaps."

Then Juliet became preoccupied with untying the gold ribbon and carefully undoing the gold silk that surrounded the slender package. She heard her great-aunt exclaiming over whatever it was she had discovered in hers.

The wrapping fell away to reveal a beautiful rosewood box underneath. She lifted the lid and there, presented against a black velvet background, was a neckchain with a small gold tube dangling from the end.

"What is it?" she inquired, intrigued.

Lawrence reached down and plucked the chain from the box. He slipped it over her head until the tiny tube nestled between her breasts. "Hold it up to your eye, turn the disk and look toward the light of a window."

Juliet did as he had instructed. "Why, it's a

miniature kaleidoscope. It is beautiful!" she exclaimed.

Euphemia called out as she held hers up to the light. "Mine is sapphire-blue."

"And mine is gold." They both knew the significance of the color he had chosen for her. "Thank you, Lawrence."

"You are most welcome, Juliet. And now I would like to see your Bronzino," he prompted.

"Of course," she said, putting the box down and rising to her feet.

"I prefer to stay here and look through my pretty glass," said Euphemia. "You two may go gawk at that funny old painting without me."

They strolled into the front hall and stood side by side before the Bronzino portrait of Eleanor of Toledo, wife of Cosimo de' Medici, Duke of Florence. It hung in perfect splendor above the Italian marble table.

Juliet sighed contentedly. "It is the perfect setting for the painting."

"Perfect," he agreed.

"The portrait is very elegant."

"Indeed."

"But the duchess seems so cold and imperious, somehow."

"Perhaps it is the mannerist style of Bronzino, or—"

"Or?"

"Or perhaps it is because she was married to a de' Medici," he said.

Juliet chewed her lip. "That point should be taken into consideration." She dared not look at the man standing beside her. "Being the wife of a duke must certainly have been serious business."

"It still is." She felt Lawrence's gaze go from the portrait to her. "But it has its rewards."

"Excuse me, Miss Juliet—"

She turned. "Yes, Brambinger."

"Tea is served in the Blue Room."

Timing was everything . . . as another Greek philosopher had noted. And his was bloody awful, Lawrence decided as he balanced a ridiculously fragile china teacup in the palm of his hand.

"Another rum cake?" whispered Juliet.

"No. Thank you," he mouthed, wondering how long they would sit there, quietly sipping tea and whispering an occasional innocuous remark to each other, all in an attempt not to waken Euphemia Jones from her impromptu nap.

"More tea?"

"No. Thank you," he said louder than he had intended.

"Shhhhh—"

"Dammit, Juliet," he growled.

She gave him a look that only a woman like Juliet Jones could give a man.

"I need to talk to you alone," he insisted.

She finally put her teacup down on the tray and indicated he should follow her. He did so eagerly.

"We will go into the library," she informed him, closing the door of the Blue Room behind her. "We should be undisturbed there."

It was exactly what he had in mind.

Once they had entered the library, Lawrence strolled over to a reading table and picked up the first book off the top of a stack. "*Eugenie Grandet* by Balzac, in the original French." He picked up another volume. "*Oedipus the King* in the original Greek." Then another, "*Pride and Prejudice—*"

"In the original English," she said saucily.

Lawrence had always thought one could tell a great deal about a man from the books he read. Perhaps the same held true for a woman. In which case, Juliet Jones was a female of decidedly eclectic tastes. It could prove interesting—before it was all said and done.

She meandered around to the other side of the desk, stopped to tidy a pile of papers, and then glanced up at him. "You said you wanted to speak to me in private."

It was time to get down to business.

He didn't mince words with her. "We need to discuss what happened on Tuesday afternoon in front of the art gallery."

She became absolutely still. "I don't know for certain. I've gone over it again and again in my mind . . ." She gave a shake of her head. "I don't know, Lawrence."

He didn't want to frighten her unnecessarily, but they had to consider all the possibilities. "I thought I saw a man behind you."

Her head shot up. "What did he look like?"

"Mean." He ran his hand along the back of his neck. "That doesn't tell us much, does it?"

"No."

He came right out and asked her: "Do you think you were pushed?"

"You mean deliberately?"

"Yes."

Juliet lifted her shoulders and dropped them again. "I may have been. I thought so at first. Now—"

"Now you aren't sure."

She nodded. "Now I'm not as certain." She hesitated, then told him. "It was crowded. The sidewalk was slippery. I was watching for David." Her voice lowered to add, "I was thinking about you."

His body immediately tensed. The lady could get to him. Easily. Too easily.

He listened broodingly. "What about the incident in the park?"

Her voice seemed lifeless. "Perhaps Hera was pricked by the thorn when she ran into the Ramble."

"It's possible." If improbable, in his opinion. "Are you saying they were both accidents?"

She drew in a long breath and let it out slowly. "It's the only logical explanation."

"You can't think of a single person who would want to do you harm?"

"Not a one."

"And no one will gain if anything happens to you?"

Juliet's voice was soft but determined. "If you're asking what I think you're asking, the answer is no. Everyone gains if I am alive."

A scowl creased his forehead. "How?"

She was candid with him. "My great-aunt is

independently wealthy. My cousin receives a very generous allowance and will soon have his own income from a trust fund. For a large number of other people—lawyers, bankers, moneymen—I will make them rich only if I stay alive." There was an edge to her voice when she added: "It was the first valuable lesson I learned from my father."

Lawrence was filled with admiration. "I would like to have met your father."

"He was a remarkable man."

"And your mother?" he said as he made his way around the massive desk toward her.

"She was an angel."

"Then you are truly your mother's daughter, as well." He halted in front of her and reached out to cup her chin. "I can't get that night out of my mind."

"Neither can I," she confessed.

They both knew what night. It was the night of Mrs. Astor's annual ball. It was the night they had decided to escape to the small salon, only to be caught in a far more dangerous trap than a noisy, crowded ballroom.

"I think about kissing you, Juliet."

She swallowed hard and appeared to be studying the cleft in his chin.

"I dream about touching you."

That brought a small strangled sound from the back of her throat.

"I imagine all of the wonderful things I can teach you about men and women."

"Lawrence—"

"What is it?"

"I'm frightened," she admitted, raising her eyes to his.

"What are you frightened of?"

"You. Me." She added in a barely audible voice; "The way I feel. I'm a stranger to myself."

"I'm glad."

That apparently startled her. "Why?"

"Because I feel like I'm not in control of myself, and I don't particularly like the feeling." Hell, even as his hands came to rest nonchalantly on her shoulders, he could detect the first signs of his own sexual arousal. He sighed. "But there doesn't seem to be a bloody thing I can do about it."

"Why aren't you in control?"

"Because you make me lose control."

"I don't understand."

He blew out his breath expressively. "I know you don't understand. That is what makes it so hard." Then he laughed roughly.

Juliet was suddenly incensed. She stabbed his chest with her finger, punctuating each word. "There. You've done it again. It's that secret language, that private code you men use. You will explain yourself, Lawrence."

"Explain myself?"

"Yes."

"Here and now?"

"I absolutely insist."

"Are you certain you want to know?"

"I am positive."

"It may not be what you think."

"I have no idea *what* to think and I never will unless you explain it to me," she stated.

The lady had a point. Still, she was a lady and an innocent. And he was a gentleman.

"This is not a good idea," he declared, aware that his body was responding to the slightest movement on Juliet's part, to the slightest suggestive thought of his own. His manhood was growing heavy. It was thickening. The tip was beginning to throb as it pressed against the front of his trousers. He was nearly ready to explode. "This is definitely not a good idea," he repeated tightly.

She stood her ground. "It is."

His smile was crooked. "Trust me, it isn't.

"Lawrence—"

"Juliet, you don't know the first thing about men or sex," he said bluntly.

The color came up in her face like a red flag. "I know that I'm ignorant. That is the whole point of this discussion. But as Christopher Marlowe wrote nearly three hundred years ago: 'there is no sin but ignorance.' "

"I don't think he was referring to this particular topic," Lawrence said dryly.

"Don't patronize me, sir."

"Then may I at least remind you, madam, that it has also been written: 'ignorance is bliss, tis folly to be wise'?"

"I will be the judge of that."

Lawrence wanted to choke her. "You are the most headstrong, stubborn, goddamned irritating female I have ever encountered."

She did not back down. Not even an inch. In

fact, she shot back. "And you are trying to change the subject. You are also using offensive language."

"Oh, I can be a great deal more offensive than that," he bellowed.

Her lovely little aristocratic nose went straight up in the air as she regally declared: "No doubt you can."

That did it.

"You want your explanation?" he ground through his teeth.

"Yes. I do."

"Then you will have it." Where the hell to begin? That was the problem.

Juliet tapped her foot impatiently. "I am waiting."

"I am trying to decide where to start."

"You may start by explaining why you laughed when you said 'that is what makes it so hard.'" She cocked her head at him. "What is *that*?"

He took in a deep, fortifying breath and released it. "*That* is your sweet innocence."

She wasn't fooled for a minute. "My ignorance, in other words."

Lawrence tried diplomacy. "Your lack of understanding." Then he went on as if he were giving a lecture at university. "The secret language or private code that men use is based on the concept of double entendre."

"A word may have several meanings."

He nodded. "One may be innocent enough, the other usually carries a risque connotation."

She raised an elegant eyebrow. "What is *it*?"

"*It* is several things." This was getting harder and harder. Hell, he was getting harder and harder.

"You have that peculiarly smug smile on your face again," Juliet warned him.

His smile vanished. "*It* refers to the relationship between us."

"And—" she prompted.

"And *it* also refers to a certain—appendage."

"Appendage? What appendage? An arm is an appendage. A leg is an appendage. Specifically what type of appendage are you speaking of?"

Lawrence's face was hot. So was the rest of him. "I am specifically speaking of the male appendage."

Juliet froze.

He plunged ahead. "*Hard*, of course, means the degree of difficulty involved in our relationship and the physical state of the male appendage when aroused."

She stared up at him in disbelief. "Are you telling me that men think of nothing but—?"

"Yes. No. What I mean is men think about it a good deal of the time but certainly not to the exclusion of everything else."

"I am amazed."

"I thought you would be."

"I am dumbfounded."

"Understandably."

"I am speechless."

"I did not notice."

Juliet wrinkled her forehead. "But I still don't fully comprehend—"

He cut her off. "That is enough discussion for today, Juliet. We have other things to do."

"What other things?"

Lawrence reached out and slipped his arm around her waist. "For one, I am going to kiss you."

"Why?"

"Because I will go insane if I do not."

"I think it is too late."

"You, madam, have a quick tongue." He could not prevent the corners of his mouth from turning up.

"Lawrence—"

"You have been left to your own devices too long. What you need is the firm hand of a man."

"Lawrence—"

"I know. That is two more double entendres in a row. But I will explain them to you another time."

She opened her mouth to protest. He took advantage of the situation and covered her parted lips with his.

God in heaven, she was enticing. She tasted slightly of sweet rum cakes and tea and that same indefinable something he had noted the night of Mrs. Astor's ball. He decided it was simply Juliet. He dipped his tongue into her mouth and took a longer, deeper taste of her. He felt her surprise, then her curiosity and finally her response.

He wanted to race to the nearest mountaintop, throw his head back, beat his chest and give a warrior's victory cry. He wanted her, yes. He desired her, yes. But she wanted and desired him, as well.

Miss Juliet Jones was his for the taking!

Lawrence slowly slid his hands from her waist to her ribcage. It registered vaguely somewhere in the back of his mind that the usual barriers a man encountered seemed to be missing. A woman's clothing was normally such a confounded nuisance. It was not until his palms were directly beneath her breasts—indeed, he was supporting their weight with his thumbs and forefingers—that it dawned on him.

The lady was wearing no underwear.

He could think of no logical reason for this phenomenon. He simply considered it extraordinarily good luck for him. He moved his right thumb one inch higher and scraped his blunt nail across the tip of her breast.

Juliet jerked as if a bolt of lightning had coursed through her body.

He raised his left thumb and flicked it back and forth once, twice, three times, and felt both of her nipples curl up very prettily beneath the soft material of her dress. It was immensely satisfying.

Lawrence could contain herself no longer. He thrust his tongue even deeper down her throat, covered her breasts with his palms and ground his hips against hers. There was no mistake about it: he was more aroused than he had ever been in his life. Business before pleasure be damned!

Then, beneath his sensual onslaught, he became aware of Juliet moaning. It was not strictly a moan of pleasure; it was the sound of someone in pain. Admittedly the line between pleasure and pain was often obscured, but something niggled at him.

Lawrence raised his head and gazed down at her. His voice was deep and husky. "Juliet, what is it? Have I hurt you in some way?"

Her eyes were dark blue. "You were not to know. Indeed, you had no way of knowing."

"Knowing what?"

"I was bruised," she said in a whisper.

His breathing stopped. "Bruised?"

"In the accident."

"In the accident?" he repeated dumbly. Then it dawned on him. "The accident on Tuesday?"

"Yes."

"When I grabbed you?"

Her eyes flew to his face. "When you saved me," she insisted.

"I was too rough."

"You had no choice."

His heart was thudding in his chest. His innards were tied up in a knot. "How badly are you hurt?"

"Nothing is broken," she said after a slight hesitation.

His lips thinned. "Have you been examined by a doctor?"

"That was not necessary."

He loosened his grip until he was barely touching her. "Yet you were bruised to the extent that you could not wear a corset or any tight-laced undergarments."

She blushed bright red. "I didn't think anyone would notice. I had planned on staying home for a few days."

"And you did not plan on me assaulting you."

Juliet shook her head with vehemence. "You did not assault me."

He stared at her fixedly. "What would you call it?"

"Kissing."

"We did more than kiss."

"Touching."

His stance relaxed slightly. "Caressing."

"It was wonderful."

He still felt like a first-rate bastard. "I didn't mean to hurt you."

"I know."

"I would never deliberately hurt you," Lawrence declared, and he suddenly realized it was true: he would never wish to deliberately harm this woman.

"I would like to try it again."

His head came up. His eyes focused on the beautiful and determined face in front of him. "Exactly what do you mean by that statement, young lady?"

She took a deep breath. It seemed to require all of her considerable courage for Juliet to admit: "I mean that I would like us to kiss and touch and caress again. Once my bruises are healed, of course."

Lawrence bent over and leaned his forehead against hers. "Oh, my dearest girl, do you have any idea of what you're asking for?"

She swallowed hard. "I think so."

"You will be the death of me yet," he muttered under his breath.

Juliet took his remark seriously. She gripped his hand, digging her fingernails into his skin. He would find the small moon-shaped scratches later. "Oh, please, Lawrence, don't say that. I couldn't bear to be the cause of any harm to you."

"Do not distress yourself, madam. I was merely making a jest."

She arched her brow and made a slight inarticulate sound that was a little like a lioness's growl. "It was another of your damned double entendres, wasn't it?"

The expression he turned to her was decidedly sheepish. "Now, Juliet—"

"Don't you 'now, Juliet,' me, Deakin."

He found himself retreating a step or two until he felt his shoulders hit something solid. His back was literally against the wall.

She marched up and planted herself in front of him. "You have a great deal of explaining to do."

"You are referring, I assume, to the secret language and private code of the human male."

"Of course."

"It may take some considerable time."

"So be it."

"I will be required to call upon you frequently."

He saw her lips twitch in an effort not to smile. "Then I will make every effort to be at home to receive your frequent calls."

"I must warn you, my intentions in this matter may not be what you think."

Her smile mocked him. "Is it your intent, sir, to seduce me?"

He smiled right back at her. "It is my intent, madam, to court you."

12

SHE was infatuated.

She could not possibly be in love with the man, Juliet decided as she gazed at herself in her boudoir mirror.

Why, she had only known Lawrence a mere three weeks, perhaps four.

"It has been exactly twenty-four days," she informed her reflection.

And this evening she and Aunt Effie would be dining as guests aboard his private yacht. The very thought of what might occur sent a thrill coursing through her.

Tonight could be the night.

For the past week—since the afternoon Lawrence had paid them a social call and enchanted her great-aunt, her housekeeper, even her butler—he had shown up on her doorstep each afternoon for tea. And each time he had come bearing gifts.

First, of course, the miniature kaleidoscopes.

Next, there had been a pair of yellow canaries in a gilded cage for her, and a small slender blue parrot in a blue wicker cage for Euphemia.

One day it had been fresh flowers. Dozens of them. Like sunlight brought indoors.

Another day she had received a book of love poetry in the original French, and her great-aunt a box of playing cards.

Only yesterday it had been candies and sweet cakes.

The gifts were never elaborate and never expensive. They were always appropriate, always thoughtful and always appreciated.

But since that first afternoon in the library Lawrence had not tried to be alone with her. He had not tried to kiss her or touch her or caress her. And he had not explained even a single example of the secret language and private code used by men. In fact, he had been a perfect gentleman.

Oh, he was a clever devil. The less he did, the more she thought about him.

She was waking even more frequently in the night: feverish, restless, her nightdress damp and disheveled and wrapped around her legs, her hair undone from its braid and twisted into a mass of wild tangles, her skin sensitive to the slightest touch, her heart pounding, her lips swollen as if she had been kissed again and again, her hands trembling, her breasts aching, her nipples distended, her body quivering.

Dreams.

He came to her in dreams. He was tall and dark, powerful and dangerous. Only now she saw his face; it was no longer obscured in the shadows. The mysterious lover in her dreams was Lawrence.

It was the same dream every time. He hovered over her, whispering sweetly erotic words to her that she could not remember later upon awakening. He leaned down to kiss her, to touch her, to caress her, to love her. She felt his hands on her, his lips, his mouth, his tongue, his body.

Juliet groaned aloud and pushed herself away from the dressing table. She rose and paced back and forth across the floor of her boudoir, the skirt of her silk evening gown softly sweeping the Aubusson rug underfoot with every step.

She recalled a bedtime story her mother had often told her when she was a little girl. It was about a beautiful lady who was imprisoned in an ivory tower of her own making. One day a handsome prince rode up on a white charger, climbed the steep walls of the tower, vowed his eternal love, and rescued the lady from a life of loneliness. They galloped away together and lived happily ever after.

It was only a fairy tale.

It was merely a schoolgirl's fantasy.

It was nothing more than the "stuff as dreams are made on."

Juliet knew it didn't work that way in real life.

In real life her parents had been killed in a senseless carriage accident.

In real life Great-Aunt Effie's young man had run off and married another woman because he was shallow and greedy, a cad and a bounder.

In real life a handsome and wealthy English duke did not sail to America aboard his own ship, fall madly in love with an heiress of a "certain" age, make her his duchess and return with her to his ancestral home to live happily ever after.

Or did he?

She recalled their conversation in the library.

"I must warn you, Juliet, my intentions in this matter may not be what you think."

She had mocked him with her smile. *"Is it your intent, sir, to seduce me?"*

He had smiled right back at her. *"It is my intent, madam, to court you."*

Juliet sighed heavily. Miss Jane Austen had been right all along: Men *were* altogether a different species.

A tentative knock at her boudoir door interrupted her reverie. "Yes?"

"It is I," came the sweet, dearly familiar voice of her great-aunt.

"Please come in, Aunt Effie."

The door opened. "Oh, the blue silk is perfect!" exclaimed the older woman as she clapped her bejeweled hands together. "The color matches your eyes. Why, you look like a queen, my dear." She paused to add meaning to the last part of her statement. "Or a duchess."

"Aunt Effie, you are matchmaking again," she warned.

"Am I?" she said, appearing momentarily confused.

Juliet relented, as she always did. "You are beautiful in the yellow silk."

The tiny woman did a pirouette. "Do you truly think so? I was afraid that I might look like one of your yellow songbirds," she chirped.

"Ladies," came the inimitable voice of Brambinger from the doorway. "His Grace has sent a carriage for you. It is at your disposal whenever you are quite ready."

Juliet picked up her gloves and matching silk bag from the dressing table. "I believe we will be quite ready, Brambinger, once we collect our evening wraps."

"It is cold out tonight, miss."

"Then my great-aunt and I will each require a fur cloak for the ride."

Brambinger nodded and added, "The footman has informed me that His Grace has provided lap robes and foot warmers inside the carriage."

"His Grace has apparently thought of everything," Julie said with a nonchalance she was not feeling.

"I must confess I am a trifle nervous," said Euphemia Jones once they were comfortably settled in the duke's carriage and on their way. She peered at Juliet across the seat. "You seem very calm, my dear."

Which all went to show how deceptive appearances could be, Juliet supposed. She was certain she would not be able to consume even one bite of her dinner.

She brightened and told a tiny fib. "I wish that Cousin David were here to join us for dinner tonight."

"Are the ladies at home tonight, Brambinger?" David inquired as he removed his hat, his gloves, his overcoat and handed them to the butler.

"You have just missed them, sir. They left not more than a half hour ago," he replied.

"Are they dining out?"

"Yes, sir."

"With whom are they dining?"

"With His Grace."

"His Grace?"

"The Duke of Deakin."

"Where are they dining?"

"Aboard the *Alicia Anne*."

David felt a growing impatience with the old man. "And what is the *Alicia Anne*?"

"The duke's private yacht."

"I see."

"Miss Juliet wasn't expecting you back tonight, sir."

The slightest hint of disapproval had crept into the longtime butler's tone. David did not fail to recognize it for what it was: he knew damn well he was still considered an outsider, an interloper, a distant relation, not quite one of the Joneses. Especially by the staff.

Time, he reminded himself. Anything worthwhile took time, and time was on his side.

"Yes. I know my cousin wasn't expecting me."

"Miss Juliet told the staff to prepare for your return on Saturday. This is Thursday."

He realized it was Thursday. He wasn't a bloody idiot. And he didn't like being reprimanded by a underling. The master did not explain himself to the servant. Of course, he wasn't the master.

Yet.

David deliberately instilled a touch of warmth and cordiality into his voice. "I finished my business in Boston sooner than I thought. I saw no reason to stay among strangers. So I decided to return home early to my family."

"That is your prerogative, of course, sir." Brambinger said with all due respect. "There is a fire laid in the library."

"Thank you, Brambinger." He straightened his lapel and took a step toward the library door. "Would you be good enough to send in a bottle of brandy and a glass?"

The butler gave a nod of his head. "Will you be requiring anything else, sir?"

Stroking his jaw, David commented, as if he had just thought of it: "I am rather hungry after my journey. The food served on trains these days is abominable. Perhaps a simple tray with some bread and butter, and a slice of cheese. I wouldn't want to put the staff to any trouble."

"I believe there is some beef left over from last night, Mr. David, and a lamb chop or two, as well. Perhaps you would enjoy a slice of cook's incomparable meatpie. I know it's one of your favorites."

He made certain to show his humble gratitude and express his appreciation. "That would be splendid. Thank you, Brambinger."

"You're welcome, sir. I'll have the housemaid bring you something nice."

If there was one thing David Thoreau Jones had learned growing up in an orphanage, it was the fact that you caught more flies with honey than with vinegar.

He liked to think of it as his own special brand of charm. He had certainly been told often enough over the years that he could charm the birds right out of the trees. Charm, and his blond good looks, had, to a great extent, gotten him where he was today.

Which was exactly where he had always wanted to be, David reflected as he made himself at home in front of the fire. It was no accident that he was sitting in an overstuffed leather chair in the library of one of New York's largest and finest mansions.

It was all part of his Grand Scheme.

Of course, *everything* had not quite gone according to his plans. But that was to be expected. There were always adjustments and changes to be made to any plan. Flexibility was the key. If at first he didn't succeed, he must try and try again until he did.

The first two "accidents," for example, had gone slightly awry, due to the intervention of the devil Englishman. The duke was turning out to be a confounded nuisance.

He was the one cast in the role of Sir Galahad: pure, noble and unselfish. *He* was the one who was destined to rush in at the last minute and save the fair damsel. *He* was the one to whom the lovely Juliet was supposed to be eternally grateful. *He* was the one she would find favor with and make her consort.

But David had a second rule: always be on the lookout for unexpected opportunities.

He slowly rubbed his hand back and forth along his chin. If he were smart—and he was—he would find a way to make use of Lawrence Grenfell Wicke.

Where there was a will, there was a way. He had the will and he always found a way. He always got what he wanted, sooner or later. He was young. He was clever. He was charming. He was also patient. He could wait.

For a while.

After all, David reminded himself, as he took a sip of the fine Napoleon brandy from the crystal snifter Brambinger had left for him on the table, someday this would all be his.

13

DINNER was over. They were strolling along the deck of the *Alicia Anne* for a breath of fresh air. Juliet had her fur wrap draped around her. Lawrence was wearing his formal black evening clothes.

They had been speaking of insignificant things: the position of the constellations in the night sky, the chances of an early spring, the best breed of dog, the oriental art of producing trees in miniature, the difficulties in cultivating a proper wildflower garden, their favorite music. She preferred Mozart, or a Strauss waltz: "The Blue Danube" or "Tales from the Vienna Woods." He favored the traditional English airs.

As they passed the ship's lounge, they could hear the sound of laughter and deep masculine voices, occasionally punctuated by a feminine trill. Juliet glanced back over her shoulder. "Do you think Aunt Effie will be all right?"

"Euphemia is having a wonderful time conversing and playing cards with Miles, Captain Chandler, and the ship's officers. A woman likes her share of undivided masculine attention, regardless of her age."

"You know a great deal about women," she observed.

He shrugged. "I watched my mother and my grandmother: two of the greatest ladies to grace this earth."

"And what did you discover?"

"It is possible to understand women. It is difficult, if not impossible, to understand one woman."

"The same may be said of men, for that matter."

They walked in silence, then. They stopped by the ship's railing and stared at the stars overhead. It was so peaceful and so serene, Juliet hated to bring up an unpleasant subject. But it was necessary.

"Lawrence," she began solemnly.

"Yes, Juliet."

She shivered and clutched her cloak more closely around her. "We have become the subject of gossip."

"That's nothing new." He seemed totally unconcerned. "Next week the gossip mongers will turn on the Vanderbilts again, and we will be forgotten."

"I do not think so. In fact, it seems to get worse every day, not better. Our names are being bandied about from the most respectable society matron to the lowest housemaid. Upstairs *and* downstairs."

He turned his head and stared searchingly at her. "How do you know?"

"My maid told me."

"And how did your maid come by this knowledge?"

"She has it on the best authority from a friend whose sister is a chambermaid for Mrs. Astor."

He seemed to take into account what she had told him, then inquired: "Do you mind very much?"

Juliet snuggled luxuriously down in her fur. "I accept it. That does not mean I like it." She rested her gloved hand on the ship's railing for a moment, and gazed out across the harbor to the twinkling lights of the city. "You should stop bringing me gifts."

"I like giving you gifts."

"I like receiving them."

"Then we will do as we like and not as others would dictate to us," he said as they began walking again.

They strolled past several deckhands who nodded their heads and murmured respectfully: "Good evening, Your Grace. Good evening, miss."

Juliet sighed. "This is a beautiful ship."

"My grandfather had excellent taste and an endless supply of funds."

"It will be a shame to sell her."

His mouth curved humorlessly. "Keeping the *Alicia Anne* for sentimental reasons would be the height of folly."

"I suppose so."

They continued in companionable silence. It was at least five minutes before Juliet realized they were in an unfamiliar and deserted section of the yacht. There was not one other person in sight.

Without turning her head, she asked him, "How do you always manage to get me alone?"

Lawrence shrugged his broad shoulders and smiled into the night. "It is a talent."

She laughed lightly; she could see her breath. "I have never heard of this talent."

"It is a talent peculiar to the Wicke family," he advised her.

"You mean peculiar to the *men* of the Wicke family." His broadening smile was all the confirmation she needed.

"Where there is a will, there is a way. It is our motto," he said.

"Is it truly?"

"Only unofficially. The motto chiseled in stone above the fireplace in the Great Hall of Grantley Manor when the house was built in the late fifteenth century reads: *Pro rege, lege, et grege.*"

" 'For the king, the law, and the people,' " she translated.

"You know your Latin."

"I once had a tutor who felt that anyone who did not know their Latin was uncivilized."

"I must have had the same tutor," he said dryly.

"Your family motto is a commitment, isn't it?"

He nodded. "Sworn by each Duke of Deakin in his turn."

"He pledges to support his sovereign, the law of his country, and its people."

"It is more than just a pledge, Juliet. It is a sacred trust and a sacred duty," he stated.

"Handed down from father to son, from one generation to the next."

"For four hundred years and more."

It was a little while before Juliet ventured: "Sometimes it must be a burden."

"Sometimes." He frowned and looked across the harbor. "One is not always free to do what one might like."

"That's true for all of us."

"I suppose it is," he said with an air of pre-occupation. "My brother Jonathan refers to it as the pressures of privilege."

"But think of it, Lawrence," she said passionately. "All that history, all that heritage, all that family behind you: it must be wonderful."

"It can be."

"I have so little family history and even less family. I find it fascinating that you can trace your ancestors back hundreds of years."

Lawrence's expression was slightly self-conscious. "Legend has it—and in a family like mine there are countless legends—that we came over with the Conqueror."

She felt her eyes grow huge. "William the Conqueror?"

"The very one."

"Why, that would mean that your family has been in England since the year 1066."

"Give or take a week. Of course, we were not given the titles and lands of a duke until several centuries later."

Juliet gave him a look of polite inquiry. "And

are there paintings and portraits of all these icons hanging somewhere at Grantley Manor?"

"In the Long Gallery."

"It must be very long, indeed," she murmured, not altogether seriously.

"I have seen longer."

"But not often."

"No. Not often. There is a portrait of every duke and duchess from the first to the last, excluding myself, of course."

"I don't suppose you've had time for sittings."

"I haven't had the time or the patience."

"And, if I have not lost count, you are the eighth Duke of Deakin?"

"I am. My wife will be the eighth Duchess of Deakin. After we are married, suitable portraits will be rendered and mounted with the others. One day our firstborn son will become the ninth duke." He was very quiet for a moment. "In addition to the portraits in the Long Gallery, there are a number of others in the Reynolds Room. Those are mostly of the fifth duke and duchess and their offspring, however."

"The Reynolds Room?"

"Sir Joshua Reynolds."

"I surmised as much. How many paintings do you have by Reynolds?" she asked enthusiastically.

Lawrence frowned. It was almost as if he were counting the individual portraits in his head. "Six. No. I am wrong. It is seven. I forgot the small picture of the youngest son, William."

"Your home must be filled with many beautiful and wonderful things."

"Just as yours is."

"But mine have not been a legacy handed down from generation to generation. The Louis XIV furniture, the Boucher tapestries, the Boulle cabinets, the Rembrandts, and my prized Bronzino, were all acquired by my parents or by myself."

"It is always refreshing to find someone who has both money and good taste," he said diplomatically.

He took her by the elbow and steered her around an obstacle on the deck.

She looked at him out of the corner of her eye. "Aren't you feeling the least bit cold?"

"Not in the least."

"It is the middle of the winter."

"I am a hot-blooded man," he said and she could see his mouth curl up in the light cast by the lanterns along the ship's deck.

"That was a double entendre, wasn't it?"

"Now you are beginning to understand."

"Barely."

He grinned again.

"You are impossible." But Juliet wasn't offended. Indeed, she was amused. The night was too lovely and the champagne had been too delicious to take offense at every little thing Lawrence said or did.

"Would you like to see the portrait of my grandmother?"

"Yes. Very much."

"This way," he said, guiding her down a private corridor. There were a set of carved double doors at the end. He opened them. "This was Alicia Anne's stateroom."

Juliet stood in the entrance and exclaimed, "Oh, Lawrence, it's splendid."

The walls were wainscotted with a delicate floral design on the top portion and polished rosewood on the bottom. The draperies were woven of the same floral pattern. The furniture was vintage Chippendale. The carpets were soft and thick and luxurious. There was a small French writing desk beneath a window and a pair of Louis XV chairs on either side of an occasional table. The woodwork had been carved by a true artist, no doubt the same man who had put his hand to the doors.

Beyond what had been Alicia Anne's boudoir was the bedroom. Juliet was suddenly aware of how alone they were, how isolated from everyone else aboard the yacht.

"It seems warm in here," she said.

"Let me take your wrap," he offered.

She allowed Lawrence to slip the fur from her shoulders and lay it across the back of a divan.

"This way," he indicated and they walked into the adjoining room.

Someone had been there before them. The lamps were burning low. Lawrence placed his hands on her shoulders and turned her around. And there, opposite the elegant bed that was covered in floral brocade, was the portrait.

"My grandmother," he announced with reverence and affection, "Alicia Anne, Duchess of Deakin."

Juliet stood and stared at the painting. The girl—for she was certainly young enough to be called a girl—was as lovely as her name. Her hair was dark brown in color, nearly black, and swept up into the traditional style of the early Regency period. Her complexion was flawless. Her nose aristocratic. Her eyes dark, intelligent, sparkling with humor. Her mouth was turned up slightly at the corners, as if she were enjoying some private little joke at the expense of the world.

"How old was your grandmother when the portrait was done?" she asked quietly.

"Nineteen."

"So young." Juliet sighed. Five years younger than she was on her last birthday. "Do you have memories of her?"

"Yes. She didn't die until I was eight. She was an old woman by then, of course, but she was still beautiful. She still had that mischievous glint in her eye."

"You loved her very much."

"Of course." Juliet could feel his eyes on her. "You haven't mentioned her jewelry."

"Her jewelry?"

"The jewelry my grandmother is wearing in the portrait."

"I was preoccupied with her face, her eyes, her expression. The jewelry seems very nice, though."

"Nice?" Lawrence laughed as if she had said something quite funny and outrageous. "Grandmother is wearing the world-famous Deakin Diamonds."

"World-famous? I have never heard of them." Juliet peered at the black stones depicted in the painting. "They do not look like diamonds to me. They look like jet."

"Jet?" the man roared as if it were the most preposterous idea he had ever heard. "Jet is nothing more than polished coal. These are rare black diamonds. Priceless black diamonds," he informed her.

Juliet took a second look. Alicia Anne was adorned in a necklace and earrings, a bracelet, an elaborate brooch, and a large ring, all made up in the stones that Lawrence called the Deakin Diamonds. "I'm sure the black diamonds show to great advantage, especially on a woman with your grandmother's dark eyes and hair."

Lawrence gave a grunt. "You are the most unusual female I have ever met."

"I assume, sir, you meant that as a compliment."

"I do," he assured her.

"Then I thank you."

He tapped his fingertips together. "I believe you are the only person, certainly the only woman, who has ever seen this portrait and not noticed the Deakin Diamonds first."

"That doesn't seem very likely to me. Surely not all ladies are interested in fancy baubles."

Lawrence shook his head. "Fancy baubles."

"As you well know," she said, "I prefer to

leave the wearing of jewels to my great-aunt and to the other ladies who enjoy such things."

"But you have no personal interest in them, yourself?"

"A certain curiosity, if there is historical significance attached to the jewelry. I am rather keen on history."

"As I have discovered," he muttered.

"Beyond the ancient Greeks, I might add—although that is my first love. I am also fascinated by the period in your own English history and literature dating from Chaucer to Milton. And I am currently reexamining certain aspects of the Italian Renaissance."

He cut her off short. "As I said, Juliet, you are most unusual."

She faced him squarely. They may as well reach an understanding here and now. "My father was a self-made man, Lawrence. He started with nothing and built himself the greatest fortune in America. He was flamboyant. He was colorful. He was brilliant. But the single greatest achievement of his life was marrying my mother, and he would be the first one to tell you that if he were alive today."

"You told me she was an angel."

"But she was not perfect. She was not the prettiest woman he had ever met. She was not the smartest woman he had ever met. She was anything but the richest since she was the daughter of a humble schoolteacher. Mama was beautiful where it really counted. She was beautiful on the inside."

"My mother often said the same thing about physical beauty," he murmured.

"I would have liked your mother," she said quietly. Then she returned to her original point. "My parents understood the ultimate truth and they made sure that I understood it as well."

"Which is?"

She paused to lend emphasis to what she was about to say. "Money means nothing at all."

The expression on his face was priceless.

She went on. "I know what you are thinking."

"Do you?"

She nodded. "You are thinking that it is an odd thing for an heiress to say."

"That's something of an understatement," Lawrence suggested smoothly.

"I watched my parents. I remember them well since they were not killed until I was eleven years old. Their greatest wealth and their greatest joy was the love they had for one another. Without that love, they would have been poor, indeed."

He heaved a great sigh and reached out to caress her cheek. "Oh, my dearest Juliet, you are a romantic."

"No, Lawrence, I am first and foremost a realist." She glanced back at the portrait. "The Deakin Diamonds are obviously worth a king's ransom. But what is the sense in owning something that must be stashed in a secret hiding place, or locked away in a bank vault somewhere?" Juliet shook her head. "Besides," the businesswoman in her noted, "the insurance on them must be exorbitant.

"They were uninsured."

She went very still. *"Were?"*

His eyes narrowed to two dark slits. "The Deakin Diamonds disappeared in 1828."

She drew a breath and spoke slowly. "They were lost?"

"They were stolen."

"How did it happen?"

He spoke without anger, but with a kind of cold finality. "I only know a portion of the story from my father and from Nanny. My grandmother could never bear to speak of it since she blamed herself for their loss."

Juliet studied the face of the innocent young woman. "Poor Alicia Anne."

"Yes, poor Alicia Anne," he sympathized. "Apparently my grandparents were giving a gala house party to celebrate the restoration of the chapel and some of the older sections of the Manor. The house was filled with friends, family, neighbors, even royalty. It was during that weekend nearly fifty years ago that the Deakin Diamonds disappeared. They vanished without a trace."

"Vanished without a trace," she echoed.

"Despite everyone's efforts at the time, they were never found and never heard of again. No one was accused of the theft, of course. That would have been a disgrace, a stain of dishonor upon the Wickes that my family would not have allowed. But it is unlikely the gems were misplaced."

"I am so sorry, Lawrence."

"As you say, they were only fancy baubles."

"But the loss must have been devastating to Alicia Anne, especially since the stones were uninsured."

A dangerous glint showed in his eyes. "At this moment I have only one regret regarding the Deakin Diamonds," he said in a husky voice.

Juliet held her breath. She was almost afraid to ask—but, in the end, she did, of course. "What is your one regret?"

"That I will never see you standing in this room wearing the Deakin Diamonds—and nothing else."

Juliet suddenly existed in a universe occupied only by her own heartbeats. She found herself drawn to Lawrence like a moth to a flame, and the danger be damned!

He took a step toward her. "I have never wanted to kiss a woman as much as I want to kiss you at this moment."

"And are you?" There was no coyness in her manner, merely feminine curiosity.

"Am I what?"

"Going to kiss me?"

"I have to."

"You *have* to?"

"If I don't kiss you I think I shall die," Lawrence declared, seducing her with his words.

Her hands made a supplicating gesture. "I wouldn't want your death on my conscience."

He leaned toward her and Juliet could feel his hot breath wafting across her face: her eyes, her nose, her mouth. The anticipation was almost more than she could bear.

Why didn't he take pity on her? Why didn't

he put her out of her misery? It had been a full week since he had kissed her, held her, touched her.

Why didn't he swoop down and ruthlessly take her lips as he had before? Why didn't he thrust his wonderful tongue down her throat and overwhelm her with his passion?

He did none of these things.

Instead, she felt the tip of a wet tongue delve into her ear, then circle the sensitive outer shell, once, twice, three times. A soft breath blew across her damp skin, and she shivered. She was covered in gooseflesh from head to toe. Then serrated teeth sank into her earlobe and her legs buckled beneath her.

"Lawrence, what are you doing to me?" she gasped.

"I am kissing you," he said huskily as he supported her full weight.

"But that is my ear," she pointed out faintly.

"Yes, it is. You have lovely ears, Juliet."

Then he brushed his lips along her bare throat, leaving a trail of scorching kisses behind that did strange and wonderful things to her insides.

"Lawrence, that is my throat."

"I know that. I am well-acquainted with human anatomy. You agreed that I could kiss you. You did not specify *where* I had to kiss you."

Her voice was a rasp. "I thought you meant my mouth."

"You were mistaken." There was something in his voice that caught her attention. "I intend to kiss you, my dear Juliet, in each and every place you would be wearing the Deakin Diamonds if they adorned your body tonight."

She could feel his hot gaze on her. Her heart began to slam against her chest. "Each and every place?"

"I have touched upon the earrings and the necklace, although I may come back to them again later." He raised her wrist to his mouth and, with eyes darkened to midnight, licked the sensitive flesh of the underside.

She held her breath.

"This is the bracelet."

"Of"—she slowly let out her breath—"course."

He carefully selected the third finger of her right hand and slipped it into his mouth, and began to suck on it. His suckling drew it farther and farther in until she feared that he intended to swallow her finger whole, and somehow her along with it.

"The ring," she groaned, never imagining that anything so seemingly innocent could be so erotic.

Lawrence released her hand and mumbled against her mouth: "You have set my whole body on fire. I am burning up."

"And I am melting like candlewax," she confessed.

He made a strangling sound that rumbled deep in his chest. "The last piece in the collection was a brooch that was always worn on the left breast."

Juliet's evening gown was lowcut, and she was wearing only the flimsiest of bodices beneath it since her skin was still tender, but she never foresaw what would happen next. Nor did she try to stop it.

Lawrence found the row of tiny buttons down the front of her dress and managed to undo them one by one. He pulled the top of her evening gown down her arms, pushed her undergarment aside and bared her breasts.

"Lawrence!" She tried to cover herself.

"No!" He captured her hands and held them away from her body. "I have imagined you this way so many times. I want to see you. I must know."

"Must know what?"

"If your breasts are beautiful."

Her cheeks flamed. "And are they?"

"Your breasts are perfection itself," he concluded after careful and meticulous study.

Her body seemed to react to his words alone. Her breasts swelled. Her nipples became hard and erect, darker around the centers, engorged.

"I ache—" she cried out. "Help me!"

Lawrence was more than willing to help. Indeed, he seemed eager. He stuck out his tongue and licked the tip of her breast. Juliet watched as her nipple curled up into an even tighter bud. It was exciting. It was forbidden. It was wonderful.

"But I still ache," she moaned. "Worse than before."

He took pity on her, then, and took her fully between his lips. He suckled on her nipple as he had earlier on her finger, drawing it deeper and deeper into his mouth, until she wondered if he were going to eat her alive. He reached up with his thumb and finger and captured the other nipple between them and pinched, softly at first and then more intensely.

Somewhere in her lower body, Juliet felt a corresponding erotic pull that felt very much like a major "disturbance" of the womb. She had never imagined that her body could feel this way, could *or* would react this way.

When Lawrence finally came up for air, he praised her. "These are magnificent jewels, indeed," he murmured, covering her breasts with his palms.

"Do you have any jewels?" she inquired innocently.

"Jewels?" His laugh came from the back of his throat. It sent a shiver spiraling down her spine.

"Have I said something I oughtn't?"

"No." But he was still laughing in that same manner. "As a matter of fact, my dear Juliet, I have the family jewels on me at this moment."

She frowned. "You do?" She wasn't certain she believed him. She arched a skeptical brow. "What do they consist of?"

"A sceptor and two very large pearls."

"How large?" she asked suspiciously, thinking of the anatomy of the big, black stallion in the park.

"They change size."

"The scepter, as well?"

"Even more so," he confessed.

"I am not sure I believe you," she murmured,

taking a step toward him. "You will have to prove it to me."

His eyes widened. "Are you sure you want tangible proof?"

"I am sure."

"Unbutton my coat, put your hand out and touch my waist," he instructed.

She did as she was told. "I see nothing. I feel nothing." But a firm muscular body and a lean waist. Lawrence was a superb physical specimen.

"You must look lower," he suggested.

Juliet dropped her eyes. "There is something in your dress trousers."

"Indeed."

"It is large."

He nodded and said nothing.

"It is huge." The breath caught in her lungs for a moment. "It is growing."

"It is growing because of you."

"Am I permitted to touch it?"

He flushed a dull red. "I don't think that would be a good idea."

"Why not? You have touched me."

"It is not quite the same thing."

"Why not?"

He heaved a great sigh. "Because I cannot reciprocate the favor."

"I don't understand."

"I know you don't, my dear Juliet."

"What is stopping you from explaining, from demonstrating?"

"Your armor for one."

"My armor?"

"Your confounded clothing," he said in a hard, dry voice.

"Oh—" It had taken the help of her maid to get her into the silk dress and she was not even wearing the usual full regalia of corsets and boned stays and bodices.

"And the fact that you are an unmarried lady and a virgin."

She wrinkled up her brows. "I thought those traits were considered desirable."

"They are."

"But in this case they are detriments."

"Let us say, they are obstacles."

She sighed and announced: "I do not feel satisfied."

Lawrence rolled his eyes. "That makes two of us."

"Indeed, I feel frustrated. One might even say irritated."

"You are not alone, madam."

Her gaze zeroed in on him. "Are you also unsatisfied?"

"Yes."

"Frustrated?"

"In the extreme."

"Irritated."

"Beyond belief."

"Good."

Black brows knitted together. "Good?"

Juliet smiled at him sweetly, too sweetly, she knew. "There is some satisfaction in simply knowing that you are suffering, as well."

"Madam, the hour grows late," Lawrence

growled. "Put yourself to rights. It is past time we rejoined the other members of our party."

"And you, sir?"

"I will button my coat and think of Queen and country."

They eventually left the stateroom and wended their way back to the lounge where Euphemia Jones was enjoying her card game with the gentlemen.

Before he opened the door, Lawrence paused and addressed her in a formal manner. "Madam, may I call upon you tomorrow?"

He had been calling upon her every day for the past week. She wondered why his request was so stilted this time.

She shrugged and said: "Yes."

Little did Juliet realize at the time how much that one word was going to change her life.

14

"MADAM, I would be speaking to your father this morning, if he were living, or to your guardian, if you had one, but as neither is the case, and since your male cousin is a mere boy, himself, and your only other living relation is your great-aunt—I must address you directly. I beg your pardon for doing so."

"I quite understand, sir. There is no need to beg. You are pardoned."

Was Juliet Jones having a bit of sport at his expense? Lawrence had to admit he couldn't tell.

They were not in the Blue Room which was typically used for morning visits. Nor were they in the library, where they had taken afternoon tea on numerous occasions. At his request, they were in the rarely used formal drawing room.

Serious matters called for serious surroundings.

After her departure from the *Alicia Anne* last night, under the chaperonage of her great-aunt, Lawrence had decided that the best and *safest* approach to take in this affair was an appeal to Juliet's logic and intelligence—since she was a most logical and intelligent female. She would understand that there were certain conventions, certain proprieties, a certain decorum that must be observed.

Business before pleasure, Lawrence reminded himself, as he seemingly had several hundred times since their initial encounter in Central Park.

He paced the floor, his hands linked behind his back. "If I may, madam, I would like to ask you a question."

"Of course. Would you care to sit down first?" she inquired, gesturing toward the sofa.

"I prefer to stand at the present time, thank you. But please do take a seat yourself, Miss Jones."

She plunked down, folded her hands in her lap, and looked up at him expectantly. He suddenly wished that her eyes were not quite so blue or her mouth so diverting. It made it difficult for him to concentrate on what he had to say.

"You wished to ask me something—" she prompted.

He cleared his throat. Actually he wished to ask her a great many things. "It is a personal question."

She sighed and plumped the tasseled pillow at her back. "I am beginning to think that's the only kind there is. Oh, do go on, Lawrence. We are hardly strangers."

"I would like to know"—he paused and then said in a different voice—"why a woman with your means, your social position and your beauty has reached a certain—ahem—age and has declined to marry."

She didn't blink an eyelash. "In other words, you want to know why I am an old maid."

He frowned and said with a hint of reprimand in his tone, "That is putting it indelicately, madam."

"That is putting it straightforwardly, sir." She gave it about thirty seconds of thought before answering. "I do not wish to be a widow."

Based on the reports he had had from Miles's and Bunter's discreet investigations upon their arrival in New York some weeks ago, that was the last thing Lawrence had expected her to say. "I'm sure no woman desires to be a widow."

"I wouldn't bet on it," she muttered under her breath as she straightened the pleats in her skirt.

"Would you explain?"

"Of course." She looked up. "There is more to life than eating, drinking, and making merry."

"Yes, I know. We have had this conversation before," he pointed out testily, his impatience surfacing as it seemed to with increasing frequency these days. "There is also more to life, if I recall your exact words, than balls."

"You do. And there is."

"I believe broad-shouldered, empty-headed dancing partners were also mentioned in passing."

"They were. You have an excellent memory, sir."

"Thank you, madam." He gave a small but

polite bow of his head. "But we stray from the subject—"

She stiffened her back and announced: "Men of Society die young."

He was confused. He tried to see the logic of it from her viewpoint. "And, therefore, presumably, young wives become young widows."

"Precisely." There was an intractable expression on her face. "It is little wonder."

Lawrence sighed and attempted to follow her train of thought. "What is?"

"That men of Society die young, of course. On the average they smoke an entire box of cigars each day." Juliet wrinkled up her nose and declared: "A disgusting habit."

His hopes rose. "I do not smoke."

"That is to your credit."

"That cannot be your only objection to young gentlemen, however."

"They also consume lengthy dinners of eight and ten courses and more. They grow rotund, short of breath, and more interested in food than in their wives."

His hopes soared. "I eat reasonably and as a soldier—"

"As an ex-soldier."

"And as an ex-soldier I am in excellent physical condition," he told her.

"You are to be commended. Nonetheless—"

"There is more?"

"There is definitely more. Young men—indeed, it seems men of all ages—do a great deal of drinking."

"I drink sparingly."

The lady studied him for a minute, head cocked. "Moderation in all things."

"It is my motto."

"I thought your unofficial motto was 'where there is a will, there is a way'?"

"Surely a man may live by more than one motto."

"Apparently the Wicke men do," she said, looking at him in cool appraisement. "My last objection to young men of Society is the most serious of all."

Lawrence waited. He knew Juliet would tell him when she was good and ready and not before.

She wet her lips with her tongue and drew in a deep breath. "It is a question of fidelity."

He frowned. "Fidelity?"

"When it comes to the marriage bed."

Lawrence choked on his saliva. "Juliet!"

The image she presented, sitting on the formal drawing room sofa, pretty as you please, was one of utter innocence. "Have I put it wrongly?"

He began to pace again. "There is no right way of putting it. There are simply certain matters that should not be discussed between a man and a woman."

"Why not?"

That stopped him dead in his tracks. "It is not done."

"Why is it not done?"

"It is—inappropriate."

"Balderdash!" She was on her feet in an instant. "Men want to have their cake and eat it, too."

Lawrence felt the heat of discomfort creep up his neck and onto his face. Those were the exact words Miles had used not long ago in describing Helena, the wayward Lady Deerhurst.

Juliet began to pace back and forth in front of him, waving her arms animatedly. "You have doubtless heard that Miss Jones has vowed never to marry, that Miss Jones has certain 'notions,' that Miss Jones is a hopeless romantic." She paused and chewed on her bottom lip for a moment. "Indeed, it was only last night that you called me a romantic in a most patronizing fashion, yourself."

He supposed he was guilty as charged. "I was not quite myself last night."

She speared him with fierce blue eyes. "Then *who*, pray tell, were you?"

"Well, for one thing I was a sexually aroused male who did not get any sleep," he thundered.

She stared at him in stunned silence.

Hell and damnation, this was not the proper way to present his suit to a lady. The woman got him going in circles until he met himself coming and going!

She apparently recovered from his outburst and then had the audacity to wag a finger at him and go on with her lecture as if nothing had happened. "I know that love and fidelity between husband and wife are not the fashion in Society, that they are considered incidental—if they are considered at all. But if that is marriage, sir, I will have none of it."

The lady was infuriating.

The lady was unconventional.

The lady was magnificent.

The lady was utterly irresistible.

Miles had been right: Juliet Jones would be a challenge and she would never bore him.

Lawrence planted himself in her path and when she turned around the next time, she ran directly into his chest. His arms went around her. He held her firmly but gently to him. Her lips were pressed to the front of his jacket, making speech difficult, if not impossible.

"Wrence—" she mumbled.

"Hush, my darling," he crooned to her. "No more words. No more logic. No more arguments. No more rantings and ravings. And no more discussions." He stood there, enfolding her within his embrace, realizing that he had done it all wrong.

There was only one way to a woman's heart. . . .

Lawrence finally felt her heave a great sigh and sink against him. He leaned over and buried his face in her hair, nuzzled her neck, breathed in her scent.

"I love the way you smell," he murmured, brushing his lips softly across her skin.

"I don't wear perfume," she said dazedly.

"I know." He drew her nearer. "I love the way you feel in my arms. I love the way you feel in my hands."

He slid his hands up and down her body, spanned her slender waist, and finally covered her breasts with his palms. Her nipples rounded into two perfect pearls.

"Lawrence—" she began, her voice faltering.

"I especially love the way your body reacts to my touch, to my caress," he confessed. It was indefinably sweet to sense her response through his mouth and fingers. "And I love what you do to me."

Juliet put her head back and gazed up at him. The gesture revealed a surprisingly long, slender neck with the merest hint of blue veins beneath the surface of the skin. A faint pulse throbbed at the base of her throat. Mesmerized, he caught himself counting her heartbeats.

"What do I do to you?" she murmured.

"You make me forget where I am, who I am, what I am. You make me forget every other woman I have ever met. You make me feel both weak and strong, like a fool and a wise man."

It was true, he realized. It was all true.

He went on. "I want to make love to you, Juliet. I want to take your body. I want to give you mine in return. I want us to be as one." Lawrence took a fortifying breath. "I want us to be husband and wife. I am asking for your hand in marriage. Will you accept my offer?"

There was one suspenseful moment when he feared she would laugh in his face and refuse him outright.

When she did not laugh, Lawrence heard himself start to ramble nervously: "Naturally, you will want time to think about my offer. I did not mean to rush you. There is a great deal to consider. You must, of course, weigh the advantages and disadvantages of a match between us. You must take inventory of your feelings for me, whatever they may be, to whatever degree you may or may not hold me in regard. You will be residing in a foreign country, leaving behind your home, your friends, the life you have known. I realize it is no small matter. Indeed, it will be a monumental undertaking."

Juliet went up on her tiptoes and whispered against his astonished mouth: "Lawrence."

"Yes?"

"I accept your offer."

She was in love with him.

Juliet had known it for some time, she acknowledged it to herself in that moment before she accepted Lawrence's proposal of marriage.

It was not sensible. It was not logical. It was certainly not rational.

It *was* foolish. It *was* impulsive. It *was* a little crazy. And it *was* very probably dangerous.

But her heart had decided for her: Lawrence was the man she wanted. He was the only man she had ever wanted. Now he would be hers, and she would be his—heart and soul and body.

"We must seal our bargain with a kiss," he muttered huskily as he leaned over her.

"Promise me one thing," she said, once she had caught her breath again.

His black eyes were indulgent. "Anything."

She caught the tip of her tongue between her teeth. "Will you please finally explain all those delicious double entendres to me?"

Lawrence put his head back and laughed

without constraint. "I will not only explain them to you, my dearest Juliet. I will show them to you."

She blushed right down to the tip of her toes.

"I hope you won't want a long engagement," he said, after a brief pause.

She shrugged. "I hadn't given it a thought."

"Then I would like to be married soon and sail for home." He gazed down into her eyes and quoted: " 'Oh, to be in England now that April's there.' Mister Robert Browning."

"April, it is, then."

"It means we must be ready to leave in a month."

"Six weeks?" she bargained.

"Six weeks," he agreed.

Juliet took him by the hand and urged him toward the door. "We must go and tell Aunt Effie straightaway. She will be so surprised."

Lawrence shook his head good-naturedly. "Somehow I don't believe Euphemia is going to be nearly as surprised as you were."

15

It was her wedding night.

Juliet, the Duchess of Deakin, sat in front of the toilette table and gazed, unseeing, into the mirror. She was dressed in the finest nightgown of embroidered lawn and temporarily wore a combing sacque over the top. She had sent her maid away, preferring to take down and brush out her own hair tonight. She needed a few minutes alone.

Drawing the brush through her hair with long, even strokes, Juliet thought about the hectic day that had started before dawn. There had been a great deal to be done: she was scheduled to be bathed, dressed, coiffed, and transported to the wedding chapel by nine o'clock.

She had arrived on time.

They had decided to be married in a small, private ceremony with only Aunt Effie, Cousin David, Miles, Bunter, Brambinger, Mrs. Hudson, and the other longtime staff in attendance. Neither she nor Lawrence had been interested in turning their wedding day into a circus or a public spectacle.

Her dress had been of ivory satin; the long

train of Brussels lace. Lawrence had chosen the bridal bouquet, himself: a cascade of white roses.

"Roses," he had whispered to her just before they exchanged their vows, "because their scent always reminds me of you, my dearest Juliet."

Roses would remain her favorite flower throughout the rest of her life.

At her request, her wedding ring was a plain gold band with their names engraved on the inside along with the date of their marriage.

Juliet held up her left hand and gazed at the gold ring. She was a married lady now. She was no longer "Miss Juliet" or "Miss Jones." From this day forward she would be Juliet, Duchess of Deakin.

She was quickly learning the pecking order of the British aristocracy. Miles was permitted to call her Juliet, of course. He was a marquess, himself, and her husband's best friend. But the ship's crew, the staff, even her own maid referred to her as "Your Grace."

Thank goodness she had several weeks to get used to the idea before the *Alicia Anne* docked in England.

England: her new country and her new home.

The arrangements had all been made. Brambinger and Mrs. Hudson had chosen to retire to the horse farm in Kentucky where the weather was more amenable to their various physical ailments. The New York house was getting too much for them to handle and the prospect of moving to a faraway land, especially one with a damp climate, held no appeal for either of them.

The rest of the staff was staying on at 665 Fifth Avenue. David was going to continue living there and oversee the property, but he had promised to visit them in Northumberland later in the summer.

Besides the necessary business papers and files, Juliet was taking only her most cherished things with her: her favorite books, her Bronzino, the birds that had been a gift from Lawrence and, of course, Aunt Effie. Indeed, the ladies' clothes trunks—they had numbered in the dozens—had been packed and put aboard the yacht several days ago.

Putting her hairbrush down, she turned and gazed up at the portrait of Alicia Anne that hung in what was now *her* stateroom. "I hope I'm half the duchess you were, Grandmother, even without the Deakin Diamonds."

Then she blushed to think of the evening Lawrence had kissed her in this very room, touching upon each and every place where the famous diamonds would have caressed her skin.

How did a woman handle the intimacy of her wedding night? Juliet rose and began to pace back and forth in front of the toilette table. Did she sit and wait until there was a knock on the connecting door between her stateroom and Lawrence's? Was she somehow supposed to signal to him that she had changed for bed? Or was she to go to him? Unfortunately the proper protocol and etiquette for the occasion had never been explained.

Juliet felt half sick. There was a loud rumble, then another from the very depths of her being. Then she suddenly realized it was not apprehension. It was not fear.

It was hunger.

The wedding breakfast—it was more of an early luncheon—had been held aboard ship hours and hours ago. But she had been too nervous at the time to do anything more than push the food around on her plate. They had set sail immediately afterward.

Dinner had been an intimate affair served in Lawrence's stateroom. She had once again been unable to swallow a bite. She noticed that he had eaten very little himself. The meal had concluded a half hour ago with her husband's declaration that he was going for a stroll on deck and she undoubtedly would like to return to her own adjoining stateroom to prepare.

To prepare for what?

Once she had undressed, put on her nightgown and combed her hair what was she supposed to do with herself? How was she to "prepare" for her wedding night, when she had only the vaguest notion of what was going to transpire?

There was another loud rumble of protest from her midsection. Perhaps the staff had yet to clear away the dinner table. Perhaps Lawrence had not returned from his walk. Perhaps she could slip into his room, unobserved, and sneak a slice of meat or a piece of bread to fill her very empty stomach.

Juliet crept to the connecting doorway and

put her ear to the wooden panel. She listened intently. She did not hear a sound. Gingerly she turned the brass knob. Slowly she opened the door.

Lawrence's stateroom was deserted.

Indeed, it appeared to be just as they had left it some thirty minutes ago. Luckily no one had cleared away the remnants of their meal. The table was still laden with covered dishes of tender fillet of beef, savory breasts of partridge, baked quail, buttered sole, bowls of exotic fruits, plates of succulent lobster salad and stewed oysters, glazed pears, honeyed dates, and sugared nuts.

It was a feast fit for a king.

In her bare feet, Juliet scampered across the carpet to the table, grabbed a fork and speared a bite of lobster salad—all the while keeping one eye and one ear tuned to the outside stateroom door. She had a piece of fruit next, then a mouthwatering slice of beef, followed by several sweet nuts.

She picked up the glass of champagne she had left untouched earlier and took a swallow. It was still cool, still bubbly. It tickled her nose and made her want to laugh.

What a ridiculous sight she must make! The new Duchess of Deakin sneaking around in her night rail and bare feet, stealing food from her own wedding feast. Nevertheless, Juliet helped herself to another bite of lobster salad and tried a little of the tomato aspic. It was all delicious.

"I must remember to give my compliments to

the chef in the morning," she mumbled, her mouth full. "The man is an absolute jewel."

Voices.

She hear voices, masculine voices, right outside the stateroom door.

She froze.

Then, when it became evident that the voices were not coming any closer, she tried to swallow the mouthful of food. She ended up washing the last of it down with the champagne from the bottom of her glass.

Juliet considered returning to her own bedroom, of course, but curiosity drove her in the opposite direction. She tiptoed to the door of her husband's stateroom, opened it a crack and peered out.

It was Lawrence and Miles St. Aldford. The two gentlemen were standing by the ship's rail, brandies in hand, drinking what appeared to be a nightcap.

Juliet was quite certain, in the beginning, that she'd had no intentions of eavesdropping on their private conversation. Indeed, she would have quietly closed the door again and slipped off to bed at that point if she had not heard mention of her own name.

"A toast," purposed Miles.

"A toast," repeated Lawrence.

"To our Juliet—"

"To *my* Juliet," corrected Lawrence.

"To *your* Juliet," slurred Miles, who was obviously slightly in his cups, "who is not only very beautiful and very intelligent, but very, very rich."

"Here, here," agreed Lawrence as they touched glasses.

The heat rushed to Juliet's face. She inched closer and listened to every word.

"Another toast," suggested the marquess. "To the Great American Heiress: long may she live and prosper."

"Long may she live and prosper," echoed the duke.

They seemed very pleased with themselves, Juliet thought with growing suspicion.

"To His Royal Highness, who first conceived the idea, with a little help from yours truly."

"To Bertie," Lawrence said with somewhat less enthusiasm than his companion.

"It was a brilliant scheme, my friend, and it was brilliantly executed," Miles declared, pounding the taller man on the back in congratulation.

Warning bells went off in Juliet's head. Brilliant scheme? What was a brilliant scheme? Or should the question be: *who* was a brilliant scheme?

"Yes, I suppose it did work out rather well, in the end," muttered her husband, frowning. He did not seem altogether pleased about it. Not nearly as pleased as Miles.

"Do be kind to her, Deakin. I believe the girl is quite fond of you."

"She is more than fond of me, Cork. I don't doubt she fancies herself in love with me."

From where she was crouched behind the stateroom door, Juliet was able to catch an occasional glimpse of Lawrence's expression. Although obscured by shadows, she was quite certain she saw his mouth turn up at the corners. She would give half her fortune for the chance to wipe that smug smile off the duke's handsome face.

"When do you think it began?" inquired his countryman as he leaned one arm on the railing.

"I think Juliet started to fall in love with me the first morning in Central Park."

"And when did you realize you were in love with her?"

"Don't be a sod, Miles," he scoffed, turning to gaze off toward the inky black horizon. It was some time before he said, "Naturally, I find Juliet very attractive."

The other man shrugged nonchalantly. "Should make the whole business more agreeable in the long run."

"It will definitely make the lady more manageable and my life infinitely easier." The duke shook his head as if he still could not believe his good fortune. "To marry for money and have your wife in love with you. What more could any man ask for?"

The air was suddenly trapped in Juliet's lungs. She could not inhale or exhale. She felt as though she were suffocating. She wanted to scream and could not.

Then she wanted to scream and *would* not.

Lawrence had married her for her money.

She wanted to laugh hysterically at the horrible irony of it. She had gone to such lengths to make sure she would not be married for her fortune. And, in the end, that was her fate anyway.

She wanted to cry because her heart was breaking into a thousand tiny pieces, and she knew she would never be the same again. She had not known she could grow up in the space of a moment or two.

Then she was angry.

In fact, she was incensed.

By all the saints in Heaven, she was not going to hide behind a door and listen to one more word from the mouth of that devil Englishman!

The duchess rose to her full height, put her shoulders back, raised her chin and marched across the gentleman's stateroom to her own. She rummaged under her bed until she located a small trunk. Then she took out a special key, unlocked the trunk and removed a heavy drawstring bag made of velvet. She marched back into the connecting room with the velvet pouch just as Lawrence came strolling in from outside.

"My dearest, I see you're ready for bed," he murmured, his eyes glittering with anticipation.

"I am, sir," she said icily.

His black eyes narrowed warily. "The door was ajar when I came in just now."

"Was it, indeed?" she responded haughtily.

"Yes." Lawrence took a casual step or two into his room and sauntered over to the dinner table. "I noticed you did not have an appetite earlier. Would you care for something to eat?"

"I have already helped myself."

He dropped his hand and stepped away from the table. "What is it that you have there, Juliet?"

"It is yours," she said, her eyes snapping with feeling. She tossed the bag of coins at him.

He caught it easily. "What is this?" he inquired with what sounded like genuine reluctance.

"Payment."

"Payment?"

"Or should I say the first of many payments?"

"I do not understand."

Her voice rose. "You married me for my money. Well, there is some of it. In gold, of course. And it is a tidy sum, if you care to count your booty."

Lawrence swore savagely. "You were listening at the door."

Her eyes burned with unshed tears. "It was unintentional, believe me."

"It was also not quite what you think."

"I have ears. I know what I heard. Do not try to lie your way out of this one, Your Grace."

Lawrence looked directly at her. "I have never lied to you, Juliet."

"You cannot seriously expect me to believe that."

"I can and I do, madam. I am a gentleman of honor. I have never deliberately told you a falsehood."

She glared at him. "You walk a very fine line, then, Your Grace, between truth and lies." She turned and regally made her way toward her own stateroom.

He tried to reason with her. "Let us at least talk about it."

Her mind was made up. "There is nothing left for us to say to each other."

"Juliet, this is our wedding night and you are my wife," he pointed out.

How dare he bring up *that* business now! Was that all men ever thought about? Was that all *he* ever thought about? Surely he did not expect to claim his "rights" as a husband after what had just transpired between them?

Juliet was trembling from head to toe. She was furious with Lawrence. She didn't care if he was a duke: the man had all the brains, all the manners, all the finesse of a jackass.

She paused with her hand on the doorknob and condescended to glance back over her shoulder at him. "You, sir, have made your bed and now you must sleep in it . . . alone."

The next sound Lawrence Grenfell Wicke heard was the click of the lock on the door between their staterooms.

"Damn it all to hell," he swore as he glared at the seemingly insurmountable barrier he had just erected between them.

Something, or someone, was pounding on the outer door of his stateroom. It felt like they were pounding on his head with a sledgehammer.

Lawrence rolled over and groaned: "Go away,

damn you, and leave me alone." Then he buried his head under several pillows.

"Deakin, it is Cork."

"Cork who?"

There was a brief pause. Then: "Lawrence, it is Miles."

"What do you want?" he growled.

Hell and damnation, his head was killing him. It hurt even to talk.

The door to his cabin opened and his best friend casually strolled in, very bright sunlight streaming in behind him.

Lawrence turned over, put a hand up to shade his eyes and complained, "The sun is very bright this morning."

"The sun is very bright this *afternoon*," corrected Miles St. Aldford. He took a handkerchief from his pocket and held it to his nostrils. "Gad, the smell in here is disgusting, Lawrence. It's like a distillery. Or worse." He walked around the room and commented: "Little wonder. Empty champagne bottles. Mounds of spoiling food. A plate of what once must have been a rather nice lobster salad, a bowl of stewed oysters, a tureen of . . ."

"Say one more word and I will be sick," warned Lawrence.

The marquess shook his head. "I knew you were never much of a sailor, but you didn't seem to have this problem on the voyage over. Perhaps Juliet is right."

"Perhaps my wife is right about *what*?"

"She thinks it may be a case of 'nerves.' "

"Nerves?" he roared. He should have grabbed

his head first, Lawrence realized an instant too late. "And exactly when did you and my dear wife discuss my health?"

"At luncheon," Miles answered offhandedly. "I must confess I missed breakfast myself, but Juliet said it was superb. She described the fare to me in great detail. I believe she said the kidneys and the poached eggs were especially delicious."

"I think I may throw up."

"Poor chap. You are feeling that poorly, aren't you? Juliet told us you had been forced to take to your bed."

Lawrence ground his teeth together and ignored the pain. "Did she? I suppose this was at luncheon, as well."

"No. Actually it was while we were taking a brisk hike around the deck before luncheon. Nothing like a breath of fresh sea air to make a man feel better after too much self-indulgence, hey?" Miles stopped himself. "Of course, you wouldn't feel that way since you're suffering from a nasty case of *mal de mer*, would you? I must say, Deakin, you do look like the very devil."

"Thank you. That is slightly better than I am feeling," he said dryly. "Where is my lovely bride now?"

"Having a chat with the chef, I believe. She wanted to extend her personal compliments about last night's dinner. Said the filet of beef, the buttered sole, the aspic, the salads, the fruits, the sugared nuts, the stuffed partridges were some of the best she had ever eaten."

Lawrence rolled off the bed and staggered into the adjoining accommodations. He returned several minutes later, face pale, stomach empty, wiping his mouth with a damp cloth.

"You're not a sailor like the sixth duke, are you, Deakin?"

Lawrence ignored his friend's comment and demanded, with a gesture toward the rotting food: "Why in the hell hasn't this mess been cleaned up?"

Miles shrugged. "Haven't the foggiest, old chap. But I'll stick my head out the door and summon a steward for you."

He was as good as his word. Within a minute or two, a young uniformed servant appeared.

"Yes, Your Grace?" he said with all due respect.

"Why hasn't this been cleared away?" he demanded.

"We were not allowed to disturb you, Your Grace."

"Not allowed to disturb me?"

"No, Your Grace. We all know how seasick you've been. We were not to enter this stateroom. Those were our strict orders."

"Who gave these strict orders?"

"Why, Her Grace, of course," the young man said as if it were the Queen herself who had issued them and they were nothing less than a royal decree.

"I would like this room cleaned up immediately."

"Of course, Your Grace." The steward quickly went to work. When he was nearly finished, he inquired: "Shall I inform Her Grace that you will be joining her for tea?"

Lawrence rubbed his hand back and forth along the rough stubble of his beard. "I don't believe I'll be up for tea. By the way, where is Her Grace?"

'The captain is giving Her Grace a guided tour of the ship, Your Grace." The young servant paused and delivered one final message. "Her Grace said to be sure and tell you that the menu for dinner tonight will include cold tongue, sliced rare beef, and sweetbreads."

"Out!"

"Yes, Your Grace."

Lawrence began to strip off his slept-in shirt and pants. He turned to Miles. "And how does my wife look this morning?"

"Like a million dollars," exclaimed Lord Cork. "Or should I say, one hundred million dollars?"

Lawrence did not find the allusion amusing. He sank down on the edge of the mattress and put his head in his hands. "I have made a stupid mistake, Miles."

"I thought we agreed you weren't going to."

"It is about Juliet."

Miles groaned. "Now what have you done?"

"She overheard our conversation last night."

"Our conversation?"

Lawrence refreshed his friend's memory. "We were out on the deck, toasting the success of our brilliant scheme."

"Damn and blast!"

"My sentiments exactly."

"Now what will you do?"

He sighed and stood up. "First, I will bathe. Then I will have to start over from scratch."

Miles St. Aldford shook his head. "Not from scratch, I fear."

"You're right. Juliet is very proud, and it is her precious pride that has been sorely wounded."

"You have your work cut out for you, Deakin."

"She is going to lead me on a merry dance, isn't she, Cork?"

"A very merry dance." The other man laughed, shook his head, and sauntered to the door. "Watch your back, my friend. Your dear wife will be out for revenge. And you know what is said about revenge."

Lawrence looked up. "What?"

"It is a dish best served cold."

16

"THE duke has married an old maid," announced a pretty young thing who had recently turned eighteen and regarded anybody over the age of twenty as having one foot in the grave.

"I've heard that she is thirty, perhaps even thirty-five," volunteered the daughter of a cabinet minister who was in London for the preseason, having failed to make an advantageous match for herself the summer before.

"She is an heiress," allowed another as she sipped her tea daintily.

"My maid was told by her young man, who works as a steward aboard the duke's yacht, that the new duchess hasn't a single piece of jewelry to her name. That doesn't sound like an heiress to me. Furthermore"—the ladies leaned forward slightly so as not to miss a word of what was being said—"she wears a plain gold wedding band. Nothing more."

"No!"

"Yes!"

"You mean the duke hasn't given her a single token of his affections?"

"Not so much as a garnet ring or a pearl brooch," claimed the well-informed source.

"She is an American," pronounced one very grand lady whose claim to fame was being the third daughter of a baronet. "She must be uncouth."

"Rumor has it she is pockmarked and bucktoothed," burst out an indiscreet newcomer.

"I've heard that she is short and fat," said a pleasantly plump young matron as she gobbled down a cake.

Another, with a pinched nose and a pinched mouth and a pinched face, immediately contradicted her. "She is tall and thin."

"It is doubtful that the new Duchess of Deakin is both short and fat *and* tall and thin," interjected Helena as she sipped a cup of tea secretly laced with her favorite "restorative." It had become her custom to allow herself a little pick-me-up at this time of the day. The afternoons could be so interminably long and boring.

"Someone said that the lady is pale and sickly. Perhaps she suffers from consumption and hasn't long to live."

The well-informed source turned to their hostess. "You have a country house not too distant from Grantley Manor, do you not, Lady Deerhurst?"

"We do, but I thrive on town life. I rarely spend more than a few weeks a year in the north," she told her guests as if that were all she knew concerning the matter.

Helena preferred gathering gossip to giving

it away free. Information was a useful and valuable commodity in Society, and she collected it with determination and skill.

It was one of the reasons she deliberately never mentioned that her husband loved country life and, in general, loathed the city. Sidney and their children, lived at Deerhurst Hall nine or even ten months out of the year. He only came down to attend Parliament when some issue of import required his presence in the House of Lords.

Otherwise, the earl avoided London—and his wife—like the plague.

Still, it was not Sidney who occupied Helena's thoughts. It was Lawrence.

Damn his soul!

He had gone and done it. After refusing to take her along, he had sailed to America, found himself an heiress and married her. Thanks to H.R.H. or Miles St. Aldford.

What was the new duchess really like? That was the question that ate at the countess like a wasting disease. She would not, could not rest until she had her answer.

"From a friend's recent letter, I do know this much," Helena began, and the drawing room full of second-string and even third-string society ladies instantly fell silent, as she had known it would. All eyes were on her. "The Duke and Duchess of Deakin have been at their estate in Northumberland for a full two weeks and no one has yet to meet the bride."

Helena took another sip of tea and allowed herself a brief and somewhat smug smile behind her china cup. That would set tongues wagging. The tidbit of gossip would be all over London by nightfall.

"See to the drawing room immediately," Helena instructed her housemaid after the last guest had departed.

"Yes, Lady Deerhurst."

Her voice was all business. "The leftover teacakes are to be saved and served again tomorrow."

"As you wish, Lady Deerhurst."

"Take care with the plates and cups, you foolish girl," she admonished. "If you break any of the china I will deduct it from your wages."

"I'll be careful. I promise."

"See that you are." Helena was suddenly quite weary of it all. "I am going to my boudoir. I do not wish to be disturbed," she said.

She made her way to her private rooms on the second floor of the fashionable house off Berkeley Square. Her personal maid, Lilla, was waiting to assist her out of the *princesse* dress of cream-and-white striped India silk trimmed with cardinal red bows and cream-colored lace. She wore rubies at her ears and throat. They had been a gift from a certain foreign ambassador.

"The tea party was a success, milady?"

Helena shrugged her shoulders and stood waiting patiently as her longtime companion undid the row of tiny buttons down the back of her costume. "It was reasonably successful. The regular Season has not yet begun, so one is reduced, of course, to inviting the lower echelons of society."

Lilla shook her head and clicked her tongue in sympathy. "Did you learn anything?"

"A little useful information."

Information was their stock in trade: she and Lilla. Well, it was one of them . . .

"Is it true what we hear about the duke and his new duchess?" inquired the other woman eagerly. There were no secrets between maid and mistress.

Helena sank her perfect, white teeth into her bottom lip. "Perhaps some of it." She sighed, moved in front of the full-length mirror and watched herself being undressed. "The truth is illusive, Lilla."

"Yes, milady." She smiled at her mistress in the mirror. "Thank God."

"I am afraid, Lilla, that I am beginning to look my age," she speculated, turning her head from side to side to study her chin and profile from various angles. She had been twenty-eight on her last birthday.

Her companion countered with a very *au contraire* sort of sound. "Pah! It is not so, milady. You look like an eighteen-year-old."

"You are too kind," she said, laughing without being amused. "But we both know that is not true."

Lilla raised and lowered her hands in an animated gesture. "If not eighteen, then certainly not a day over twenty-one. And *that* is the truth."

Helena squinted at her reflection as she

stepped out of the India silk and its corresponding petticoat. Lilla went off to deal with the voluminous yards of cream-colored material and soft muslin while she remained where she was, in her tightly laced corset.

She kicked off her high-heeled silk slippers, untied her lacy drawers and let them drop unceremoniously to the carpet. Then she executed a full turn in front of the mirror.

Peering over her shoulders, she studied her bare buttocks. "Perhaps I can still pass for twenty-one from a certain vantage point," the countess murmured to herself, "or in a flattering light."

Planting her hands on her lips, Helena assessed her figure with a critical eye. Her waist was only marginally larger than it had been at eighteen, despite the fact that she had given birth to two children: two sons. Lord Deerhurst had his "heir and a spare," which was all he cared about, anyway. His children and that huge, moldering old house in the country.

Her breasts were still good: full, firm, high on her chest, even without artificial supports.

She raised her arms high over her head and watched as her nipples popped out of the low-cut corset. Her nipples were excellent: perfectly shaped, not too large and not too small, and the aureoles a natural deep ruby red color that men found fascinating. She was often accused of using rouge on them. The truth was, she didn't have to resort to cosmetics.

Her hips flared just the right amount. Her thighs were firm and the left one was accented high on the inside with a beauty mark. Her lovers were always wanting to kiss her there, for some reason.

Her legs were reasonably long for a woman who was of average height—her one regret. She would have liked to have been taller than the other ladies. Her ankles were one of her best features: slender without being bony.

Helena had completed her self-examination from head to toe. She couldn't complain.

"Tsk, tsk, let me unlace you," scolded Lilla as she returned from the wardrobe room.

The countess stood and allowed her maid to strip her down to the last garter and silk stocking—as she had a thousand times before. Once she was naked, she slipped her arms into the loose dressing gown offered to her.

"Are you tired, milady?"

"Yes. I am."

"Do you wish to have any more tea?" inquired the other woman, knowing full well its "restorative" powers.

"Perhaps just a little," said Lady Deerhurst as she stretched out on the divan in her boudoir. "You may put it there on the table beside me. Then you may leave. I will ring if I need anything else."

"Of course, milady."

Once she was alone, Helena opened a small secret drawer in the table and took out several items. The first was an envelope. The second was a photograph.

She turned the envelope over and carefully removed the single piece of paper inside. It was a letter of sorts. She had read the letter before. Indeed, she had gone over it again and again. Unfortunately, the rambling confessions of the dying man who had written it made no more sense now than they had when she'd first discovered it several months ago.

She had been going through her late great-uncle's desk, looking for anything that might be of value: deeds, stocks, forgotten bank accounts, information. That was when she had come across the letter. What had intrigued her were the instructions scribbled on the outside: *To Whom It May Concern. Please give this envelope to the Duke of Deakin.*

Of course, she had not done so.

"You always were a bloody awful fool, Great-Uncle George," slurred Helena as she sipped her tea. "Great-Uncle George, king of the fools."

She peered at the shaky handwriting. The letter opened with a few ink scratches she assumed were some form of salutation. He had gone on to apologize to the duke and to beg his forgiveness. Then there was a sentence or two she could not make out, followed by a phrase she could read, but which made no sense to her.

The least George Frewen could have done was make it clear what he meant by "the terrible stain of dishonor I must remove before I go to meet my Maker."

"What terrible stain of dishonor, you old goat?" There was not an ounce of sympathy in the countess's overripe body. "You were paralyzed for most of your adult life until the day you had the good sense to die."

The paper went on to say that he wished to return them to their rightful owner, without explaining what *they* were. The short missive ended with a cryptic message: "You will find that beauty is in the eye of the beholder."

Helena sighed and returned the letter to its hiding place. She supposed she should not have had more "tea" this afternoon. Her head was not clear and she needed a clear head. She had a great deal of thinking and planning to do.

She lay back on the divan and held up the photograph in front of her. It had once been a group picture, but the others had been cut out with a pair of sharp scissors so that all that remained was Lawrence Grenfell Wicke.

"So you're back, my dear Lawrence, and you have brought a bride with you. Not that she's going to stop me. Certainly not if what I hear about her is half true. If you did, indeed, marry the bitch for her money—then you will be wanting some proper diversion. And I know just where you can get it," she purred, running one hand down her lush body.

All Helena had ever wanted was Lawrence from the time she was old enough to know the difference between boys and girls.

Well, Lawrence and the title Duchess of Deakin.

Where there was a will, there was a way. She had the will and she always found a way. She always got what she wanted sooner or later. She was young. She was clever. She was female and she was pretty.

She was also patient. She had waited for

years . . . what was another day or two, another week or two?

After all, she reminded herself, as she took a sip of tea laced with Napoleon brandy, someday Lawrence and Grantley Manor would be hers.

Meanwhile, she was between lovers and had to take care of her own wants and needs. She slipped the photograph back in the secret drawer. Then she unbuttoned her dressing gown and pushed aside the flimsy material. She caught her nipple between her thumb and forefinger, and pinched hard. She enjoyed giving herself pleasure that bordered on pain. Her breasts hardened. She licked her fingers and went to the other and flicked it back and forth until it, too, was erect.

She gave a low moan of arousal. She parted her thighs and touched herself; she was wet and ready. She manipulated her body for its own pleasure. She finally raised her hips off the divan and reached her climax, cursing Lawrence, cursing her weak husband, cursing all men.

17

IT was love at first sight.

Juliet fell in love with Grantley Manor even before she saw the house.

It had been nearly three weeks ago, on their first drive down the eighteenth-century beech avenue: tall majestic trees lined either side of the road, forming a canopy of dappled sun and shade, their bark silvery gray in the light of late afternoon. Brightly colored rhododendrons had been in bloom everywhere, cascading over ancient stone walls, creeping between huge boulders, growing to heights of thirty feet and more. Then they had turned the corner and there was a green lawn stretched out before them like a lush carpet and the natural park and blue lake designed by Capability Brown serving as a backdrop.

That's when Juliet knew. She had come home.

She adored everything about Grantley Manor from the overgrown rose gardens to the vast, sprawling house that was a hodgepodge of architectural styles and periods, from the newborn lambs in the field to the smallest child in the village, from the ancient chapel dating to the fourteenth century to Nanny, who was eighty and had her rooms in the East Wing.

Indeed, Juliet adored everything and everyone . . . but her husband.

There was, however, no going back. She had wed Lawrence Grenfell Wicke for better or for worse. She was now the Duchess of Deakin. And she was determined to be the very best duchess she knew how. When she took on a job it was simply not in her makeup to shirk her responsibilities.

"The key," Juliet lectured herself aloud as she swept down one long hallway after another on her way to a prearranged meeting with Bunter, "is to pretend that the man simply doesn't exist."

It was easier said than done.

Lawrence was turning out to be a formidable adversary. He was very clever. He managed to put her in impossible situations where she could not ignore him: consulting her at every possible opportunity about the improvements he was making to the stables, the cottages, the farms; taking her by the elbow as they visited the tenants on the estate; and touching her hand, her arm, her waist as they sat down to dinner, sometimes even dropping a kiss on her bare shoulder.

Yes, it was difficult—if not downright impossible—to pretend that her handsome devil of a husband did not exist!

"Good morning, Your Grace," greeted Bunter as she entered the library: an octagonal room whose Gothic arches soared two stories and more toward a ribbed ceiling. A room of dusty, leather-bound books and heavy, oppressive furniture. A room of collections: miniature furniture, seashells and rocks gathered by the third duke on a trip to the Mediterranean, and a variety of viewing glasses and kaleidoscopes. A room of unpolished brass railings and threadbare carpets.

It was the least of numerous evils, in Juliet's opinion.

"Bunter," she began in grave tones, "it is a crime."

"A crime?" the duke's valet repeated, somehow maintaining a neutral expression on his face.

Juliet paced up and down the threadbare carpet. At one time, she supposed, it had been red. Now it was a faded shade of pink. "In fact, it is a disgrace."

Bunter continued to stand at attention. "What is a disgrace, Your Grace?"

She paused and ran her hand along a massive, rectangular table; her fingertips came away covered with a fine powdery soot. "Grantley has been allowed to go unscrubbed, uncleaned, undusted, unpolished, unpainted, unpruned, and unkept."

"Yes, Your Grace."

"I have made a cursory examination of the house and gardens," she stated, taking a notebook from the pocket of her dress. In truth, she had inspected every nook and cranny, from the attic to the cellar, from the orangery to the vegetable patch outside the kitchen door. It had given her something to do during the past three weeks.

She had reached one irrefutable conclusion: Grantley not only needed a woman's money; it desperately needed a woman's touch.

Bunter waited patiently.

Juliet flipped to the first page of her little black book. "The roof leaks in the East Wing."

The man didn't blink an eyelash. "Indeed, Your Grace."

"The tapestries in the Great Hall appear to have last been aired sometime in the past century."

"Very possibly, Your Grace."

"The stone steps are crumbling."

"They are, Your Grace."

"The kitchen is outdated and outmoded. The food arrives at every meal stone-cold."

"I feared as much, Your Grace."

"The linens are moth-eaten and full of holes."

"The housekeeper would know more about that than I would, Your Grace."

She blew out an expressive breath. "We have no housekeeper, Bunter. The temporary sent up from an agency in London seems to have disappeared while you, the marquess, and the duke were in America."

For the first time the valet appeared to be in danger of losing his composure. "Oh dear, Your Grace."

She stopped and looked him straight in the eye. "What is worse, we have no butler."

Bunter quickly explained. "The old butler retired when the seventh duke died, Your Grace.

Norton was nearly seventy and the responsibilities of a large country house were getting to be too much for him to handle."

"I am well aware of the facts surrounding Norton's retirement. But that was over a year ago. Why has a new butler not been hired to replace him?"

"The duke has been a busy man, Your Grace."

"That is no excuse."

"No, Your Grace." Bunter frowned and corrected himself. "Yes, Your Grace."

Juliet snapped her notebook shut and tapped the edge against her bottom lip. Then she told him, "We have our work cut out for us."

Bunter seemed to wholeheartedly agree with her. "We do, Your Grace."

"It is time to roll up our sleeves and get to work, as we say in America."

"Roll up our sleeves and get to work. Figuratively speaking, of course, Your Grace."

There was steely determination in her tone. "Figuratively *and* literally, Bunter."

The man permitted himself a small sigh. "As you say, Your Grace, figuratively *and* literally."

"We'll start at the beginning."

"An excellent plan, Your Grace."

"Grantley must have a first-class butler."

"It deserves no less."

"We will need someone who is young and energetic, yet who possesses the necessary maturity to be in charge of a large and historic house."

"Young, energetic, yet mature," he noted.

"It would also be a great help if the person were familiar with Grantley."

He nodded thoughtfully. "It would help, Your Grace."

"We must have someone whose loyalty is unswerving, who is willing to dedicate himself to the task of bringing a once-great house back to the greatness it deserves. Nay, the greatness it demands."

"The greatness it demands." His voice rang out in the vast room like a clarion call.

"How old are you, Bunter?"

He appeared momentarily confused, then responded: "I am thirty-four, Your Grace."

"How long have you been at Grantley Manor?"

The man furrowed dark brown eyebrows above intelligent, dark brown eyes. "All of my life, Your Grace." A short explanation was added. "My late father was personal valet to the seventh duke. I began as a young boy in the kitchens and worked my way up to footman."

"And how long have you been valet to His Grace?"

"Nearly eight years."

"Do you consider yourself an ambitious man?"

"I do."

Juliet pondered the information he had given her, then, in a burst of frankness, announced: "It's time you were promoted, Bunter."

"Promoted, Your Grace?"

"It is a concept, perhaps, better understood in my native country than here in England." She bestowed a confident smile upon the astonished man. "Nevertheless, I believe *you* would make a first-class butler for Grantley."

"I-I am surprised, Your Grace."

"You shouldn't be."

"I am honored, Your Grace."

"You should be." Then she inquired, "Do you accept the position?"

"Am I given a choice, Your Grace?" The freedom to choose seemed to be an entirely new concept to Bunter.

"Naturally." She circled the table slowly, speaking all the while. "If you do not wish to take on the challenges and the accompanying prestige of butler, then you may remain as valet to His Grace. In that case, I will simply have to search for someone else to fill the position."

Bunter snapped his heels together and gave an appropriate bow of his head. "You need search no farther, Your Grace. I accept."

Juliet clapped her hands together in delight. "Excellent. Of course, your promotion will include a corresponding raise in salary."

She named a generous figure and watched as the realization spread across Ian Bunter's features: he would not only be *their* man, he could be his *own* man now, as well.

He fixed his gaze on her. "Thank you, Your Grace."

"Thank *you*, Bunter."

He swore his allegiance. "I will serve you and Grantley as long as you need me."

"That will be a very long time," she assured him.

Then he cleared his throat awkwardly. "There is just one small problem, Your Grace."

"And what is that?" she asked.

He seemed reluctant to tell her.

"What is the one small problem, Bunter?" she insisted.

He swallowed hard. "His Grace."

"His Grace?"

"How are we going to tell His Grace? *Who* is going to tell His Grace?"

Juliet firmed her posture and her resolve. "You need not worry about His Grace. I will inform the duke of your promotion myself."

Bunter seemed immensely relieved. "Thank you, Your Grace."

She opened her notebook again and looked down the list she had made earlier that day. "The next order of business is finding a suitable housekeeper for Grantley. Do you have any personal recommendations?"

Bunter stood a little taller. "There is a highly capable young woman currently in your employ, Your Grace."

"What is her name?"

"Margaret Bunter."

That brought her head up. "Your sister?"

His jaw squared. "My wife, Your Grace."

"I did not know you had a wife, Bunter."

"We have tried to be discreet, Your Grace."

"In other words, you have kept your marriage a secret," she said plainly.

"It seemed for the best, Your Grace."

"I quite understand." That sort of liaison was always highly discouraged downstairs. Juliet thought about it for thirty seconds. No more. "Well, that does make a difference, of course."

"I was afraid it would," he murmured dejectedly.

"You must have accommodations fit for a married couple. It will be at the top of our list for the East Wing, after the roof is repaired. You will need privacy and adequate space: a sitting room, a small kitchen of your own, a bedroom, and a bathroom. At least to begin with."

The man was speechless.

Juliet went on. "I will speak to Margaret—Mrs. Bunter—next and you may officially begin your new duties by arranging for the head gardener to meet with me this afternoon at two o'clock in the orangery. I will wish to have a serious discussion with him about the appalling condition of the greenhouses and the grounds."

"May I have permission to speak plainly, Your Grace?" he said with all due respect.

"Of course."

"The head gardener has done his best with severely limited resources and staff."

"In other words, there have not been enough funds allocated to maintain Grantley inside or out," she said disapprovingly.

Bunter quickly sprang to Lawrence's defense. "It is not His Grace's fault. He loves Grantley. He would give up his life for Grantley."

"I know that," she finally said softly.

In her heart of hearts Juliet realized it was true. Lawrence had married her for her money, but could she blame him now that she had seen

Grantley Manor with her own eyes? Would she not have done the same if she had been in his position?

"I will speak to the head gardener this afternoon about taking on additional workers."

"Thank you, Your Grace."

Juliet continued. "You will oversee all the menservants, of course, as part of your duties as butler. You have my permission to hire as many as are required to do the job properly. We will also need an architect, an expert at furniture restoration, another to examine the paintings, not to mention carpenters, tilers, and bricklayers." She paused, handed him a small black book identical to her own and pointed to an inkwell and pen on the table. "You may wish to take notes, Bunter."

"Certainly, Your Grace." He quickly picked up the pen and began to do just that.

"I would like a master horologist to inspect and clean our incredibly large number of antique timepieces. I must have both a personal and a business secretary: we will make up a separate list of requirements. After I have met with Mrs. Bunter, and assuming that our interview goes well, she will doubtlessly need additional household staff."

"Doubtlessly, Your Grace," he said, writing as fast as he could.

Juliet gave a satisfied nod. "I believe that will do for this morning, Bunter."

"Yes, Your Grace."

"Would you please ask Mrs. Bunter to join me here in the library?"

"Immediately, Your Grace."

Once Bunter had gone, Juliet walked across the room to what appeared to be a specially built bookshelf. It contained row after row of red leather volumes. She leaned over to read a title or two, and discovered that there were none. Only dates were embossed in gold leaf on the spines. "1825. 1826. 1827. 1828," she murmured.

Taking out the volume stamped 1828, she carefully opened to the first few pages. It took her a moment to understand what she was looking at. It was a record of all the dinners and weekend house parties given by the sixth duke and duchess, including guest lists, assigned bedrooms, menus, personal preferences when it came to flowers, food, liquor, cigars, firmness of mattress, number of bed pillows.

Juliet shook her head in amazement. Someone—perhaps the butler, or the housekeeper, or perhaps even Alicia Anne, herself—had entered, in precise handwriting, an accounting of each and every detail of the occasion. As a successful businesswoman who believed in making lists and checking them twice, she was duly impressed.

"1828?" Juliet repeated out loud.

There was something about that date that rang a bell. Then she remembered: 1828 was the year the Deakin Diamonds had disappeared during a weekend house party.

"This could make for interesting bedtime reading," she remarked to herself, tucking the book under her arm.

After all, there was little for her to do once she retired to her bedroom for the night—which she did as soon as Aunt Effie began to nod off in her chair.

The truth was, Juliet did not want to be left alone with her husband. She had locked the door between her rooms and Lawrence's upon her arrival at Grantley. The door remained locked. As had the door between their staterooms aboard the *Alicia Anne*.

Juliet felt the heat of anger—or was it merely embarrassment now?—rise to her cheeks. It had been six weeks since her ill-fated wedding night. Six weeks since she had overheard the damning conversation between her husband and Miles St. Aldford. Six long weeks since her heart had been broken and her pride sorely wounded. And, still, she was not prepared to forgive Lawrence.

Would she ever be?

A knock at the library door interrupted her thoughts.

"You must be Mrs. Bunter," she said to the handsome young woman who entered the room.

"I am, Your Grace."

"Then I would like to discuss the position of housekeeper with you. . . ."

18

LAWRENCE heard his valet quietly enter his bedroom and begin to lay out what he required for another day of hard work overseeing the renovation of the stables. It was early morning, the time he usually rose.

He kept his back to the room, aware that he had been dreaming of Juliet again, aware that his body was longing for her: he was rock hard. He finally willed himself to relax, sighed, and rolled over in bed to greet Bunter.

It was not Bunter.

There was a stranger rummaging through his wardrobe.

"Who are you?" Lawrence demanded to know, coming up on his elbows.

"I am Jenkins, Your Grace."

He immediately smelled a rat. "What are you doing here, Jenkins?"

"I am your new valet, Your Grace."

"Where in the bloody hell is Bunter?"

"Assuming his new duties, Your Grace," came the unflappable reply.

Lawrence narrowed his eyes and dropped his voice half an octave. "His new duties as *what*?"

"Butler, Your Grace."

"Butler?" he thundered.

"Yes, Your Grace."

Lawrence knew the answer to the next question before he asked it, but he asked it anyway. "And who, pray tell, hired you to replace Bunter as my personal valet?"

"Her Grace, Your Grace."

He suddenly stopped and inquired: "How do you know where everything is, Jenkins?" The man was a picture of organization and efficiency.

"Her Grace was most anxious not to disrupt your routine, so she instructed Bunter to draw me a diagram of your dressing room and bureau drawers. I have memorized the exact location of all of your belongings, Your Grace."

"How very expedient of you, Jenkins," he said dryly.

"We have Her Grace to thank, Your Grace. It was entirely her idea."

He just bet it was.

Lawrence drove a hand through his hair. "Don't you think a little chaos is beneficial to the soul?"

A blank expression appeared on Jenkins's features. "There is order and there is disorder, Your Grace. A large country house like Grantley must operate on a system of order."

"Her Grace again, no doubt," Lawrence muttered under his breath.

Jenkins's hearing was excellent as well. "Her Grace is the most organized person I have ever had the privilege of meeting," he declared with genuine admiration.

Damn the woman! Lawrence swore silently as he reached for his robe. She had turned his life upside down. She had disrupted his entire routine, whatever Jenkins claimed to the contrary. She had invited total strangers into his house; they were always milling about underfoot. And now she'd had the audacity to steal his valet!

A man's home was supposed to be his castle. His had become a veritable beehive of activity. There were people everywhere: scrubbing, polishing, sweeping, painting, measuring, cutting, sawing.

It was bloody inconvenient!

His wife was, indeed, getting her revenge and it was a dish served *ice* cold, Lawrence fumed as he later strode through the Great Hall on his way to the library. It was the one place he was assured of finding Juliet these days.

He threw open the library door and nearly ran over a young man and woman as they were coming out. They each had a small black notebook in one hand and a fountain pen in the other. He had never seen either of them before in his life.

"Who are you?" Lawrence demanded to know, not caring if he sounded rude and out of sorts. By God, he was feeling rude and out of sorts! It was his privilege. He was lord of the manor, after all.

"I am Her Grace's personal secretary," replied the young woman.

"And I am Her Grace's business secretary," answered the young man.

"Humph!" Lawrence swept his gaze around the library. The room was empty. "And where is Her Grace?"

"She is meeting with the architect in the East Wing, Your Grace."

"Why?" he inquired curtly.

The two exchanged glances. The young woman responded. "I believe they are trying to determine which walls must be knocked down."

"Which walls must be knocked down?" he roared, seeing red. The woman took too much upon herself. Grantley was his ancestral home. It had been in his family for generations and she intended to waltz in and begin to knock down walls. Not if he had anything to say about it!

"Rabbit hutches!" mentioned the male secretary.

"Rabbit hutches," agreed the female secretary, nodding her head.

"Rabbit hutches?" Lawrence mouthed, frowning. He did not understand.

"According to Her Grace," said the young man.

"According to Her Grace," echoed the young woman. "And Her Grace is always right."

"Always."

As they scurried off to do their mistress's bidding, Lawrence took a deep breath and bellowed at the top of his lungs: "Juliet!" He took the steps two at a time. "Juliet!" His stride down the long hallways of the East Wing was twice that of the average man. "Juliet!"

Juliet heard him coming one flight of stairs and two hallways away.

The architect, a talented man from Dartmoor, lifted his head from the plans they were studying and scowled. "What in the world is that noise, Your Grace?"

"That noise, Mr. Lloyd, is my husband."

The color came up in his face. "I-I'm sorry, Your Grace," he stammered.

"There is no need to apologize. The duke is a large man with a large voice, which is often required in this very large house. He is simply trying to find me."

Bravado. That was the key to dealing with a man like Lawrence Grenfell Wicke, Juliet had decided. A man who tended to be overwhelming, overbearing and, at the moment, overloud.

Her name rang out again. "Juliet!"

They both turned their heads toward the door. The breadth of Lawrence's shoulders filled it from frame to frame. On this fine spring morning he was dressed in black trousers, black boots that reached to the knees and a white shirt open at the neck. He was collarless, coatless, and hatless. He wielded a riding crop in his left hand.

His black hair was slightly longer than he usually wore it, and slightly mussed. His black eyes glittered like diamonds. His black expression foretold his mood. Indeed, he was fairly bristling with indignation.

"What is this business about rabbit hutches?" He sounded almost savage.

"Good morning, sir," she called out cheerfully, ignoring his question for the moment.

She heard him give a snort of mirthless laughter. "Good morning, madam."

"Are you going riding?"

Lawrence glance down at the small whip in his hand. He seemed unsure of how it had gotten there. "I must be," he said sardonically.

"It will be a lovely morning for a ride," Juliet pointed out pleasantly.

"Juliet—" he growled, visibly impatient.

She dared not delay him much longer. "This is our architect, Mr. Lloyd."

Lawrence focused his eyes on the man standing beside her. "Mr. Lloyd."

"Your Grace."

Juliet suggested: "Perhaps we can continue our discussion at a later time, Mr. Lloyd."

"As you wish, Your Grace." He appeared only too willing to remove himself from the premises.

As soon as they were alone, Lawrence demanded to know, "What in the hell is going on here, Juliet?"

"We are doing a little renovation in the East Wing," she explained calmly.

"A little renovation?" he ranted, swinging his arm in a wide arc. "I have heard that you're planning to knock down half the walls."

"Only one or two," she said placatingly.

"Only one or two?" he repeated in a sarcastic tone.

"Yes. You see," she said, indicating the architectural drawings spread out on the table in front of them, "the servants' quarters are too small. They simply will not do. For example, three maids are expected to share this bedroom. I do believe you could stand in the center of it, sir, and touch the walls on either side."

Lawrence looked around him for what seemed the first time. "My dressing room is larger than this."

"Indeed, it is." She assumed so. She had never actually been in his dressing room.

"*Three* maids, did you say?"

"Three. On occasion as many as four."

He wrinkled his forehead, considering the logistics. "How? There is barely enough room for two narrow beds and a minimal space between them."

"They either sleep in shifts or two—" Juliet held up her first and second fingers—"to a bed."

He gave her a long measuring look. "Two to a bed?"

She nodded.

He put his hand on her shoulder with apparent casualness. "There would be only one way to accomplish that with any degree of comfort."

"How?"

"If one were a man and the other a woman. With one on top and the other underneath."

The room suddenly seemed even smaller than before—and warmer. Juliet quickly rattled on: "We also need to create a decent suite of rooms for Bunter and his wife."

Lawrence reached out and entwined a strand of her hair around his index finger. "Lucky man to have a loving wife to share his bed."

Juliet shivered in spite of herself. "I-ah-I believe you mentioned rabbit hutches when you first came into the room, sir. Well, that is how I would describe the servants' quarters as they currently exist."

"Now I understand," he murmured, his breath stirring the wisps around her face. He swayed toward her.

"Sir, you forget yourself," she said sharply.

He sighed and drew back. "Madam, if only I could."

"I think it would be best if we adjourned to the library." She did not wait for his consent, but turned and marched out of the tiny bedroom.

The first thing Lawrence said to her once they reached the library was, "Speaking of Bunter—"

Juliet put the width of the rectangular table between them before she responded. "Grantley desperately needed a new butler. Bunter seemed the logical choice."

Lawrence propped one leg up and sat on the corner of the table. He looked intently into her eyes. "I agree with you."

She exhaled in relief. "I thought you were angry with me."

He folded his arms across his chest. "I am."

She blinked owlishly. "Oh—"

There was an underlying edge of steel to her husband's voice when he spoke next. "I have gone along with your plans for Grantley because it is my fondest wish to see this house restored to its former greatness. But make no mistake about it, madam, I am the master here. And, as master, I retain certain privileges, among them the right to choose my own valet.'

"Yes, Lawrence."

"I do not like waking up to find a stranger in my bedroom."

"No, Lawrence."

"You could have told me."

Her eyes met his for an instant only. "I meant to."

"But you didn't."

She sighed. "But I didn't."

"It will not happen again, will it?"

"No."

Lawrence unfolded his arms and picked up a large nondescript rock used as a paperweight on the library table. He tossed it into the air and caught it again. "When do you intend to unlock the door?"

The question caught Juliet off guard. "Unlock the door?" she echoed faintly.

Black eyes bored into hers. "Between our bedrooms, wife."

She held her breath.

When she did not answer, Lawrence stood and walked toward the library door. With his fist wrapped around the brass knob, he turned and recited to her. " 'O! A kiss long as my exile, sweet as my revenge!' "

Her heart began to pound. "Spenser?"

"Shakespeare."

"Antony and Cleopatra?"

"Coriolanus."

"I have never read it," Juliet admitted, sinking her teeth into her tongue.

"It is the last of Shakespeare's tragedies," he told her, "although few would claim it is his greatest."

She tried to swallow the lump that had formed in her throat and found she could not. Hot, bitter tears burned inside her eyes. Dear Lord, she suddenly realized how much she missed Lawrence!

He seemed to read her mind. "I know they say that revenge is sweet, but I wish you could forgive even if you cannot forget. I miss you, Juliet."

Then he was gone and she was left all alone.

19

"AUNT EFFIE, what are you doing all alone in this part of the house?" Juliet inquired as she took a shortcut through the ongoing renovations in the East Wing.

The elegant little woman, dressed all in bright pink silk, appeared momentarily confused. "I don't know," she said at last. "I suppose I am lost."

Dear, dear Aunt Effie. She had made the move from New York to Northumberland rather better than Juliet had expected. But there were times when she wondered if it had been wise, or even kind, to bring her along.

"Where were you going, Aunt?"

Euphemia Jones straightened a bright pink feather that was drooping over her right eye. Originally it had been one of three artfully arranged in her coiffure; the others were still in place. "To have tea with Nanny."

"You took a wrong turn two hallways back." Juliet took her gently by the arm and guided her in the right direction. "I'll show you the way."

"You need a map to get around Grantley," grumbled the tiny creature beside her.

"Why, Aunt Effie, that is an excellent idea." Juliet stopped and took out her notebook. "I will have my secretary work on it with Bunter. Everyone will be issued detailed maps of the house and the surrounding grounds. One of the new footman was misplaced last week and nobody found the poor man until the following morning. By then, of course, he was quite beside himself."

"Well, we wouldn't want to 'misplace' any more footmen or housemaids or great-aunts, now would we?"

"Naturally, not."

"Perhaps you should issue a small bell for everyone to wear around their necks—rather like a flock of sheep or a herd of cattle—just in case anyone does go astray."

Juliet glanced down at her great-aunt to see if she were making a joke. It was difficult to tell. Euphemia Jones managed to keep a straight face better than anyone she had ever known.

The diminutive woman pursed her small pink lips. "You keep very busy, my dear."

"Indeed, I do."

"All hustle and bustle."

"Yes, all hustle and bustle."

"You are amazingly well organized."

"Thank you, Aunt Effie."

"An island of calm in a sea of chaos."

"I try to be."

Her great-aunt added: "You don't think one can be too organized, do you?"

A crease appeared between Juliet's eyes. "Too organized? I don't see how." She stopped in front of a door. "Here we are."

"Why don't you join us for tea?"

She glanced down at the watch hanging from a chain at her waist. "I really should . . ."

A carrot was dangled in front of her. "Nanny is a fascinating woman. She knows everything there is to know about the Wickes and about Grantley."

"Well, perhaps for a while."

"Nanny, look whom I have brought with me today," announced Euphemia as they knocked and entered the elderly woman's sitting room.

Leaning heavily on her cane, Nanny started to rise from her chair. "Your Grace—"

Juliet quickly went to her. "Please, do not get up, Nanny."

"You are most kind, Your Grace."

"Not at all."

Their hostess gestured toward the only other two chairs in the room. "Won't you both be seated?"

They took a minute to settle in. Afternoon tea was already prepared and waiting on a tray on the round table in the center of the room.

Nanny said familiarly, "Perhaps you will pour, Miss Jones."

While her great-aunt saw to the dispensing of tea and milk, small sandwiches and rounds of shortbread, scones and crumpets with strawberry jam, Juliet gazed around the room where Nanny spent most of her waking hours.

There were knickknacks and mementoes everywhere, including a great number of photographs and tintypes. A magnifying glass lay atop a book on a reading table at the old woman's elbow. A collection of china dogs gathered dust on a shelf affixed to the wall. A stack of postcards and letters were kept in a chintz-covered box, its lid open. There was a faint smell of lavender sachet in the air, and a bouquet of fresh spring flowers on the mantel.

"Your flowers are very bright and cheerful," commented Juliet. It was raining out. It had been raining for several days, in fact.

"His Grace brought those when he came to visit me yesterday. He is always bringing me little gifts: flowers, candies, another dog for my collection." She gestured toward the shelf. "From the time they were boys, Lawrence was the thoughtful one, the serious one. Jonathan was the mischief maker." She sighed, no doubt remembering the brothers as they had once been. "I am very fond of both of them," she said, her voice trailing off.

"I am particularly fond of rum cakes, myself," spoke up Euphemia Jones.

"Are you?" said Nanny, her attention diverted for the moment. "I haven't had rum cakes in ages. They sound delicious. Perhaps we could ask cook to bake us some."

"Do you think she would?"

Nanny seemed certain of it.

"Tell us about some of your pictures," Juliet requested once the subject of rum cakes had been exhausted.

Nanny was only too happy to oblige. At the

advanced age of eighty, reminiscing had become her favorite pastime. "This was taken with the duke and duchess when we all went to Brighton once." A slightly faded photograph was handed to Juliet for her inspection. "The boys were nine and seven at the time. They are all grown up now, of course." She paused. "Lord Jonathan does not come to see me as often as he used to."

"Lord Jonathan is married now. He and and his wife, Lady Elizabeth, have an estate in Essex," Juliet reminded her. "But I'm sure they will be coming for a visit soon."

"Both of my boys married." The old woman sighed contentedly. "I am pleased that they married for love. The duke and duchess were very much in love, too. Yes," she said, making a kind of bobbing movement with her head, "I am especially pleased that my dear boys listened to their hearts and not their heads." She reached out and placed a wrinkled hand over Juliet's. "Forgive an old woman, my dear, but you do love Lawrence very much, don't you?"

Juliet was not offended—it was impossible for Nanny to offend anyone—but she was taken aback by the personal nature of the question. She finally admitted in a soft voice: "Yes, I love Lawrence very much." There was no sense in denying it to either Nanny or her great-aunt, or even to herself. She blinked several times and said: "Tell me about this drawing."

"That is a picture of me when I was a young girl," explained Nanny. "It was sketched by a wandering artist some sixty-five years ago when

I first came to Grantley Manor with the sixth duke and duchess."

"Then you knew Alicia Anne?"

"The sixth duchess was the one who brought me to this house as an assistant nanny when I was barely fifteen. She would have been in her mid-twenties at the time."

Juliet leaned forward eagerly. "That means you were here when the Deakin Diamonds disappeared."

She nodded. "I remember that fateful night as if it were only yesterday. Have you seen the portrait of Her Grace wearing the black diamonds?"

"Yes, I stayed in her stateroom aboard the *Alicia Anne* on our trip from America."

"Rightly so. Rightly so," murmured the woman.

"I have also recently discovered a red leather volume in the library that has all kinds of fascinating details concerning the dinners and weekend house parties given by the sixth duke and duchess. I've been reading the book in the evenings."

Nanny said respectfully: "Her Grace was very particular about that type of thing. Very organized. Not unlike yourself, Your Grace."

"Thank you, Nanny."

The old woman lifted her sagging chin and peered at Juliet with still-bright eyes. "I've heard that you are doing splendid things for this house. It desperately needed a woman's touch."

"It did."

"Is it true that you are knocking down walls in this wing to expand the servants' quarters?"

"It is." Juliet bit the inside of her mouth against a smile. For someone who rarely ventured outside the privacy of her own rooms, Nanny didn't miss much.

"You're going to make a first-rate duchess, even if you are an American," she blurted out.

"Thank you."

The longtime retainer lowered her voice. "I must warn you, Your Grace.

Juliet pricked up her ears. "Warn me about what?"

"Not about *what*, about *who*." She leaned closer. "Lady Deerhurst has returned."

"Lady Deerhurst has returned?"

"From London."

"To the area, you mean?"

Another quick nod of the white head. "She was Lady Helena Frewen before her marriage, you know."

"Actually, I didn't know."

Nanny frowned. "It is most unusual."

"What is?"

"For Lady Deerhurst to return to the Northumberland during the London Season. It is common knowledge that she despises the countryside and, in particular, Deerhurst Hall."

Juliet was driven to ask: "Why?"

"Because that is where her husband and her children reside." Nanny clicked her tongue in disapproval. "Not a maternal bone in her body."

Euphemia Jones was enthralled. She set her

teacup down and inched her chair forward. "Really?"

Nanny obviously relished having a fresh audience for her stories. "I don't like to speak ill of anyone, but the truth is Lady Deerhurst is the sort of woman who prefers Society over everything and everyone else. She revels in the gossip and the intrigue. Why, I have heard that she flits from one party to the next, from one six-course dinner to the next, from one fancy dress ball to the next, from one handsome young lover to the next with equal abandon."

Euphemia Jones turned a most becoming shade of pink. Juliet sat there in stunned silence.

Over the top of her spectacles, Nanny looked from one to the other. "I beg your pardon, Your Grace. I had forgotten how naive Americans are when it comes to such 'liaisons.' Lady Deerhurst runs with the Prince of Wales and the fashionable Marlborough House Set, and dalliances are expected of a woman if she socializes with that group."

Juliet sat up straighter in her chair. "Then it is highly unlikely that this Duchess of Deakin will ever be part of the fashionable set."

"Nevertheless, Your Grace, mark my words: stay away from that one. The countess is pure poison. Why, she has been after Lawrence and the title of Duchess of Deakin since she was old enough to walk."

"You said Lady Deerhurst was married."

"She is married to the Earl of Deerhurst, and

they have two sons. That does not stop a woman like Helena."

Juliet confessed to a certain curiosity about the notorious Lady Deerhurst. She would like to meet the woman Nanny believed had been chasing after Lawrence since childhood.

She wasn't only curious, Juliet realized. She was jealous. Lawrence was *her* husband. No one else was permitted to form a "liaison" with him. She simply would not have it!

Then it occurred to her that her husband must have certain physical needs. After all, he was a healthy male with healthy male appetites. Appetites that were not being satisfied by his wife. His wife had locked him out of her bedroom . . . and out of her life.

Juliet sat back in her chair. She felt as if the breath had been knocked out of her.

What if Lawrence were seeking from another woman what she had been denying him? What if he were kissing another woman as he had once kissed her? What if he were touching another woman, caressing another woman, whispering sweet words of desire into another woman's ear?

She would strangle him, if it were true. But in her heart of hearts, she knew it wasn't.

Not yet, anyway.

She had some serious thinking to do when she retired for the night, Juliet reflected. She loved her husband. They were man and wife until death parted them. Revenge was not sweet; it was cold and bitter and lonely. Perhaps it was time to forgive and move on with their lives as Lawrence had suggested that day in the library.

Juliet gave herself a good shake and realized that Nanny was still speaking.

"It's in the blood," she said.

"What is?" Euphemia queried.

"Helena has fancied herself in love with Lawrence all these years—with no encouragement from him, I might add. And it was her great-uncle, George Frewen, who was equally obsessive about the sixth duchess."

"You mean Alicia Anne?"

"Yes. He claimed he would have no other, and he never did. In the end, the poor man outlived everyone of his generation. He died just last year."

"George Frewen—" Juliet tapped a finger against her lip. "The name seems familiar."

"If you've been reading the sixth duke and duchess's social records, then you would have seen his name mentioned frequently. George Frewen was a guest in this house many times in the early days—before the accident."

"What accident?"

Nanny was more than willing to relate all the lurid details. "He got roaring drunk, caused an embarrassing scene and insisted on riding home in a downpour—even though his estate is some distance from Grantley. Apparently he tried to get his horse to jump over a fallen tree and the poor animal tripped, breaking its neck instantly. Helena's great-uncle was trapped under the weight of his dead horse for hours. He wasn't found until the following morning."

Euphemia's hand fluttered to the pink pearls at her throat. "Oh, dear me."

"They say George Frewen was never the same again. Both of his legs were crushed, and he was forced to live out the rest of his life in a wheelchair. He was a broken, bitter man in body, in spirit, *and* in mind."

"Do you remember when the accident happened?" asked Juliet.

"I could never forget. It was the same weekend as the treasure hunt party."

"The treasure hunt party?"

"That was when the Deakin Diamonds disappeared, my dear."

Juliet's heart began to pick up speed. "Please tell me more, Nanny. Whatever you can recall."

"Well, Their Graces had been renovating Grantley for months. They decided to throw a grand party to celebrate and to show off the Manor to their friends."

"What a splendid idea!" Euphemia Jones interrupted. "A coming-out party for a house. You and Lawrence should do the same, my dear."

"Perhaps we will, Aunt."

"I will have to carefully plan my wardrobe," the woman said aloud.

"Please continue, Nanny."

"The weekend included numerous festivities: shooting and archery contests, wonderful teas, elaborate dinners, a fancy dress ball, and as the grand finale, a treasure hunt. It was after the treasure hunt that Her Grace returned to her bedroom and discovered that someone had rifled through her jewelry. The only pieces missing were the Deakin Diamonds. We searched everywhere, of course, but they seemed to have vanished into thin air. No one ever saw them again. No one has seen them since."

"And no one was accused of the theft."

Nanny sniffed. "The house was filled with titled folks and royalty. His Grace could not search the likes of them or their belongings. It was a matter of pride."

"Indeed." If there was one thing Juliet understood, it was the high price one paid for pride. "The diamonds seemed very pretty on the portrait of Alicia Anne."

"They were far more than pretty, Your Grace. They were magnificent. I have never seen their equal. I don't expect I ever will."

"I imagine you've seen quite a few stunning gemstones during your years in this household," prompted an interested Euphemia Jones.

"Everything from the grandest tiaras to the crown jewels is all. But to my knowledge the Deakin Diamonds were the most spectacular black diamonds ever unearthed." Nanny put her head back and sighed. "Only the Black Heart would have been larger."

Juliet's head came up. "The Black Heart?"

"Hasn't Lawrence—His Grace—told you the legend of the Black Heart?"

"No, he hasn't."

"Then you must insist that he do so. I told the story to him over and over again while he was growing up." Nanny fell silent and then said: "When I look back now I can see that the financial fortunes of the family changed after the diamonds disappeared. Of course, then the old duke died and then his son and there were all those inheritance taxes—" She made a gesture that spoke for itself. "You have brought life and hope back to this house, Your Grace, and to more people than you will ever know. There is no way we can ever thank you."

"There is no need for anyone to thank me, Nanny. I love Grantley."

"You love Grantley and you love Lawrence."

"Yes, I love Grantley and I love Lawrence."

"Just what every husband likes to hear," said a voice from the doorway behind them. Lawrence sauntered into Nanny's sitting room. His presence seemed to fill the small space to overflowing. He warmly greeted the two older women: "Nanny. Euphemia." Then he bent over and kissed her.

It was a bittersweet kiss. A soft-turned-hard kiss. It was the kiss of a hungry man. It hinted at the desire, the longing, the need he had for her. Juliet wasn't sure which surprised her more: the passion in Lawrence's kiss, or her passionate response to him.

"Lawrence—" she said breathlessly.

"Good afternoon, my dearest," he murmured against her mouth.

"Good afternoon," she responded, her lips throbbing.

He reluctantly stepped back. "Have my three favorite ladies been having their tea and a good chat?"

"Indeed, we have," replied Nanny. "We have been discussing the Deakin Diamonds."

"My lady wife is not interested in gemstones, Nanny."

"Nonsense. Every woman is interested in gemstones. And you are a naughty boy for not having told her the legend of the Black Heart."

"The Black Heart is not a legend, Nanny. It is a fairy tale." Lawrence gazed down at her and Juliet could see it in eyes that glittered like black diamonds: he would make her his wife in every sense of the word and *soon*. His voice dropped half an octave and took on subtle undertones. "But a fairy tale makes a good bedtime story."

It was a turning point. There would be no going back now, Juliet realized. It was possible—indeed, quite probable—that after tonight she would no longer be the virgin Duchess of Deakin.

20

WHEN Juliet entered her bedroom that night, she found a single white rose on her pillow, the evening dew still fresh on its petals. She picked up the rose and inhaled its fragrance: the scent was subtle yet unmistakable.

So was the message.

A cascade of white roses had been her bridal bouquet chosen by Lawrence. Before they had exchanged their wedding vows on that beautiful morning nearly two months ago, he had whispered to her: *"Roses, because their scent always reminds me of you, my dearest Juliet."*

The message was unmistakable: this was to be her wedding night.

Juliet bathed and slipped into a sheer lawn nightdress and combing sacque, then she sent her maid away and, as she had on that other fateful night, took her own hair down and brushed it until her arms ached.

It was time to face facts.

She might be the Duchess of Deakin, but she was a wife in name only. She was twenty-four-years old and she was still an old maid in the very real sense of the word.

She had glimpsed passion briefly, had tasted sexual desire for a moment, had experienced the erotic stirrings and urgings that happened between a man and a woman, but there was so much more she did not know about Lawrence, about herself, about the intimacy of the marriage bed. There were so many questions she did not have the answers to.

Juliet stared at the connecting door between their rooms. It was still locked. Yet she knew Lawrence—and her answers—were waiting just on the other side. All she had to do was walk over to the door and turn the key.

Juliet swung back and gazed at her reflection in the mirror. "Damn. Damn. Damn."

What was stopping her?

Anger? It seemed to have burned itself out sometime during the past several weeks.

Pride? She was a proud woman, but she was not going to let pride stand in the way of her own happiness. There was a point, she realized, when pride ceased to be a virtue.

Fear? Yes, she was afraid. She was afraid of the unknown, afraid of losing herself in emotions and circumstances she could not control, afraid of revealing herself, afraid of learning who she might really be.

"You are a coward, Juliet," she whispered to the pale young woman in the looking glass.

Did she want the man?

Yes.

Did she need the man?

Yes.

Did she want to be a real wife to him?

Yes.

Then she couldn't just sit there. She had to put her hairbrush down, rise to her feet, walk across the room and unlock the door.

It was that easy . . . and that difficult.

Juliet vigorously drove the brush through her hair two more times, slammed it down on the dresser, marched across her bedroom, and emphatically turned the key in the lock.

Lawrence had finally gotten rid of Jenkins, slipped into a dressing gown, downed a quick brandy—not that he was nervous, of course— and sat down in his favorite chair with his favorite book. He didn't bother opening it since he had no intention of reading tonight. He knew what he was waiting for: the sound of a key turning in a lock.

Click.

He wasn't aware that he'd been holding his breath until he exhaled. His lady wife, it seemed, had at last unlocked the door between their bedrooms.

Lawrence was not a patient man, but he was also not a man who would ever force himself on a woman, any woman. He had sorely wounded Juliet's pride. It had been necessary to give it time to heal.

The time had come.

He strode across the room and clasped the doorknob in his hand. "Slow and easy, Deakin. Slow and easy," he reminded himself as he opened the door between their bedrooms.

Juliet was sitting at her dressing table,

brushing her hair; it was like pure gold in the lamplight. As he came toward her, she watched his every step in the looking glass. Her eyes were a startled blue. Her expression was unreadable. Her hand had frozen in midair.

"I will finish that for you," he offered, taking the hairbrush from his wife's grasp.

He began to stroke through the long, blond tresses that hung halfway down her back. She sat bolt upright at first, her spine stiff, her posture perfect. She gave no indication if he were bestowing pleasure or pain upon her.

Then, very slowly, little by little, he could feel Juliet begin to relax. Her eyes finally fluttered shut as she surrendered to the pleasure, the purely physical sensation, of having him brush her hair.

Lawrence observed her reflection in the mirror. Her lips parted slightly and the tip of her tongue darted out to moisten them. Her complexion went from ghostly pale to a rosy glow. Her body took on a softness, a willingness, an openness it had not had when he'd first entered her room.

He leaned over and put the hairbrush down on the dressing table. At the same time he nudged the combing sacque aside and trailed his lips along one shoulder. He knew she could feel the caress through the material of her nightgown. A shiver ran the entire length of her body.

Her eyes opened and she gazed up at him. She took a deep breath and released it. Then she seemed to make up her mind about whatever it was that troubled her. "Lawrence," she began, her voice low and tremulous, "I have something to tell you."

He placed his hands on her shoulders. "What is it, Juliet?"

She blew out another soft breath and quickly confessed, "I am very nervous."

He made a kind of amused sound in the back of his throat. "Juliet, I have something to tell you."

Her eyes appeared even bluer. "What?"

"I am nervous, too," Lawrence admitted.

"You are?"

"I am."

"Why? You know all there is to know about a man and a woman," she pointed out.

Oh, his sweet, innocent Juliet!

"But I don't know everything about you, wife," he told her. "Indeed, I know very little."

"I know even less about you," she lamented, studying the solid gold wedding ring on her finger.

"Then we will regard each other as a gift that is about to be opened for the first time. Neither of us have any idea what the surprise is going to be. We will slowly undo the ribbon, carefully remove the wrapping and take our time discovering what is inside."

Juliet seemed to like the idea. She leaned back against him and covered his hands with her own. "I remember you once said to me that the pleasure a man and woman give each other is a kind of gift."

"It is a wonderful gift," he told her, measuring out his self-control.

As her slender body brushed up against his, Lawrence felt the reaction in his groin. He was already becoming aroused. A fine sheen of perspiration broke out on his upper lip. His heart began to thud in his chest. His manhood stirred, thickened, grew heavy with need.

Slow and easy, Deakin.

"You have given me many lovely gifts in the past," she reminded him.

"But nothing like this, my dear Juliet. This is a gift you give and receive at the same time."

"Where do we start?"

"At the beginning, of course."

"At the *very* beginning?"

He frowned. "Perhaps not at the very beginning."

"Especially since the very beginning for us was a rather hair-raising ride through Central Park," she said, with a self-amused smile.

"I believe we can also skip the formal introductions, the first dance, the first dinner engagement, the first walk—" he ticked the items off one by one on his fingertips.

"Lawrence—" she interrupted.

He blinked. "Yes, Juliet."

"Why don't we start with a kiss?"

Slow and easy, Deakin.

"An excellent idea," he said, bending to press his lips to that soft, inviting spot just beneath her earlobe.

She shivered. "When you kiss my neck it gives me gooseflesh, but I am not cold. Indeed, if anything I feel a trifle warm. I wonder where my fan is."

"Your fan will be of no consequence tonight, my dear Juliet." He bit the inside of his mouth and then, with a wicked grin, said it anyway: "Before long, I think I can guarantee you will be feeling quite hot."

She stood up and faced him, her hands on her hips. The action drew attention to the fact that her combing sacque had slipped off her shoulders and her lush body, covered only by the fine nightdress, was revealed. "That was a double entendre, was it not, husband?"

"It was, wife," he said, staring at her breasts. There were the most perfect, the most beautiful pair of breasts it had been his privilege to behold. And they were his, all his. Lawrence found himself licking his lips.

"What are you staring at so intently, sir?"

"You, madam," he muttered, not welcoming the distraction of conversation.

"Yet your eyes are not meeting mine when I speak," she had cause to note.

"Nevertheless, I find I cannot tear my gaze away from you, lady wife."

"From exactly what part of me, husband?"

He raised both of his hands in front of him. Her glorious breasts were a mere inch or two from his fingertips. He was itching to touch her. He was dying to touch her. "Your crowning jewels," he exclaimed. "They are the shape, the color of the largest, rarest, and finest pearls. Their tips are pale rubies. No, I am wrong. They are plump, luscious berries. They make my mouth water. They arouse my appetite. I must taste them. I must satisfy my hunger."

Face flushed with excitement, Juliet swayed toward him and he captured her breasts. Her nipples puckered up, tickled, teased, skimmed along the sensitive surface of his palms.

It brought Lawrence to his knees. He found himself on the cushioned seat before the mirror, his face level with those rare pearls whose virtues he had so recently extolled.

It was most fortuitous.

He did not bother with the endless row of tiny buttons down the front of her nightdress: he had neither the time or the patience to deal with them. Instead, he buried his face between those twin globes and inhaled Juliet's scent. "Ah, wife, no one smells as you do."

"I take it, husband, that is a compliment," came a breathless whisper from above.

"Summer roses and golden sunshine," he murmured, nuzzling her through the nearly transparent material.

"A moment ago I was lush berries," she said with a mystified laugh.

"You are all these things and more," Lawrence declared as he took her breast into his mouth.

He was rewarded with a feminine gasp that soon became a moan of sensual arousal. He had once made the mistake of thinking that Miss Juliet Jones was his for the taking. He would not make the same mistake twice. He had wed her. Now he must woo her, win her, and bed her.

In that order.

"Lawrence. Lawrence. Lawrence." His name became a litany upon Juliet's lips as he went back and forth from one breast to the other, licking, tasting, nipping, biting, suckling until her gown was thoroughly drenched and transparent as it clung to her skin.

When he came up for air, she glanced down and saw what he had done. "I may as well be naked," she choked.

"My sentiments exactly," he muttered, his fingers fumbling with the tiny buttons. Unsuccessful, he swore vehemently: "Slow and easy be damned!"

"Are you angry, sir?"

"I am frustrated, madam. I am too eager and too awkward to make a success of it. I require your help."

"I can only try." Juliet's hands were trembling but somehow she managed where he had not.

Then he reached down and whisked the gown over her head, and she stood before him: Venus come to life.

He stepped back and admired her for a moment. "Egods, you are magnificent!"

Juliet burned under his intense scrutiny. No man had ever seen her without clothes. She had to keep reminding herself that this was her husband, that this was the way it was intended to be between man and wife.

A frown creased her forehead. "But—"

Lawrence displayed immediate concern. "But what, my lovely Juliet?"

"There is something wrong here."

His manner became wary. "What is wrong?"

"It is unfair."

His impatience surfaced. "What is bloody unfair?"

"I am standing here without a stitch on, while you are still wearing your dressing gown."

She watched as a smile of understanding slowly spread across Lawrence's handsome features. "That can be easily remedied." His hand went to his waist.

Then his fingers froze on the silk sash. She waited. He gave her an odd look.

"Is something amiss, husband?"

"Nothing is amiss, wife." He cleared his throat. "It has occurred to me that you may never have seen a grown man without his clothes before."

"Of course, I have never seen a grown man without his clothes," she conceded. "What woman has before marriage?"

"The answer to that question is best reserved for another time and another place," he said.

She felt the heat of embarrassment rise in her face. "I am not totally ignorant, Lawrence. I know the kind of woman you are referring to."

"Yes . . . well . . ."

"Why do you not remove your robe?" she persisted.

"You may recall a conversation we once had on the subject of the male member."

How could she forget? "I do."

Lawrence folded his arms across his chest—he seemed to take up most of her sizeable bedroom, but Juliet knew that was not possible; it had to be an illusion. "I explained that certain physical changes take place in a man's body when he is sexually aroused."

Her husband was trying to tell her something. Juliet wondered what it was. Then it dawned on her. He was aroused at this very moment. The changes in his body had already occurred.

" 'That is what makes it so hard,' " she quoted him verbatim.

"You have an amazing memory," he commented in a sardonic tone.

"Thank you."

"Madam, I am trying to prepare you."

"Sir, for what?"

"The sight of an unclothed, fully aroused male," he blurted out.

Bravado—that was the key. She imitated his arrogant stance by folding her arms under her naked breasts. "I am prepared."

Lawrence untied the sash around his waist, shrugged off his dressing gown, nonchalantly tossed it across the cushioned seat beside him and stood before her in all his natural glory . . . and then some.

Juliet sucked in her breath. She was wrong. She was not prepared.

"I did try to warn you," Lawrence said with a crooked smile.

It was huge. It was hard. It protruded. In fact, she could have sworn it moved.

It was smooth and satiny in appearance. It was strong, yet vulnerable. It was taut as a bow, yet she knew it was human flesh. Indeed, once Juliet had recovered from her initial shock, she also found it was fascinating.

"I don't know what to say," she murmured at last.

"Are you repulsed?"

"Repulsed?" she repeated, not comprehending.

"By the sight of me in this aroused state."

Her eyes flew to his for an instant. "You are my husband. Nothing about you could ever possibly repulse me."

"I am, of course, gratified to hear that."

She couldn't tear her eyes away. "I have never seen anything like it."

"I certainly hope not."

"It is amazing."

"All men are essentially the same," Lawrence said dismissively.

"It is astounding."

"Although, perhaps, not all men are so large," he said, as an afterthought.

Juliet gave him a final measuring look and announced: "Sir, it is *you* who are magnificent!"

With that, Lawrence Grenfell Wicke put his dark head back and laughed with uninhibited delight. "Oh, my dearest, dearest Juliet. I should have known."

She blinked. "You should have known *what*?"

"That you would be as unconventional in the bedroom as you are in every other room of the house," he said.

She was bubbling over with questions, brimming with curiosity. Indeed, it seemed that the sight of her husband naked only served to whet her appetite for knowledge, not satisfy it.

"Am I allowed to ask questions?"

"Naturally."

"Does it hurt when you are hard?"

"It is both painful and pleasurable."

"I do not understand."

"You will," he promised.

"When does it return to its normal size?"

"When I am no longer aroused."

"How long will that take?"

"With you staring at me as you are now, wife: forever."

Juliet moistened her bottom lip with the tip of her tongue. "May I touch it?"

She heard Lawrence suck in his breath. "Of course."

Juliet took a step toward him. She stopped, reached out and tentatively touched her index finger to the very tip. His manhood jumped. "It moved!"

"Yes."

She eyed him warily. "Is that normal?"

"Perfectly normal."

She tried again. This time she drew a line down one side of his hard shaft and back up the other, then circled the tiny hole at the very end. "Your skin feels like silk," she announced with wonder.

Lawrence groaned.

"Is that a groan of pain or pleasure, sir?" she inquired.

"Pleasure, madam," he gritted through his teeth.

"You do not look to me like you enjoyed it."

Beads of perspiration formed on his forehead. "Trust me, I did."

"Shall I try it again?"

That quickly he reached out and grasped her hand in his. "I think not."

"Why not?"

"There is a point of no return for a man."

Juliet was puzzled. "For a woman, too?"

"Yes."

"What is the point of no return?"

There was a look in Lawrence's black eyes that she couldn't decipher. Indeed, she did not think she had ever seen it before.

"I could explain . . ."

She pursed her lips. "But you won't."

"I would rather show you, Juliet, than to try to explain the unexplainable."

"But—"

The next word was cut off by his mouth taking hers. She was drawn into his embrace and for the first time she knew what it was to feel bare flesh against bare flesh. Where he was hard, she was soft. Where he was muscular, she was rounded. Where his skin was covered with a smattering of dark hair, hers was blond.

His hands and lips and teeth seemed to be everywhere at once: nibbling on her ear, sucking on an aching nipple, leaving a trail of scorching kisses from her neck to her waist.

She felt his hand glide lower to cover that most private and vulnerable place on a woman's body, and she suddenly could not draw her breath. "Lawrence—"

"It is all right, my sweet Juliet. I won't hurt you. I promise," he murmured against her lips.

Then he plunged his tongue into her mouth, and somewhere in the midst of the overwhelmingly erotic kiss, his hand urged her thighs apart and he slipped a finger into her.

Her knees buckled. She was vaguely aware of being swept up into Lawrence's arms at some point. Then she felt the bed give beneath their weight, yet his tongue still dipped into her mouth even as his fingers drove into her body faster and faster.

Something was happening to her that she didn't understand. It began deep inside her, in a place she had not known existed. It was like a spring coiled so tightly it would, it could, never come unwound.

It was both painful and pleasurable.

Then an exquisite tension began to build until Juliet was certain she would go quite mad. She cried out loud: "Dear God, help me!"

"I will! I am!" Lawrence vowed, rubbing his thumb back and forth across a throbbing nub that proved to be the most sensitive flesh of all.

Something was overtaking her. Every nerve

ending in her body was atingle. She was spiraling higher and higher. She was about to explode. She was out of control. She had reached the point of no return.

As she shattered into a thousand infinitesimal pieces—the impact was felt from the finest hair on her head to her aching teeth to the curled tips of her toes—Juliet shouted hoarsely, "Lawrence!"

It was some time before she stirred, before she could even manage to open her eyes. When she did, her husband was watching her.

"Do you understand now why I could not explain?" he asked.

She nodded but did not speak.

It was even later—she had been nestled comfortably in his arms, her head resting on his chest—that Juliet became aware that Lawrence's body had undergone no change: he was still huge, still hard, still protruding. In fact, she could feel his manhood pressing against her leg.

"Lawrence?"

"Yes, my sweet."

"You have not returned to your normal size."

"No, I have not."

"You are still aroused."

"Yes, I am."

"You have not reached the point of no return."

"But I am very close," he confessed.

She pushed herself up on one elbow. "Shall I touch you with my fingers until you do?"

His eyes were very dark. "That is one way to make love."

She was learning fast. "But there is another way you would prefer."

"You will prefer it one day as well."

"And you could explain it to me, but you would rather show me," she said with a smile that deliberately teased and taunted him.

Lawrence stared down at her. "It will be different from the first time, Juliet. It will not be my fingers that I put inside your body."

She went very still.

He added: "You will no longer be a virgin."

She blushed but said what was in her heart. "I do not wish to be a virgin, husband. I wish to be a real wife."

"And I want you," he declared as he drew her closer. "I want you more than I have ever wanted anyone or anything before in my life."

Lawrence kissed her then, gently, enticingly, persuasively, passionately, fiercely. He drove his tongue into her mouth. She responded by flicking hers along the serrated edges of his teeth.

He parted the delicate folds of her skin and insinuated his fingertips into the tight channel. She instinctively arched her back and he sunk his fingers in all the way.

"You said it would not be your fingers this time," she said, gasping for air.

"I am trying to open you little by little, so as not to cause you any more pain than I must. You are so tight and so new. I may be too large, too hard, too close to the point of no return. I don't want to lose control."

"But I want you to lose control," she whispered huskily, "as I did. I want you to forget everything and everyone else in that moment but me."

Lawrence hovered over her. "Are you certain that's what you want?"

"I'm certain."

Then he removed his fingers, damp with her honeyed dew, and guided his shaft to the entrance. He entered her, slowly easing into her, filling her inch by inch until she could bear it no longer.

"Lawrence, I want all of you now!" she cried out.

"Juliet!" He lost control and drove into her, long and hard and deep, burying himself to the hilt.

She had all of him, then, and as the first shock wave began to recede, he moved faster, thrust longer and deeper and harder, again and again, until Juliet felt as though her world was coming apart. Somewhere in the back of her mind she realized it was happening to her a second time.

She heard Lawrence give a shout of masculine triumph, of ultimate relief and release, as he exploded inside her. Then she felt herself going over the edge, past that exquisite point of no return.

It was the strong, steady rhythm of his heart beating within his breast as they lay together in her bed that prompted Juliet to say, "You promised me a bedtime story, husband."

"A bedtime story, wife?" he laughed softly.

She could feel his laughter through her fingertips as she rested her hand on his muscular chest, as she wound her fingers through the smattering of silky black hair that encircled his small, brown, male nipples and then pointed southward, like an arrow, toward his crowning glory.

She thought for a moment. "Tell me the legend of the Black Heart."

" 'Tis not a legend. 'Tis a fairy tale," he scoffed.

She loved fairy tales. Indeed, at times, Juliet thought she believed in them. "Then tell me the fairy tale of the Black Heart."

Lawrence pulled the covers over them—it was late and the night had turned cool—settled her within the circle of his arms and began with: "Once upon a time . . ."

"Once upon a time . . ." she murmured, snuggling closer to his warmth.

"There was a handsome, young, black-haired duke of the realm named Deakin," he told her.

"How long ago?" she interjected.

"Long, long ago," he said indefinitely. "Anyway, the duke was a mighty warrior. He was without equal in battle. He was as strong as ten ordinary men."

Juliet chuckled. "This is beginning to sound more and more like a fairy tale."

Lawrence sniffed. "I'm only telling the story

to you the way Nanny told it to me as I was growing up."

"Go on," she prompted, when she feared he might stop.

"As I was saying, the duke was as strong as a dozen ordinary men. One spring he stormed his archenemy's castle and captured all who dwelled within its walls. One of those he took captive was a beautiful flaxen-haired lady. She was as light as he was dark."

Juliet intertwined a long strand of her own blond hair with one of Lawrence's black locks.

"For the sake of peace between the two warring nobleman, the king ordered the duke to take the beautiful lady as his wife. He was an obedient servant of his sovereign and soon after the couple were wed."

Juliet began to hum the traditional wedding march under her breath.

"The lady was a good wife who did all that was required of her, but the duke wanted more. He wanted to win her love. He began to shower her with attentions and gifts, fine cloth from the East and chests filled with silver and gold. And, still, she did not love him. He searched the countryside for rare gemstones and had them made into elaborate rings and necklaces and, still, she did not love him. Then he went on a faraway quest for a fabled treasure of black diamonds; the largest was reputed to be a stone called the—"

"Black Heart," Juliet finished for him, utterly enthralled.

Lawrence nodded and added: "Because it was the size of a man's heart."

"And, still, she did not love him."

He looked at her askance. "Are you sure you have not heard the story?"

She shook her head.

"Anyway, the duke, in his despair, gave away all his worldly possessions and wandered the realm as a beggar, seeking the answer to his question. He finally returned to his lady wife and offered her the only thing of value he had left. His wife smiled upon him and at last declared her love."

Juliet was holding her breath in anticipation. "What did the duke offer her?"

Lawrence gazed down into her eyes. "He offered the lady his heart."

She sighed and exhaled. "What a lovely story."

"Yes," he commented dryly.

"Did they live happily ever after?" she asked.

"Naturally." Then he went on. "Of course, they were very poor. . . ."

"I'm sure it did not matter."

"Not in fairy tales."

Juliet pressed her cheek to his chest and listened to the strong rhythmic beat of that which gave him life. "What became of the Black Heart?"

"It became part of the fairy tale—the legend, if you will—and passed into the annals of history."

She dropped a kiss on Lawrence's chest, another on the jut of his jaw, a third on his mouth. "Thank you for telling me the story, husband."

His eyes were glittering as he drew her atop his torso. "You are most welcome, wife."

A crease appeared between her eyes and she remarked to him: "There seems to be something poking me, sir."

"Poking you, madam?"

Juliet bit the corners of her mouth against a smile. "One might even say prodding me."

The expression on his handsome face was one of complete innocence. "Pray tell, where?"

She moved against him and said breathlessly, "Between my legs."

He seemed to have a bright idea. "Perhaps it is a gift."

"Another gift?"

He shrugged.

She inquired with a raised brow: "So soon?"

Lawrence was suddenly serious. "Do you mind?"

Juliet brought her mouth down to his and murmured against his lips: "You know what they say."

"What?"

" 'Never look a gift horse in the mouth.' "

The part-laugh, part-groan seemed to come from the back of his throat. "One of your damned ancient Greeks, again?"

She shook her head and tried to retain her train of thought. It was easier said than done since Lawrence was doing wonderful things to her body. "St. Jerome," she gasped. "Fourth . . . century," she barely managed. "In his

Epistle to the ..." Juliet never finished the sentence.

Lawrence was still smiling as he buried himself deep within her warm and willing body.

21

"LADY DEERHURST, Their Graces are still sleeping," objected Jenkins in a tone that managed to be both polite and insistent at the same time.

"Nonsense!" she said, waving him aside with an ecru kid-gloved hand. She had chosen a fashionable visiting costume of strawberry satin with alternating pleats of black velvet and black lace, a black lace bonnet with a face trimming of strawberry faille and an ostrich plume posed low behind.

"But—"

"I know His Grace," she declared in a voice that would brook no argument. "He never stays abed after daybreak. It's one of the reasons why he was never any good at Society parties. The man is the Duke of Deakin, and yet he insists upon acting like a bloody farmer. Up with the damned chickens, to bed with the damned cows."

Helena swept into the front hall of Grantley Manor, paused to survey her surroundings, caught a glimpse of the library through an open door—she noticed that the faded red carpet had been replaced and the furniture rearranged—and headed straight for Lawrence's bedroom.

She was going to have this business settled once and for all. Rumors had been flying through every rung of London society and the local countryside: the Duke and Duchess of Deakin were man and wife in name only.

For God's sake, Lawrence had gone and married the American bitch and apparently couldn't even bring himself to bed her!

She started down the hallway of the West Wing, calling out in a coquettish voice: "Lawrence . . ."

Jenkins ran to keep up with her, his hands raised in supplication. "I beg of you, Lady Deerhurst. Keep your voice down. They are asleep."

Helena flung open the door of the duke's bedroom. "You are mistaken." She pointed to the bed. The covers had been turned down, but it had obviously not been slept in. "His Grace is not even here."

It was just as well that Bunter was also not there. Helena didn't think she could have forced her way past him, especially since his elevation to butler. This new valet, Jenkins, was formidable enough—although he was no match for her, of course. Not when she had her dander up. And her dander was definitely up.

"His Grace is asleep in Her Grace's bedroom," whispered Jenkins, his face red.

Helena did not know whether his florid coloring was a result of running up the stairs after her, or a fit of temper—but she found it amusing, nonetheless.

The valet turned and waved a curious house-maid to be on her way.

"*His* Grace asleep in *Her* Grace's bedroom," she mimicked. "Don't be an ass, my good man. Why would Lawrence be asleep in *her* bed?"

Jenkins bit his tongue. It was not his place to correct a lady like the countess. She was his social superior, after all. She was also head-strong, determined, in a flying rage and, he sur-mised, somewhat tipsy. He had learned a long time ago that his kind survived *downstairs* by scrupulously turning a blind eye to those who drank to excess *upstairs*.

Still, his first loyalty was to Their Graces. They had been very kind to him. His wages were half again as much as any other personal valet in service, and he and the duke were beginning to adjust to one another. The duchess was, of course, a saint.

If only he knew what to do about Lady Deer-hurst.

"If you will wait in the drawing room, I will ascertain if either His Grace or Her Grace is available to see you," Jenkins suggested, trying to get out of the most awkward situation of his career.

"Unless you want your head on the chopping block, Jenkins, you would do well to turn around and leave while there is still time," the countess warned him, brandishing in ever-widening circles her satin parasol with the black lace trim.

The young man retreated.

It had been eating at her for weeks, Helena

acknowledged. She would have her satisfaction at last: What was the new Duchess of Deakin really like?

Perhaps she would have waited, *could* have waited, until Lawrence and his "bride" appeared in London—even the Duke of Deakin occasionally came to sit in the House of Lords—but only last week a pretty young man had arrived in town. He called himself David Thoreau Jones, and he claimed to be the cousin of the former Miss Juliet Jones, now the Duchess of Deakin.

It was whispered that there was a strong family resemblance between Mister Jones—David to her now—and his distant female relation.

If so, then Lawrence may not have married a cow after all. She had to see for herself, Helena had decided that very morning as she sipped several cups of her "restorative" tea for breakfast. She had several more for luncheon. Then Lilla had dressed her in one of her most fashionable visiting gowns, arranged her hair, artfully done her makeup so that it appeared that she wore none, and was even now sitting outside in her carriage, waiting.

Helena threw open the connecting door between Lawrence's bedroom and that of the American witch.

"Lawrence, are you in here?" she said, trying not to slur her words.

Somewhere in the deepest recesses of her brain it must have registered that someone was asleep in the duchess's bed. Helena assumed it was the duchess herself.

There was movement under the covers and a girl sat up in the massive four-poster. Still half-asleep, she stretched her ivory arms high above her head.

It was not the duchess.

It could not *possibly* be the duchess.

The girl's face was soft and young; her features perfectly proportioned. Her complexion was flawless. Her hair was the consistency of silk; it fell around her shoulders in a cloud of gold dust.

Her breasts were breathtaking. The rest of her figure, at least what could be discerned of it, was equally divine. The creature was, Helena realized, her mouth unconsciously dropping open in amazement, one of the most beautiful human beings she had ever beheld, male or female.

The girl yawned, showing perfect white teeth. She blinked and slowly opened her eyes. They were a startling shade of blue. Then she blinked several more times in rapid succession, gave Helena a look of utter bewilderment, and grasped the sheet to cover her nudity.

She finally found her voice. It was low and husky. She spoke in a whisper. "Who are you?"

Good Lord, Juliet implored silently as she sat up and grabbed the sheet to cover herself, there was a stranger in her bedroom!

She came awake instantly.

It registered somewhere in her consciousness that a housemaid, even a new housemaid, would not be dressed in bright red satin with accents

of black velvet and black lace. Nor would a servant be wearing a black lace bonnet with a face
trimming of red silk and an ostrich plume
coiled around her hair. This was a lady from
the top of her lace-and-silk hat to the tips of her
matching silk slippers.

Still, what was a lady doing standing in the
middle of her bedroom in broad daylight staring at her as if she had grown a second head?

"Who in the bloody hell are you?" demanded
the woman, her face going from white to red to
an enraged purple in a matter of moments.

Juliet was taken aback, to say the least. "I
beg your pardon, madam."

"Are you hard of hearing, girl? I asked who
you are."

"I-I am Juliet."

"Juliet?" came a coarse snicker. "Are you a
new housemaid, Juliet?"

"No, I—"

The woman cut her off rudely. "No, you
wouldn't be a housemaid, would you? I'll war-
rant that those soft, lily-white hands of yours
haven't seen one day's hard physical labor. Perhaps you are a new toy that Lawrence is amusing himself with? Or an actress? You are pretty
enough to be an actress." The stranger's tone
turned ugly. "Or are you simply some doxy he
picked up on the streets?"

Juliet tried to maintain as much dignity as
she could under the circumstances. "I am a
duchess."

The woman snorted. "A duchess? You?"

She sat up straight in the oversize bed and

tucked the covers around her to retain some semblance of modesty. She was determined not to awaken Lawrence, who was still sleeping soundly behind her. The poor man needed his rest. It had been a most exhausting night for him. Indeed, they had not fallen asleep the last time until the birds began to twitter at dawn. She pitched her voice to a clear whisper and announced regally: "I am Juliet, Duchess of Deakin."

There was stunned silence in the room.

"You are not an old maid," came the accusation.

"Not any longer," she said with a satisfied smile.

The woman's catlike eyes narrowed to two green slits. "You are not even old."

"Should I be?"

There was an inelegant sniff from her unwelcome visitor. "I was told that you were thirty-five, perhaps even forty."

"You were told incorrectly. I am twenty-four."

The green eyes widened in surprise. "You do not even look twenty-four."

"Thank you. I think," Juliet added, wondering if she should awaken her husband, after all. Perhaps Lawrence would know what to do with the demented woman questioning her in her own bedroom.

"You are not short and fat," was whirled at her next.

"I am not short or fat," she verified.

"Neither are you tall and thin."

Juliet felt she had to point out: "I am tall, actually." Naturally, under the circumstances, she had no intentions of standing up to prove it.

"I don't suppose you suffer from consumption, either."

"I am as healthy as a horse."

Bits and pieces of conversation she had heard from Nanny and Aunt Effie were replaying in Juliet's mind. She was almost certain she could guess the identity of her uninvited guest.

The woman peered at her and would have come closer if Juliet had not held up a hand to stop her. "That is close enough, Lady Deerhurst." She tilted her head to one side. "It is Lady Deerhurst, is it not?"

"It is, indeed." The words were carefully enunciated. "You do not appear pockmarked or bucktoothed, Duchess."

"I do not appear pockmarked or bucktoothed, Countess, because I am neither."

"My information is never wrong."

"Nevertheless, it seems you have been misinformed this time," Juliet said, studying her opponent.

So *this* was the notorious, the infamous, the poisonous Lady Helena Deerhurst. All Juliet could feel for the woman was pity. The countess was handsome, she supposed, in a hard, brittle kind of way—but the pathetic creature had been drinking. Indeed, it appeared that she had been drinking to excess.

Lady Deerhurst peeled off her kid gloves, opened her velvet and lace bag, and stuffed them inside. "I was also told, Duchess, that you are an heiress."

It had never been a secret. "I am."

"And you are an American."

"I am," she said proudly.

The woman nodded her head with satisfaction. "At least that much of my information is correct, then."

"That much and more has been published in every newspaper on both sides of the Atlantic Ocean, Countess."

"You cannot fool me," Lady Deerhurst claimed, opening her velvet and lace bag and taking out the gloves she had just removed. As she compulsively yanked them back on her hands, her sharp nails sliced through the ends of the fragile kid. "I have heard all about you, Duchess, from the villagers and the local gentry and even those in Society." There was a decidedly unpleasant smile on her face when she stated, "I know that you do not sleep with Lawrence."

Juliet froze in place. Her tone was icy cold as she countered: "My relationship with my husband is none of your business, madam."

The countess looked down her nose. Juliet noticed it was slightly red on the tip. "Furthermore, you are not English, and must, therefore, be uncouth."

"At least I have never barged into another woman's bedroom while she and her husband are still asleep," Juliet pointed out.

Helena swayed unsteadily. "You can't fool me, Duchess. The fact is the duke has not bought you one single piece of jewelry beyond a plain gold wedding band."

Juliet gazed down at her left hand. "My husband understands that I do not care for fancy baubles. The gold ring he placed on my finger the day we were married is more precious to me than all the gemstones in the world."

"You are a strange creature." Helena began to pace back and forth, not quite managing a straight line in the process. Then she stopped, turned, and announced, "Lawrence married you for your money."

Juliet grew weary of dealing with her. "Frankly, Lady Deerhurst, many men have wanted to marry me for many reasons. I consented to Lawrence's proposal because he swept me off my feet. I simply could not say no."

"Lawrence sweep a woman off her feet?" the countess snorted. "I have been after him for years. He turned me down flat."

Juliet quirked a blond brow. "I gathered as much."

She pointed a gloved finger at Juliet. "I don't care if you are young and beautiful and rich. I have it on the best authority that you and the duke have separate bedrooms and the door between them is kept locked."

"If it is kept locked, how did you manage to open it and walk into my bedroom?"

That stopped the countess cold. Her voice grew louder and more shrill. "You do not share a bed with your husband, with my Lawrence."

"Please keep your voice down. He is still asleep. The poor man had an exhausting night."

Lady Deerhurst blew out her breath. "Humph. You expect me to believe that the lump of pillows and bedcovers behind you is Lawrence."

"You may believe whatever you like. Frankly, I am indifferent to what you think."

Helena delivered a threat. "You shouldn't be. I know more about gossip and Society than you ever will."

Juliet sighed. "Countess, I have been the subject of gossip since the day I was born. It is nothing new to me. I have never given a fig for what Society thought of me in New York or Newport or Paris. I care even less what your kind of Society thinks of me here in England."

The woman's lower lip protruded in a childish pout. "I will get him in the end."

"Get who in the end?"

"Lawrence."

"You may not have my husband."

"You will have nothing to say about it."

"I will have everything to say about it." Juliet felt the bed behind her move, then a masculine thigh rub up against hers. "I must ask you to leave, Lady Deerhurst. You have created a scene and awakened my husband."

The woman was adamant. "Lawrence is not in your bed."

"I certainly hope it is Lawrence," she murmured as the mattress began to jiggle. The blasted man seemed to be laughing. She was somewhat less amused and tossed over her shoulder. "It isn't funny, darling."

"You are a very good actress, Duchess."

"You are wrong, Countess. I am a terrible actress. Just ask Lawrence."

"I would if he were here."

As if on cue, Lawrence Grenfell Wicke's head and shoulders emerged from beneath the bedcovers. His black hair was tousled. His expression was sleepy, satiated, and slightly bemused. He rubbed his bare chest with one hand and yawned. "What is that infernal noise, wife?"

"It is nothing, husband."

"Good morning," he murmured, dropping a kiss on Juliet's shoulder.

"Lawrence, we have company."

He squinted and stared toward the bright sunlight streaming in the window, then peered around the room. "At this hour of the morning?"

"It is not morning," Juliet informed him gently. "It is afternoon. And you no doubt remember Lady Deerhurst."

Lawrence propped himself up behind her and glared at the intruder. "Countess."

Helena laughed in the back of her throat. "Why so formal, Lawrence, when we have known each other so long and so well?"

"What the devil are you doing here, Helena? Juliet and I are not receiving visitors yet. We are still on our honeymoon."

"Your honeymoon," she hooted.

Juliet explained, "Lady Deerhurst seems to have been given false information, husband. She was under the impression that ours was a marriage in name only."

His only answer was a sensual laugh that spoke for itself.

"I do believe the countess came here today to offer herself to you as a mistress." Juliet turned her gaze upon the now livid woman. "My husband does not require a mistress. He has his hands full with me."

Under the bedcovers, Lawrence insinuated his arm around her waist and snaked his way up to cover a breast. He sighed. "She is a handful."

Juliet slapped at him playfully. "You must excuse us now, Lady Deerhurst. We are very busy."

Helena was beside herself. "Busy doing what?"

"Well, for one thing we are renovating Grantley. Then we are going to throw a gala weekend house party when the work is finished." Juliet looked back at Lawrence. "I thought we might recreate the famous treasure hunt of 1828."

"An interesting idea," he said.

"I mustn't take all the credit. It was really Aunt Effie's inspiration."

Helena frowned. "Aunt Effie?"

"My great-aunt, Euphemia Jones. She came from America to live with us." She turned back to her husband. "We could invite your brother, Jonathan, and his wife, Elizabeth. Miles St. Aldford, of course, and your other friends. David must come from America." She failed to see the dark expression that flitted across her husband's face at the mention of her cousin. "No doubt we should include some local people. We will make up a guest list. I'll have Bunter work with my secretaries.''

"I beg your pardon—" interrupted Helena.

They had both temporarily forgotten the existence of their "guest."

Juliet said as an afterthought: "You and Lord Deerhurst will be on the list, as was your great-uncle, George Frewen, during the time of the sixth duke and duchess.''

"Dear, dear Great-Uncle George." Coming from Helena it was anything but an endearment.

In tandem Bunter and Jenkins appeared in the open doorway. They were both red-faced, nonplussed and abjectly apologetic. "Your Graces."

There was a great deal of bowing and scraping. "We humbly beg your pardons for the intrusion."

"The more the merrier," Lawrence muttered under his breath.

"I am prepared to offer my immediate resignation," intoned Bunter gravely. "I was attending to a small crisis in the kitchen when Lady Deerhurst arrived and, consequently, I failed in my primary duty to you.''

"I, too, am prepared to give notice, Your Grace," spoke up Jenkins. "It was entirely my fault that the lady got beyond the front hall.''

Lawrence appeared to have had quite enough for one day. He barked his commands like the born leader of men that he was: "Your resignations are not accepted. You will both remain in your present positions. Bunter, you will escort Lady Deerhurst to the door and see to it that she is deposited in her carriage."

"Yes, Your Grace."

"Jenkins—"

His valet snapped to attention. "Your Grace."

"You will close the bedroom door behind you and make certain that Her Grace and I are not disturbed again."

"Your wish is my command, Your Grace."

Once they were alone, Juliet let out a great sigh of relief. "That was exhausting."

"Indeed, wife, it was."

She inclined her head and chewed on her bottom lip. "It was a most unusual way to start the day, wouldn't you say?"

"I would. And it is one I hope never to repeat," he said dryly.

Juliet started to push the covers back and reach for her dressing gown. "It is past noon, Lawrence. We must be getting up."

"My sweet Juliet," he murmured, pulling her beneath him on the bed, "I already am.

They did not make it downstairs in time for either tea or dinner. . . .

22

LAWRENCE watched his wife pace back and forth in front of the library table. She stopped to rearrange the items on the top for the third time in as many minutes. Then she selected a book from the shelf behind her, opened it to the first page, skimmed through the information, snapped the cover shut, and replaced it on the shelf.

Next she picked up one of the dozen vintage kaleidoscopes from his grandfather's collection, turned toward the window and held it up to her eye. She peered through it for a moment, put it down and picked up another.

When she seemed to have tired of that, she straightened her skirts, touched her hand to her hair, tucked a stray wisp behind her ear, chewed on her bottom lip, drummed her fingertips on the table top, twisted her wedding band around and around on her finger, and then began pacing the floor again.

"Juliet!" His voice rang out in the library like the blare of a trumpet.

She started. Her wide blue eyes flew to his face. "Yes, Lawrence."

He pointed to a chair. "Sit!"

Juliet sat.

Lawrence stood at ease before his wife, his hands linked behind his back, his feet planted solidly apart, shoulders back, chin up, eyes forward. "Explain, madam."

Her golden blond brows, the same color as her golden blond hair, drew together. "Explain what, sir?"

"The reason for all of this"—he made a circular motion in front of him with one hand—"movement."

"Movement?"

"Fidgeting."

"Was I fidgeting?" she said, her gaze darting from his eyes to the window and back again.

"Yes."

"Are you certain?"

"Positive."

He watched the rapid rise and fall of her breasts beneath the blue silk summer dress she had chosen for the occasion.

"I suppose," she began, "it is because your brother and his wife are due to arrive at any moment."

"*That* is why you are fidgeting? Because Jonathan and Elizabeth are coming for a visit?"

She nodded her head and concentrated on the hands folded in her lap. "I have never had a brother or a sister."

He spoke to her slowly, reasonably. "Of course, you haven't. You are an only child."

"I am very nervous about meeting your family. I must confess I haven't felt this nervous since"—she swallowed—"well, since I don't know when."

But they both knew since when.

His lady wife seemed to burst out with all her thoughts aloud. "I so want to make a good first impression."

"My dearest Juliet," Lawrence said, holding out his hands to her. She stood and placed her palms in his. "You will make an excellent first impression. You could do nothing else."

"Is your brother like you?"

"Jonathan is the same and yet very different."

She frowned and inquired: "How can he be both the same and not the same?"

Lawrence attempted to explain. "My younger brother has the same black hair as I do, the same general build, but he inherited what we call the 'wild Wickes' blue eyes."

"The 'wild Wickes' blue eyes?"

He nodded. "We seem to produce a legendary black sheep in our family every other generation, hand in hand, it always seems, with piercing blue eyes."

She was paying him the fullest attention now. "And is your younger brother the black sheep of the family?"

"He was."

"Ah, he has reformed."

"He has married."

"I understand marriage can often cure that kind of thing," she said in a perfectly serious tone.

Lawrence laughed good-humoredly. "Jonathan met his wife while they were in Egypt several years ago. Elizabeth was the daughter of the Earl of Stanhope, a renowned archaeologist. I believe that her brother has since inherited the title."

"Do you think Lady Elizabeth will be very grand? Perhaps she does not care for Americans. Some on the Continent do not, you know. She will undoubtedly be a small, delicate creature, and I will tower over her like an Amazon."

He tried to reassure her. "I think you will find, Juliet, that you have a good deal in common with your sister-in-law. She always has her nose in a book, or is attending her rose garden."

"Roses are my favorite flower," she murmured.

"Furthermore, Elizabeth is enamored of the ancient Egyptians and you of the ancient Greeks."

She seemed to find that prospect appealing.

"Now, do you feel better?"

"Yes, I do. Thank you, husband." She went up on her tiptoes and dropped a quick kiss on the jut of his jaw.

"You are welcome, wife."

Then she turned and raced to the library window. "They are here! They are here, Lawrence!"

"Yes, Juliet," he said as he watched her cheeks grow pink and her eyes sparkle.

She did a pirouette. "Do I look all right?"

It was a rare thing, indeed, for Juliet to be

concerned about her appearance. Apparently the arrival of his family meant more to her than he had realized. "You have never looked more beautiful," he told her.

She smiled and admitted, "My hands are shaking."

"It is my brother and his wife, my dear. It is not the Queen."

"I don't give a fig about meeting the Queen," she blurted out with characteristic candor.

How like his Juliet, Lawrence thought as she tried to contain her excitement and failed.

"They are getting out of the carriage," she announced. "They are coming up the front walk. Why, Lawrence, your brother looks very much like you and Elizabeth—" She was speechless for a moment. "Lady Elizabeth appears to be every bit as tall as I am!"

Somehow it did not surprise Lawrence when the four of them ended up in the library rather than in the formal drawing room. It was too late for luncheon and too early for tea, so the ladies were enjoying a glass of lemonade and sitting on the sofa, chatting like longtime friends.

He and Jonathan stood to one side and discussed the improvements that had recently been made to the stables, the cottages, the farm.

"I don't believe that Grantley Manor has ever looked better," Jonathan complimented his older brother.

Lawrence looked around him with a genuine

sense of pride. "I agree. Grantley has never looked better."

"Neither have you.

"The credit for both goes to Juliet."

Jonathan lowered his voice and inquired discreetly: "Has the food improved any?"

Lawrence grinned. "Not only is it edible, brother. It is actually delicious. Juliet has hired some fancy French chef and she has even devised a system for getting the food to the table while it is still hot."

"That is amazing."

He didn't stop there. "You should hear some of my dear wife's future plans for Grantley. She is talking about having those newfangled electric lights installed and getting rid of the gas altogether."

"Electricity is the latest thing."

"But will it last?"

Later, over a celebratory brandy, Jonathan commented: "Having an open house and gala weekend party to show off Grantley is a wonderful idea."

"It was Juliet's. Although she claims her great-aunt should get part of the credit. My wife has been reading Alicia Anne's diaries year by year. Claims they're a fascinating glimpse into the family history as well as a social commentary on the first three decades of this century."

"Sounds like something Elizabeth would come up with," said Jonathan. "By the way, who's invited next weekend?"

Lawrence began to rattle off a partial guest list, ending with the names of Miles St. Aldford and Lord and Lady Deerhurst.

The latter brought a raised eyebrow from his sibling. "I expected Miles to be attending, but Sidney and Helena?"

Lawrence shrugged his shoulders. "Juliet is generous to a fault. She seems to feel sorry for the woman."

"Sidney is the one I feel sorry for." Jonathan Wicke shook his dark head. "To be married to Helena . . ."

"I quite agree," remarked his brother.

"Gentlemen—"

Both of their heads came up.

"Elizabeth and I are going upstairs to the Small Gallery."

"Juliet is going to show me several stone sculptures she acquired on a trip to Greece two years ago. We think they may be centuries older than they were originally dated," exclaimed Elizabeth.

"Then we plan to stop and say hello to Nanny and Aunt Effie before tea time," Juliet added.

The two young women linked arms, strolled out of the library, and started up the grand staircase.

Lawrence heard his bride say to her new-found friend and sister-in-law: "You must meet my Great-Aunt Euphemia. She is supposed to be writing out the clues for the treasure hunt with the help of Nanny. But if you want my opinion, I think they're spending most of their time playing cards."

Elizabeth Wicke was amused. "Nanny? Playing cards?"

Juliet admitted with a slightly sheepish expression on her face: "I fear that Aunt Effie is not always a good influence."

Jonathan gazed after his lovely wife. "We both married kind and gentle souls."

"Yes." Lawrence watched as Elizabeth whispered something to Juliet. She put her blond head back and laughed lightheartedly. It was a wonderful sound that brought a smile to his face. "We married women who make us happy."

"Indeed, we did."

"Beautiful women."

"Each beautiful in her own way," Jonathan said, as the blond head bent closer to the dark chestnut brown one.

"Have you also observed that we both married tall women?" Lawrence said, taking a sip of his brandy.

"And intelligent women," added his brother as they raised their glasses in salute.

"To strong-minded women," was their next toast.

"They're a challenge," admitted Lawrence.

"But they're never boring."

"I'll drink to that."

"Actually, Elizabeth can be downright stubborn on occasion," confessed Jonathan.

"There are times when Juliet is like a pedigree dog with a choice bone between her teeth. She gets hold of something and she will not let go. Damned irritating."

"Elizabeth can be almost infuriating when she has half a mind to be." Jonathan Wicke sighed. "How did we both end up married to women like that?"

"Just lucky, I guess," said Lawrence as they adjourned to the billiard room for a game and another brandy.

Lady Luck was with him.

David rolled over in bed and saw that Helena had fallen fast asleep. One bare arm was flung in wild abandon over her head, the other rested just below a ruby-teated breast. The rumpled sheet was wrapped around a shapely white thigh, leaving the other, with its distinctive beauty mark, exposed.

He had to give credit where credit was due: Lady Deerhurst was imaginative in bed. She wasn't a prude like Cora. Indeed, Helena would do anything for a man. He was convinced there was nothing she hadn't tried at one time or another.

In the beginning, she had pretended to be less experienced than she was, of course. But the demure act had quickly been dropped when she realized that David preferred a woman with a certain "expertise."

Yes, the countess was very accomplished with her agile fingers and her willing mouth, her sharp little teeth and her quick tongue, her white thighs and those special inner muscles that grabbed hold of a man and squeezed him dry.

Not that she was any match for him. He was

young and virile and could keep it up for hours. He had never bedded a woman yet who hadn't pleaded exhaustion and begged for mercy before it was all said and done.

In fact, David Thoreau Jones smiled smugly, he was getting hard just thinking about his own virility.

He glanced over at the sleeping woman and was tempted for a moment to crawl between her parted thighs again.

"Business before pleasure," David whispered as he slipped out of bed.

Helena was trying to hide something from him, although it certainly wasn't her obsession with the Duke of Deakin, or her jealousy of his lovely duchess. He had known about her vendetta against Lawrence and Juliet from the start.

Indeed, it was one of the reasons he had taken up with the countess upon his arrival in London. She was the sort of woman it was useful to know in Society. She knew everything about everyone. Yes, Helena had served her purpose well.

He had kept his own counsel, of course. As he always did. Lady Deerhurst was a secret drinker. And sooner or later, all drinkers talked. They became careless. Sloppy. Indiscreet.

He could not afford indiscretion.

He had called upon Helena yesterday afternoon and found her poring over what appeared to be a letter. She had tried to act nonchalant, but she had sent him from her boudoir on the pretense that she must slip into something more presentable. Since he had seen the lady on numerous occasions without a stitch of clothing, since he'd had his hands and his mouth over every inch of her naked flesh, it had seemed a flimsy excuse to him. Still, he had retreated to the drawing room and waited.

Now was his chance.

Helena was softly snoring. He'd seen her like this before: between the sex and the spirits she would be "out" for several hours.

There was something hidden in her boudoir.

David began a systematic search of the room. There was the usual assortment of knick-knacks, china whatnots, and pictures. There were photographs of Helena with this prince and that prince, Helena with the ambassador of a neighboring country, of Helena with a king, if not a very grand king.

He went through the drawers of the countess's desk, leaving each exactly as he had found it. He checked behind the books on a small shelf; he doubted if Helena had actually read any of them. Her jewelry box was sitting on a bureau. It was locked. He had discovered in the course of conversation one day that the formidable Lilla had the only key. She wore it on a chain around her neck.

Next to the divan was a small table. Helena often kept her teacup on it. But she wasn't fooling him. David knew what was in her tea. No matter how she tried to hide it, he could always detect the brandy on her breath.

He almost missed the secret drawer. Only by

running his skilled fingers along the bottom of the wood did he accidentally trip the lock.

A small drawer slid open.

The contents were minimal. There was a picture of Lawrence, obviously cut out of a larger group photograph, and a letter. The letter was what interested him. It was addressed to the Duke of Deakin, but David was willing to bet his trust fund that the devil Englishman had never set eyes on it.

He turned the envelope over and carefully removed the single sheet of paper inside. The handwriting was shaky, illegible in places, but he could make out most of what had been written by Helena's great-uncle, the one she disdainfully called "king of the fools." He was looking at the rambling confessions of a dying man.

David was buoyed by his discovery. He smiled to himself. It wouldn't be the first time he had wrung valuable information from the dead.

He tiptoed back into the bedroom, took a small notebook from the pocket of his jacket and returned to the boudoir. He began to copy George Frewen's letter verbatim.

Helena sometimes talked when she'd had too much to drink—which was happening with increasing frequency since her return from Northumberland. He'd gathered from her mumbled complaints that her great-uncle had once been a friend of the sixth Duke of Deakin. Indeed, it seemed that George Frewen had had a lifelong infatuation with his friend's wife, Alicia Anne.

Helena had oft repeated to him what a bloody fool the invalid George had been and that the man had gone to his grave with a stain of dishonor upon his name—as if anyone gave a damn.

Rumor.

Innuendo.

Fact and fantasy.

A bit of conversation from here, another bit from there.

They were all pieces of a great puzzle.

Some of the pieces were still missing. And David wasn't sure exactly how they fit together yet—but he was a clever fellow. He had every confidence that it would all fall into place for him.

Frankly, although he had enjoyed having Juliet's Fifth Avenue mansion to himself and had reveled in being invited to the finest and grandest houses in New York, he preferred London Society. They were less biased against the *nouveau riche* and Americans were *en vogue* thanks to the Prince of Wales.

Besides, the married women of the "Marlborough House Set" were like plums waiting to be picked from the nearest tree. He could eat to his heart's content.

David carefully returned the letter to its envelope and replaced the contents of the drawer. Then he quietly made his way back to Helena's bedroom and tucked the notebook in his coat pocket.

It was time to head north, he reflected as he slipped into the bed beside the countess's sleeping form. It was time for a reunion with his dear cousin, Juliet. It was time to determine the lay of the land.

It was time to uncover the final pieces of the puzzle and put it all together.

23

"I don't have a thing to wear," lamented Euphemia Jones as she stood in front of a wardrobe filled with fashionable dresses and gowns.

Juliet tapped her fingers together. "What is wrong with the yellow lace?"

Her great-aunt scowled. "The yellow lace makes me look like one of your pet canaries."

"Then why not wear the sapphire-blue silk?" Juliet suggested soothingly.

"Too obvious."

"Too obvious?"

"Everyone knows it is my favorite color," explained the elegant little woman. "They will all be expecting me to show up in that particular shade of blue, decked out from head to toe in my sapphires."

"We are not being presented at Court, Aunt Effie," she pointed out, although her voice was reproachless. "It is simply a treasure hunt."

"Simply a treasure hunt? Have you seen the guest list? Of course, you have," muttered Euphemia Jones. "You made up the guest list."

Juliet was puzzled. "What does the guest list have to do with the color of your dress?"

"I must look my best tonight. Anybody who is anybody in English society will be in attendance. At last count there were seven dukes and duchesses—including dear Lawrence and yourself, of course—a half dozen marquesses and marchionesses, and a vast assortment of earls and countesses, barons and baronesses, gentry, and plain common folk."

Juliet bit the inside of her mouth. "I didn't realize you had developed such a keen interest in the peerage."

"Nanny."

"Nanny?"

"She says I must understand the pecking order of life if I am to reside in England."

"And when does she give you lessons on the pecking order of English life?"

"While we are playing solitaire." Euphemia Jones furrowed her delicate brows. "I was in the drawing room this afternoon, and I must confess that I could not tell the aristocracy from the gentry.

"It's very simple really," Juliet said, taking her great-aunt aside for a moment. "The dukes are like Lawrence: they are, for the most part, hardworking farmers. They are not at all the kind of dandified dukes who flit about London society. They dress in dark colors, usually black, and tend to wear somber expressions."

"Ah! Now I know which ones they are," declared the older woman.

"The marquesses, with the possible exception of Miles St. Aldford, who inherited a great deal of money with his lands, are hunting for heiresses to wed."

"They must be the gentlemen in brown tweed."

"Unfortunately, yes."

"Then *who* are those dressed in the expensive, gaily colored satins and fancy waistcoats?"

"The gentry. They are the only ones who can afford such luxuries," explained Juliet. "Everyone else is economizing to keep an expensive estate going."

"They should go to New York and find themselves a lovely young American heiress . . . like Lawrence did."

Juliet told herself she was no longer sensitive when it came to the subject of money and marriage. "I believe we may see more than one American duchess in the future."

Euphemia took out an ivory satin. "This one will do. It matches my hair."

"It will look lovely on you," said Juliet. Then she added: "Don't forget. The guests are to assemble in the ballroom at ten o'clock sharp to begin the treasure hunt. Lawrence and I will be handing out the envelopes with the clues inside to each team."

"Oh, what fun!" exclaimed her great-aunt, clapping her tiny hands together. "Nanny and I have selected our vantage point. There are two comfortable chairs at the top of the grand staircase. We intend to watch from there until it is time to eat."

"The midnight buffet will follow immediately afterwards."

Euphemia quirked a brow. "Your clues for the treasure hunt were clever, my dear. However did you think of them?"

"I confess I was able to use a few of the same quotes that Alicia Anne used for her treasure hunt in 1828. The rest I got from the Good Book or literature or common sayings."

"Yes, they were very clever, indeed. Nanny and I both said so."

Juliet sighed. "I only wish that Alicia Anne had explained in more detail. Some of the clues didn't quite make sense to me. 'Beauty is in the eye of the beholder'? I've racked my brain over that one."

"Spectacles?"

"That was my first thought." Juliet shrugged. "Anyway, I must thank the two of you again for copying all the clues. It was a great help to me."

"It was our pleasure. It made us feel a part of the proceedings. After all, you could hardly expect two old women to go scurrying about looking for treasure." Euphemia Jones dropped her voice, although they were alone in her bedroom. "Have you hidden any real treasure?"

She supposed it wouldn't hurt to tell Aunt Effie now. The secret would be out soon enough, anyway. "As a matter of fact, I have."

Sapphire-blue eyes grew as big and as round as saucers. "What?"

"Bunter and I have hidden two treasure chests. The first-place team will discover that theirs is filled with gold coins. The second-place team will find silver coins. For all our guests there will be a small souvenir silver chest at their place when they arrive for the buffet. I have had each one engraved with Lawrence's coat of arms, the name Grantley Manor, and the date. I have one for you and Nanny, too."

Euphemia was delighted. "What an inspired idea, my dear. It will be the crowning touch to a truly unforgettable weekend." She confided to Juliet: "I hear them talking, you know, when they think I have dozed off. Or sometimes they assume anyone older is hard of hearing."

"There is nothing wrong with your hearing."

"I know that. And you know that. But they don't know that," said her great-aunt.

"Who are *they*?"

"Your guests. They cannot stop singing your praises. They recite to each other all the marvels you and Lawrence have managed in a few short months with Grantley. The common folk are grateful because you have given a good many of them employment and an income. Even the gentry seem to think you are an angel because you are so generous. The only sour face is Lady Deerhurst. Do you know, my dear, I believe that she takes a nip now and then when she thinks no one is looking."

"A nip?"

"Of brandy."

"Oh—" Apparently she was not the only one to recognize that Lady Deerhurst had a problem.

"The countess drinks to excess, I am afraid. And I noticed that she was very friendly with

David at tea—although he did do his best to avoid her."

Juliet had witnessed the same thing.

"David seems to have taken an avid interest in Grantley since he arrived a few days after Jonathan and Elizabeth," Euphemia commented, her eyes shrewd. "He has been asking a great number of questions."

"What kind of questions?"

"About the history of the house and who used to visit during the old days, especially during the time of the sixth duke and duchess. He even got Nanny to tell him the entire story behind the Deakin Diamonds."

"I see."

What was David up to? For Juliet was certain he was up to something.

Well, she didn't have time to worry about it now. She had a house full of people and a grand treasure hunt and buffet to pull off before the night was over. She could think about Cousin David tomorrow after their guests had departed.

"You'd better run along and change, Juliet. You can't keep everyone waiting," admonished her great-aunt.

"Yes, I must run along."

"What gown have you chosen for tonight?"

"Lawrence has specifically requested that I wear my gold satin."

The elderly spinster smiled. "Ah, no doubt the dress you wore to Mrs. Astor's ball."

"The very one."

"What a romantic notion." Euphemia Jones

permitted herself a sigh. "It was the first dress Lawrence saw you in."

"Actually the first time Lawrence saw me I was wearing a mud-splattered riding habit and my hair was tumbling down around my shoulders and flying in my face as my hat blew helter-skelter across the Sheep Meadow."

Euphemia gave a knowing chuckle. "Well, then, no wonder the man fell in love with you."

If only her husband were in love with her, Juliet thought with a pang as she headed for the door of Aunt Effie's bedroom.

"My dear, something has just occurred to me."

Juliet paused with her hand on the brass knob and glanced back over one shoulder. "What is it?"

"You mentioned you were puzzled by some of Alicia Anne's clues, particularly: 'Beauty is in the eye of the beholder.' "

"Yes?"

Euphemia held up the tiny kaleidoscope dangling from a chain around her neck. It was the one Lawrence had given her great-aunt many months before in New York; the one nearly identical to her own. "Perhaps the duchess meant one of these little thingamabobs."

"Perhaps she did. You are very clever to have thought of it, Aunt. But I must go now." As Juliet hurried along the corridor, she took a small notebook from the pocket of her skirt and reviewed the list for the evening as she went. "Everything is under control," she murmured to herself reassuringly as she opened the door of her bedroom.

She stopped in her tracks.

Someone was in her room. Someone was standing next to the bed. Someone was reading the book she had left open on the night table.

The someone was David.

His head came up. "Juliet—?"

"David, what are you doing in here?"

He gave a melodramatic sigh. "I must"—his voice broke off in midsentence—"speak with you."

"Can't it wait?" She tried not to sound impatient. "I really must change for the treasure hunt."

His eyes were downcast. When he looked up at her she saw there were tears poised on the tips of his long, dark blond eyelashes. "I understand you are busy."

She collected herself. "I have a few minutes to spare. What seems to be the matter?"

"I have a troubled conscience."

Egods, first Aunt Effie's dress. Now David's conscience. It was one crisis after another.

"What is troubling you?" she asked.

"I am so ashamed," her cousin blurted out, his voice shaking, his hands—indeed, his entire body—trembling.

"It cannot be that bad."

He shrugged unhappily. "I don't know if I can bear to tell you. You will lose all respect and affection for me. Yet, I cannot go on carrying this terrible burden. . . ."

Juliet spoke quietly, reasonably, as she would

to a small child. "I do not believe you could have done anything so awful."

"It is awful." A tear rolled down his soft cheek.

"Don't cry, David," she implored him. "I can't bear to see you cry."

Her cousin took out his handkerchief and dabbed at his eyes. He heaved a great sigh and confessed: "I have allowed myself to be—seduced."

"Seduced?"

He nodded. "By a woman."

Juliet tried to be very grown-up about his unexpected announcement. "You are not a child, David. You are a man of nearly twenty-three. These things do happen."

"Not to me," he said in a small, dismayed voice.

"Are you in love with the woman?" she inquired gently.

"I thought I was at first."

"But now you are not so sure?"

"Now I know I am *not* in love with her." He twisted his hands together and moaned: "I have been such a fool."

"We all makes fools of ourselves, David. It is part of growing up."

"I know you are right, Cousin Juliet." He took a deep breath and let it out. "There is more."

"More?"

His face flushed a painful crimson. "The lady is titled."

Oh, dear. "I see."

He brushed his hands across his eyes as if he

could not bring himself to gaze upon her. "And I have recently discovered that she is also married."

"David!" Juliet was shocked and it showed.

"I knew you would be bitterly disappointed in me."

She could discern only his handsome profile as her cousin stood and stared out her bedroom window. Nevertheless, the agony he was suffering was apparent.

This was not the time to scold David as if he were an errant schoolboy. He was a young man and these things happened to young men all the time. Especially here in England. And that is what Juliet told him.

"I have broken it off, of course," he assured her. "I told the lady in no uncertain terms that we must not meet again except in the most public of places and circumstances. Yet—"

"Yet?"

"She may make a scene."

Juliet didn't understand. "Why?"

"I fear she was angry when I broke it off with her, and she is indiscreet."

"That is most unfortunate."

David admitted in a voice bruised with pain: "I have since discovered that the woman has had numerous love affairs. I am not the first young, unsuspecting man that she has enticed into her bed."

Juliet went to him and placed a sympathetic hand on his arm. "How dreadful for you, my dear."

"What is worse: she is in this house tonight."

Her hand fluttered to her throat. "That could, indeed, be awkward."

"It could, indeed." His mouth started to work but no sound came out. "That is why I had to confess everything. I wanted to be the one to tell you. I did not want you to find out through rumor or gossip or whispered innuendo."

"That was very brave of you, David," she said, patting his arm. "I know how difficult this has been for you."

"It is the hardest thing I have ever had to do. Your good opinion matters more to me than anything else in the world. *You* matter more to me than anyone else in the world."

"We're family, David, and family always stands together. I will help you in any way I can. I'm sure that Lawrence will do the same."

"Thank you, dearest Juliet." He self-consciously twisted the tear-dampened handkerchief in his hands. "One last admission. I must tell you the lady's name."

Her eyebrows rose frantically. "Do you think that is wise?"

"I think you should know in case the woman decides to create a scene."

Dear God, Juliet hoped she didn't intend to create a scene. "If you feel you must."

David looked at her with his beautiful and innocent face. His bottom lip trembled. His eyes were still watery. His expression was one of deep and utter shame. "The woman's name is Helena, Lady Deerhurst."

"Oh, David, no." Her hand flew to her mouth.

"Yes."

"I fear you may be right. Helena is capable of creating a scene. And I know for a fact that she is indiscreet."

David was very quiet. Then he caught a breath; it sounded like a groan. "She would not leave me be at tea this afternoon."

"I noticed."

"You did?"

She nodded. "And I wasn't the only one." Her stomach lurched. "What I am going to tell you next must be kept in the strictest confidence."

He held up his hand as if he were swearing an oath on the Bible. "I promise I will not tell a soul."

Juliet lowered her voice to a near whisper. "Lady Deerhurst has a drinking problem."

David's blue eyes, so very like her own and yet so different, widened in disbelief. "No."

"Yes."

"Are you certain?"

"I am certain."

"I-I had no idea."

"Helena has learned to hide it well. You were right to spurn her further advances. She is poison. You must stay away from her, David."

"I will, Juliet. I promise," he said earnestly. "I will never allow anything like this to happen again."

"I'm sure you won't."

"Thank you for letting me confess my sins to you. I feel like a new man."

"We all need someone we can talk to. I am your family and I am responsible for you. You can always come to me."

"You have lifted a heavy weight from my heart. Now, I must allow you to change. I know that your guests are waiting."

"Yes, I must change."

As he left her room, he turned and said quietly: "You are a saint."

"I am not a saint, David. I am just a woman like any other woman."

"You are a woman like no other woman. God bless you, Cousin Juliet."

She stood for a moment and stared at her bedroom door after he had departed. Poor, poor David. To get inadvertently mixed up with the likes of Helena. She must find some lovely young woman of good breeding and high moral character for David. A young woman who would love and cherish and keep him safe from the clutches of the Lady Deerhursts of this world.

As Juliet rang for her maid, she glanced down at the book on her bedside table. It was Alicia Anne's social diary from 1828. It was open to the pages where the sixth duchess had described the treasure hunt party of fifty years ago.

A thought popped into her mind. She wondered where it came from.

What had David been looking for?

Lawrence nervously paced back and forth in his adjoining bedroom as his wife changed for the evening.

He did not know how he was going to break the news to her. Family was so important to Juliet. He feared what he had uncovered would break her heart. He did not think he could stand to break her heart again.

Lawrence carelessly drove his fingers through his long, black hair.

Christ in heaven, how did a man inform his wife that he'd had her family investigated? How did he tell her that she had given her trust and affection to someone who didn't deserve it? How did he take her world and tear it apart?

She might blame him.

She might not even believe him.

They shared the intimacy of the marriage bed. They slept together. They laughed together. They walked together. They rode together. They planned and dreamed together. They did all these things and more together—and yet there was a great gulf between them.

They spoke of need and desire and passion. They whispered sweetly erotic words into each other's ear. Yet since that first afternoon when he had overheard the conversation between his wife and the two older women in Nanny's sitting room, Juliet had never once mentioned the word love.

More than anything in the world, Lawrence realized, he wanted to hear his wife say "I love you" directly to his face. He needed to hear the words. He needed to know that she wanted him beyond the thrill of physical excitement, beyond the passion that they shared.

Yet he had to tell her the truth.

He gave a perfunctory knock on the door between their bedrooms and entered. Her maid was just putting the finishing touches on her coiffure. Juliet was seated at her dressing table, wearing a fancy petticoat and a low-cut corset that emphasized the shape of her lovely breasts. The gold dress was spread out across the foot of her bed.

Lawrence felt a familiar stirring in the lower regions of his body. For a halfpenny he would order the maid to leave and spend the evening in this very room making love to his wife.

Instead, he said: "Juliet, I must have a word with you."

"Now? But we must greet our guests in the ballroom in a half hour, and time grows short."

"It will only take five minutes, madam, and it is of supreme importance."

Juliet indicated that her maid was to leave and return when she rang for her. Then she faced him. "What is it, sir?"

Lawrence began. "I do not like having to tell you."

"Tell me what?"

He paused for a fraction of a second before he said: "It is about David."

"Cousin David?"

"Yes."

"You need not concern yourself, then, husband. David was here within the hour and he has confessed everything to me. He has promised nothing like it will ever happen again. I believe him. After all, Lady Deerhurst is some years older in age, and many years older in experience, as we both know."

What in the bloody hell was Juliet talking about?

Lawrence frowned. "You know all about it?"

"Yes, I know all about it," she stated evenly.

How could she? He had just gotten the private investigator's report from America by special dispatch this very evening.

His wife rambled on. "Helena seduced David. It was only later that he found out she was a married woman and had had many lovers. The poor boy was stunned."

"I'll just bet he was," Lawrence said dryly.

"Now I must finish getting dressed, husband. She made a motion with her hands. "Shoo! Shoo!"

"Shoo?"

"Away with you."

He went away. But tomorrow, Lawrence vowed as he rubbed the back of his neck, tomorrow he would have to tell her.

24

THE game was afoot!

The teams had been selected. The clues had been handed out. And the treasure hunters had taken off in all directions. Aunt Effie and Nanny were comfortably settled in their seats, watching the proceedings, and the servants were busily going about their business.

Juliet found herself alone with her husband in the ballroom. She sighed and leaned a weary head on his shoulder.

Lawrence slipped an arm around her waist and exclaimed in an incredulous tone: "I don't believe that I have ever heard Lord Lundquist laugh in all the years of our acquaintance. The man is giggling like a schoolboy."

"Some of the clues are rather amusing," she said modestly.

He shook his head. "It is more than an amusing ditty or two. It is you, Juliet. You have brought joy back to this house. You have organized a wonderful, unforgettable weekend that few will ever forget."

She was gratified. "It was time to show what you have accomplished with Grantley."

"What *we* have accomplished with Grantley."

"What *we* have accomplished with Grantley," she said, basking in his approval.

"Let us drink a private toast," he said, calling for two glasses of champagne.

They touched crystal rim to crystal rim. "To Juliet, the most beautiful woman in the world."

She blushed with pleasure. "You know what they say."

"What?"

" 'Beauty is in the eye of the beholder.' " No sooner were the words out of her mouth, then she became absolutely still.

"What is it?" Lawrence inquired. "You have the strangest expression on your face."

Juliet held up a hand. Adrenaline was shooting into her bloodstream. Her mind was racing. She had to think. Bits and pieces of information, snippets of conversation, things she had read, a list of guests, a page of clues in Alicia Anne's diary, impressions, ideas: they were coming back to her, forming a pattern, falling into place.

" *'Beauty is in the eye of the beholder.'* "

"*It's in the blood.*"

"*Helena has fancied herself in love with Lawrence all these years and it was her great-uncle, George Frewen, who was obsessive about Alicia Anne. He claimed he would have no other, and he never did.*"

"*Have you seen the portrait of Her Grace wearing the black diamonds?*"

"*Grandmother is wearing the world-famous Deakin Diamonds.*"

"*What is the sense of owning something that must be stashed in a secret hiding place?*"

"*They vanished without a trace.*"

"*George Frewen was a guest in this house many times in the early days—before the accident.*"

"*Helena's great-uncle was trapped under the weight of his dead horse for hours. He wasn't found until the following morning.*"

"*They say George Frewen was never the same again. He was a broken man in body, spirit, and mind.*"

"*The accident was the same weekend as the treasure hunt party. That was when the Deakin Diamonds disappeared.*"

"*The loss must have been devastating to Alicia Anne.*"

" *'Beauty is in the eye of the beholder.'* "

"Dear Lord—" She felt a rush of emotion. It swamped her. It overwhelmed her. She couldn't seem to catch her breath.

"Juliet, are you ill?"

She shook her head and finally managed to tell her husband: "No."

"Have you forgotten something? Although, frankly, I don't see how with all the notes and lists you keep."

"I haven't forgotten anything," she said. Her voice didn't even sound like hers; it was the voice of a stranger.

This was too much for Lawrence. "Then what in the bloody hell is wrong with you?"

"Nothing." She put her champagne glass down on the table, deftly plucked his from his grasp, grabbed his hand, and urged him toward the door.

He failed to be amused by all the mystery. "What is it?" he demanded to know.

"It has become clear to me at last," Juliet told him.

"Well, that makes one of us," Lawrence remarked dryly.

Lord, she didn't have time to explain everything to the man. "Don't you see?"

"I'm afraid I don't."

She frowned and shook her head. "It is too simple."

"If you say so."

"But it does make sense in an odd sort of way," she murmured, tugging on his arm.

"Which is more than I can say for you at this moment, lady wife."

Juliet stopped in the middle of the hallway, went up on her tiptoes and whispered in his ear: "It was George Frewen."

"George Frewen?"

"Helena's great-uncle."

"I know who the man was, Juliet. He just died last year."

She hovered at the top of the staircase and gazed up at her husband. "Did you know that George Frewen was in love with Alicia Anne?"

"Grandmother?"

"Yes, your grandmother."

Lawrence stroked his jaw. "I vaguely remember Nanny mentioning something to that effect. I thought it was just another of her fanciful ideas."

"I don't believe it was just another of Nanny's fanciful ideas. I think it is in the blood."

He turned and regarded her for some seconds before he asked: "What is in the blood?"

"For the ill-fortuned Frewens to be in love with members of your family. George was infatuated with Alicia Anne. Helena has been infatuated with you all of her life."

They started down the stairs.

"I wouldn't call it love," said Lawrence.

"You're right. They are obsessive about it. It's almost unhealthy."

A faintly hard-boiled expression crept over her husband's features. *"Almost?"*

"All right, it is unhealthy." Juliet paused halfway down the Grand Staircase. "Let's pretend that you are George Frewen and it is the night of the 1828 treasure hunt party."

He lifted one eyebrow. "Must I?"

"Lawrence, this could be very important."

"All right," he agreed rather grimly. "I'll pretend to be George Frewen."

"You are drinking."

"I could use a drink," he muttered.

"You realize that Alicia Anne will never be yours."

"Alicia Anne will never be mine," he echoed.

She pulled on his arm and they continued down the stairway. "You have given up hope."

"I have given up hope."

"Alicia Anne is married to another man. Indeed, you realize that she loves him completely and utterly."

"I presume, wife, that you have a destination in mind."

"I do, husband."

"Are we on a little treasure hunt of our own?" he said with a private laugh.

"You could say that." Juliet went on dramatically, "In George's—in your—gin-soaked mind—"

"How do you know he—I—was drinking gin?"

"I don't. I simply liked the alliteration. Anyway, George has become fixated with the connection between Alicia Anne and the Deakin Diamonds. He can never have the woman. So he decides to take something of great value that belongs to her."

Lawrence stopped in his tracks. "Good God! You don't mean—?"

Juliet nodded. "I do mean."

"Hell and damnation, you think George Frewen took my grandmother's diamonds?"

"I do."

They went two more steps before Lawrence ventured: "There is a flaw in your theory."

She didn't agree, but she was willing to listen. "What is it?"

"Helena's great-uncle was found trapped beneath his horse. He had been there all night in the rain. His legs were crushed. He was unable to move. And there were no black diamonds falling out of his pockets."

Wagging a finger, she said, "That is precisely my point."

His nostrils flared. "What is precisely your point?"

"The diamonds were not on George Frewen when he was found. So either he didn't take them"—she paused for effect—"or he hid them."

Coolly Lawrence said, "It is unlikely that the man stopped in the pouring rain and stashed a cache of priceless diamonds along the road."

She gripped his hand even tighter. "Highly unlikely."

"Even improbable."

"Highly improbable."

"So—?"

"So George Frewen hid the diamonds where he thought he could come back and collect them at any time."

Lawrence eyed her sharply. "And where was that?"

Juliet delivered the *coup de grace*. "Right here at Grantley Manor."

His head snapped around. "He hid them here?"

"If I'm right," she said, "the Deakin Diamonds never left this house."

Lawrence stared at her in shocked silence. "You're telling me," he finally managed to say, "that a king's ransom in missing diamonds has gone undetected in this house for the past fifty years."

She lifted her chin. "That's what I'm telling you."

"But the idea is preposterous."

"Yes, it is."

"It is too fantastic, wife."

Juliet raised her brows and looked straight at him. "Indeed, husband."

"But—"

"But the Deakin Diamonds were never seen again. They were never heard of again. They simply disappeared. Vanished. That is what you told me."

"That is what I told you." A muscle in his face started to twitch. "*If* George Frewen did hide them in the house the night of the original treasure hunt. *If* he did intend to come back for them later . . ."

"He was prevented from doing so because he was paralyzed from that night on and confined to a wheelchair. Nanny said he was never himself again in body, spirit, or mind."

Lawrence stopped at the bottom of the staircase. "The question remains: where would he hide that much jewelry?"

"I don't think he hid the jewelry."

"What did he hide, then?"

"Just the loose stones. I think while everyone else was hunting for treasure, George Frewen was prying the diamonds out of their settings."

"Whatever gave you that idea?"

"Aunt Effie."

"Euphemia? What in the dickens does your great-aunt have to do with this?"

"I happened to mention to Aunt Effie that I was baffled by one of the clues Alicia Anne had used for the original treasure hunt."

"What was the clue?"

" 'Beauty is in the eye of the beholder.' "

"Hmm . . . spectacles?"

"That was my first thought. That was Aunt Effie's first thought. Then as I was leaving her room earlier this evening, she said something, thanks to you."

"Thanks to me?"

"She was wearing the chain you gave her in New York with the miniature kaleidoscope dangling from the end. Aunt Effie held it up and said: 'Beauty is in the eye of the beholder.' "

His jaw dropped in amazement. "You don't think—?"

"I do."

"My God, the library!" Lawrence declared, taking off at a fast clip and dragging her along behind him.

"Where would you hide something that looked like bits of colored glass?"

"With other bits of colored glass."

"And where are there bits of colored glass in this house?"

"In my grandfather's kaleidoscope collection, of course," answered Lawrence as he dashed across the front hall and headed straight for the library.

He turned the doorknob and stepped back for Juliet to enter before him.

She gasped and softly cried out as her husband closed the door behind them.

Lawrence turned around and saw Juliet standing there with her hand over her mouth. "David—"

Bending over the library table, the pieces of

a kaleidoscope spread out in front of him, a lamp shining down on his open palm, a palm filled with sparkling black stones, was his wife's young cousin.

"I can explain," David began as he straightened.

"You damn well better explain," Lawrence snapped in a voice he had often used while in command of Her Majesty's troops.

"I didn't want to say anything to either of you until I was certain my theory had some merit."

Lawrence gave him a skeptical look. "Your theory?"

"Yes, you see I met Lady Deerhurst in London," he quickly explained. "She often mentioned that her great-uncle, George Frewen, had been a regular visitor to Grantley back during the days of the sixth duke and duchess. Then I happened to see a letter she had in her possession and I noticed it was addressed to you."

"To me?"

David nodded his pretty blond head. "Written on the front were the words: *To Whom It May Concern. Please give this envelope to the Duke of Deakin.*" ·

He frowned. "I never received such an envelope."

"I know. It was obvious that Lady Deerhurst never had any intentions of delivering it to you, either. I must confess I opened the letter and read it."

Lawrence took a step toward him. "What did it say?"

"It was difficult to understand at first. But

the gist of the thing was George Frewen's conscience caught up with him before he died. He wanted to remove the stain of dishonor on his family name."

"Poor George Frewen," murmured Juliet.

David was sweating profusely. "Anyway, I managed to put two and two together, and concluded that he was the one who had taken the Deakin Diamonds back in 1828. He didn't say exactly where he had hidden them, just some babble about beauty being in the eye of the beholder." David looked from one to the other with a bright smile. "It took me a while to realize exactly what the dying man meant by that remark. It only came to me this evening: you have an antique kaleidoscope collection in this very house. That may have been where George Frewen had hidden the diamonds. I thought it would make a wonderful wedding gift if I could find the stones and return them to you."

Lawrence folded his arms across his chest and looked down his nose at the younger man. "And that is what you intended to do with the stones? Return them to Juliet and me?"

"Of course," David claimed with an air of utter innocence.

"You're a damned liar."

He turned next to his cousin. "You believe me, don't you, Juliet?"

"Oh, David—"

His handsome face suddenly turned ugly. "All right. Maybe I didn't intend to return the diamonds to you. What difference does it make? After all, they've been missing for fifty years. I figured if I was the one smart enough to find them, then I deserved to keep them. You don't need the Deakin Diamonds anymore. You have Juliet."

"That's not the point," Lawrence said, his voice and manner uncompromising.

Juliet added: "The point is the diamonds don't belong to you. They're not yours."

"They were almost mine," he whined.

"Oh, David, even I don't believe a word of what you have said," mourned Juliet. "I'm not even sure I believe that Lady Deerhurst seduced you."

"Oh, that much was true," came a sultry voice from behind them.

All three turned to see Helena, Lady Deerhurst, step into the library. She reached behind her, closed the door, and turned the key in the lock.

"I wouldn't want us to be interrupted until this unfinished business is finished," she said, her eyes glittering.

But it was not her insane, glittering eyes that had captured everyone's attention. It was the pistol Helena held in her hand. The pistol she had pointed directly at Juliet's heart.

25

FOREWARNED.

He should have been forewarned. He should have seen it coming, felt it coming, *sensed* it coming.

Son of a bitch, Lawrence swore silently as he took stock of the situation in the library.

He blamed himself. For the first time in his life his instincts had let him down.

A wave of fury swept through him.

He should have done something about Helena the day she had shown up in their bedroom. That had been his first mistake. He had known what kind of woman she was. He had even suspected for some time that she was mentally unstable. Instead, all he could think about was Juliet. Specifically, making love to Juliet.

And this business with David. He hadn't wanted to hurt his wife's feelings. He hadn't wanted to break her heart. Now she might pay a far greater price than a broken heart. She might pay with her life.

He could not allow that to happen. He would do whatever was necessary to keep Juliet safe.

Lawrence waited and he watched.

"Well, well, my three 'favorite' people all in one place at the same time," Helena drawled in a voice that sent chills down his spine.

David Thoreau Jones took a small step toward her. "Helena, my dear—"

"Don't come any nearer, you bastard." Her once-pretty mouth twisted into a caricature of a smile.

The handsome blond man spread his hands, palms up, in a conciliatory gesture. "Now, Helena . . ."

"You're the worst of the whole bloody lot, David," she said through stiff lips.

"You don't mean that," he countered.

"I do mean it. You use people and then discard them like so much rubbish when you're finished with them."

"That isn't true!" David exclaimed as if the very notion of using anyone had never crossed his mind.

"Don't try that innocent young American abroad act with me," sneered the countess. "I saw through you the first time I met you in London. You're a user."

"You're the user, Lady Deerhurst," he said contemptuously. "How many lovers have you gone through in the past year? In the past five years?"

"Shut up! Just shut up!" the woman snapped. She sashayed a step or two closer to Juliet, but the aim of the deadly pistol in her grasp never wavered: it was still pointed at the Duchess of Deakin's heart. "Shall I tell you all about your sweet, innocent cousin, Duchess? Shall I tell you the naughty things he knows how to do to a woman in bed. He has this cute little trick he does with nursery rhymes. . . ."

In an instant, David's coloring went from white to scarlet. "That's enough, Helena," he warned.

"Oh, all right," she muttered. Then she smiled meaningfully at Juliet. "You did know about David and me, didn't you?"

"I knew," Juliet said.

"So the poor boy confessed his sins and begged for your forgiveness, did he? Well, don't be fooled by him the way I was, Your Grace. He has more tricks up his sleeve than you and I ever will." The countess swayed slightly on her feet and glanced down at the library table. "So those are the famous Deakin Diamonds."

"I was going to share them with you," piped up David.

Lady Deerhurst laughed. It was an unpleasant sound. "Sure, you were."

"Just like you were going to return the diamonds to Lawrence and me," Juliet spoke up.

Lawrence waited and he watched.

"Poor Great-Uncle George. He always was a fool. He never managed to get anything right in his whole miserable life." Helena looked up at Lawrence. "He wrote you a letter. I assume the boy has told you all about it."

Lawrence nodded his head. "David told me something about a letter," he admitted.

Her voice quavered. "I'm sorry I didn't give it to you, my love. I should have. I always meant to."

"Did you?" he said softly.

"Yes."

Lawrence took a nonthreatening step toward her and extended his hand. "Why don't you give me the pistol, Helena?"

"Don't move! I don't want to have to shoot you, Lawrence, and I'm a very good shot, as you may recall."

"I do recall," he said, undisconcerted. "What are you going to do now?"

"Why, I'm going to shoot Juliet, of course." The woman's eyes grew bright with madness. "I know you married your golden girl for her money. Well, now you have her money and you don't need the bitch any longer. I'll get rid of her, and you and I can finally be together as it was always intended, as it was always meant to be."

Lawrence slowly maneuvered himself closer to his wife. "I don't love you, Helena."

Her bottom lip trembled. "I know you don't. But you will learn to love me once *she* is out of the way."

Lawrence quickly stepped in front of Juliet, shielding her with his body. "You'll have to shoot me first."

"Shoot you first?" Lady Deerhurst was suddenly confused. "I don't want to shoot you."

"If you kill Juliet, then you kill me as well anyway. I do not want to live without her. I cannot live without her," he stated.

"No!" Helena roared.

"Yes."

"You don't love her. I know you don't love

her. You're just saying that to save her," she cried out.

Behind his back, Lawrence motioned for Juliet to get down. "I'm not just saying that. I do love my wife. She is the only woman I have ever loved."

"Isn't that romantic?" sneered David.

"Shut your damned mouth, or you'll be first," threatened the countess, brandishing the lethal weapon back and forth between Lawrence and David.

"What are you going to do, Helena, kill all three of us?" Lawrence coldly inquired. "You came here intending to shoot only Juliet because she stood between what you want and what you cannot have."

Her hands began to shake. Her eyes darted wildly from one to the other. "I can have it. I can."

"You cannot. You can *never* be the Duchess of Deakin," he said bluntly, cruelly.

"I hate you!" she shrieked.

"I thought you loved me."

"I do love you," she immediately relented.

"Then give me the pistol, Helena, and let's put an end to this messy business," Lawrence reasoned. "I don't believe that you really want to hurt anyone."

"I do," she said stubbornly.

"It's me you want to hurt, then, isn't it?" he pointed out to her.

"Yes," she admitted.

"It's me you want to kill."

She nodded her head emphatically.

He scowled. "You said you loved me. How can you want to kill the man you love?"

"Stop it! Stop it!" She raised one hand to cover her ear. "You're confusing me. I can't think straight. I can't make sense of it when you keep going on and on."

"I'm not going to stop," Lawrence vowed, moving toward her while she was distracted. "I am never going to stop. I'm going to go on and on until the only sound you hear in your head is my voice."

The countess stared at him with a horrified expression on her once-beautiful, now-ravaged face. "Why, Lawrence? Why are you torturing me so?"

He spoke softly but firmly, and not altogether unkindly. "I never meant to hurt you, Helena. I want you to believe that." He took another step toward her. "You are a beautiful woman. You have a husband and two children. You should have been content with what you had."

"But I only wanted you, Lawrence." Tears began to brim on Lady Deerhurst's eyelashes and flow unchecked down her cheeks, leaving streaks in her makeup. "All I ever wanted was for you to love me."

He struck a deliberately casual pose but, like a wild cat, he was ready to strike. "We can't *make* someone love us, Helena. They either do or they don't. And I don't love you."

With that, Lawrence lunged at her. He made a grab for the pistol and managed to deliver a single blow to Helena's arm just as she fired.

The bullet went astray, whizzing past his head and burying itself in the woodwork behind him.

The countess dramatically collapsed onto the floor, sobbing uncontrollably, tearing wildly at her hair, cursing. "Damn you! Damn you! Damn all of you!"

Within a minute there was a frantic knock at the library door, then Bunter called out: "Your Grace, are you in there?"

"Yes, Bunter."

"Are you all right, Your Grace?"

"I am quite all right, Bunter."

"The door seems to be locked, Your Grace."

"I am coming, my good man." Lawrence glanced back at a pale and somber Juliet and an even paler David. "I will do all of the talking. Do you understand?"

They both nodded their heads.

Lawrence strolled to the library door as if nothing out of the ordinary had taken place in the past half hour and turned the key in the lock.

Bunter was waiting. "Are you all right, Your Grace?"

"Yes."

"Is Her Grace all right?"

"She is fine."

The butler appeared anxious. He swallowed. "I thought I heard a gunshot."

"You did. Please step inside for a moment."

The man did and nodded respectfully to Juliet. "Your Grace."

"Bunter."

"Mr. David."

David acknowledged him with a sulky glare.

They were all doing their best to ignore the weeping woman on the library floor.

Lawrence spoke slowly and deliberately. "If anyone should inquire, there was a slight accident while I was showing Mister David a new pistol. Thankfully, the bullet misfired and no one was hurt."

"I understand, Your Grace. The bullet misfired and no one was hurt."

Lawrence went on. "You will need to fetch Lord Deerhurst immediately, however. Lady Deerhurst has taken ill and collapsed. He will want to escort her home at once. Please arrange to have their carriage brought around to the front entrance after you have spoken to the earl."

"I will follow your instructions to the letter, Your Grace," he stated.

"Don't make a fuss about it, Bunter. Take Lord Deerhurst aside before you quietly speak with him. I would not want our other guests to become agitated."

"I will be the soul of discretion, Your Grace."

Lawrence gave him a nod of approval. "I knew I could count on you."

Five minutes later there was another knock on the library door. This time it was Lord Deerhurst.

The earl's mouth fell open, but he did not go to his wife. Instead, he spoke to his host. "Egods, Deakin, what has happened here?"

"Come in, Deerhurst." He took the gentleman

to a private corner of the room. "I am going to have to be brutally frank with you, Sidney."

"What is it, Lawrence?"

"Helena pulled a pistol on the three of us and threatened to shoot my wife and her cousin."

The earl lost all of the color in his slightly pudgy face. "Dear God in heaven."

"I'm sorry, Sidney. Damned sorry," Lawrence said, patting him consolingly on the back.

"I knew Helena liked her brandy. I suppose I even realized there were times when she drank to excess. But I didn't think she would slip over the edge and do something like this." Lord Deerhurst dug into his pocket for a handkerchief and mopped his brow. "I should have acted sooner. I knew she had problems. But I swear to you, Lawrence, I never once imagined that she was capable of violence."

"None of us imagined that she was, Sidney. You mustn't blame yourself. I should have seen it coming, if anyone should have." Lawrence sighed.

"I will take her home immediately."

"Your carriage is waiting out front. Bunter will assist in getting Lady Deerhurst discreetly tucked inside." Lawrence added out of friendship to his fellow peer: "Helena will need special care."

The earl gathered his sobbing countess into his arms. "I know of an excellent doctor who operates a private sanitorium in the west country. I will wire him tomorrow. Perhaps he will be able to help Helena. Either way, he has a large staff qualified to look after her."

"I'm deeply sorry, Sidney."

"So am I, Lawrence."

"Let me know if there is anything else I can do to be of assistance."

"Your discretion is all that I request."

"You must know you already have that."

Then it was just the three of them left in the library.

"You had better sit down, my dear," Lawrence said to Juliet. "You, too, David."

They both sank into chairs.

David ran a hand back and forth across his chin; it was still shaking. "Gad, I'm glad that is over. You handled yourself like a professional, Deakin."

"I was a professional," he said evenly.

"Soldier?"

"Yes."

"You sure know how to stay cool under pressure. I thought the damned crazy woman was going to shoot all of us." The young man closed his eyes, put his head back and sighed. "I'm glad it's all over," he repeated.

"It isn't quite all over, David," Lawrence contradicted him, reaching into the pocket of his evening coat. He took out an envelope. "I received this by special messenger from America. It is a private investigator's report."

David paled.

Juliet frowned and sat up slowly. "A private investigator's report? On what?"

Lawrence looked down at his wife. Maybe this wasn't the time or the place. But it needed to be done. He wasn't going to put it off again. "Not on *what*, Juliet. On *who*."

"Who, then?"

He turned to the younger man. "Do you want to tell her the truth, David. Or shall I?"

David did not move. Nor did he speak. He simply sat there and stared morosely into the distance.

Lawrence gently placed a hand on Juliet's shoulder. "I have some bad news for you, my dear. Perhaps you would like a brandy first?"

"I don't need to be coddled like a child. And I don't need a brandy. I can take whatever bad news you have to tell me," she said bravely.

He took a deep breath and stated: "David is not your cousin and his name is not David Thoreau Jones. His real name is David Whitman."

"I think I will have that brandy, after all," Juliet said, sinking back into her chair.

26

JULIET was shivering as she held the glass to her mouth and took a sip of the dark amber liquor. The brandy burned all the way down her throat and created a sensation of warmth in the pit of her stomach that she welcomed.

It was some time before she could turn her head and look at the young man who had seemed to be the mirror image of herself. "Who are you?" she finally asked.

He sulked. "You heard His Grace. My real name is David Whitman."

"But exactly *who* are you, David Whitman?"

He shrugged his slumped shoulders and replied: "I am who I am."

"And who or what is that?"

Lawrence stepped forward and answered for the recalcitrant young man. "I can tell you what he is not. He is not even a distant relation of yours, and he is not a gentleman."

David Whitman's laugh was not pleasant. Indeed, it was almost savage. "The duke is right. The duke is always right. I am not a relative and I am not a gentleman."

Lawrence apparently had more to add. "He is

a fraud. He is a cheat and a liar and a thief. And he may be, for all we know, a murderer, as well."

Juliet felt the color instantly drain from her face. She could scarcely bring herself to repeat the accusation. It was too horrible to contemplate. "A murderer?"

She saw Lawrence glance down at the private investigator's report that he still held in his hand. "There was a real David Thoreau Jones. He roomed at the orphanage with another boy named David Whitman."

"Are you *that* David Whitman?" she asked in a voice barely above a whisper.

"Yes, I am *that* David Whitman," he finally said, staring at the floor.

Juliet took a deep breath and steeled herself for the worst. "Did you—murder the real David Thoreau Jones?"

David looked up. Their blue eyes met. "No. I'm not a murderer."

"I don't know why, but I do believe you," she told him.

"Thank you for that much, at least," he mumbled.

Apparently Lawrence was not as inclined as she was to believe this David. "Do you know what happened to David Thoreau Jones?"

"Yes, I know what happened to him."

"Perhaps you would explain," said the duke. It was obvious to all three of them that he was not being given a choice. He would explain.

David Whitman blew out his breath. "I don't know who my parents are—or were—but I was shuffled from one orphanage to another all of my life. At the age of twelve I was sent to this new place in the country. It was pretty nice, actually. Anyway, I had only been there a day or two when I met another boy named David."

"David Thoreau Jones?"

"Yes." He laughed and shook his head. "It was kind of odd. Almost eerie, in fact. We were the same age. We were the same height. We were both slender in build. We both had the same shade of blond hair and blue eyes."

"In other words, you and David Thoreau Jones looked a great deal alike," verified Juliet.

He gave her a disarming smile. "Lady, we looked so much alike that people thought we were twins."

"Twins?"

"Twins." He went on. "We became roommates. Sometimes when we laid in our beds at night David would talk. He told me stories about this wonderful family he was supposed to have somewhere and how one day, when he was older, he would find them. I didn't pay too much attention at first. Orphans often make up stories about imaginary families."

Tears brimmed in Juliet's eyes. She did understand. She had always wanted a family of her own so badly.

"Anyway, the years came and went. We still did everything together, although David was smarter in school than I was. He helped me with my studies and I kept the bullies away from him." The young man looked at her. "David

Thoreau Jones was a gentle soul, but he was no survivor."

"Go on," she prompted.

"When we were sixteen, David was notified that he was going to receive a full scholarship to Harvard University. The two of us figured that he was the bastard son of some fancy gentleman, and it must have been his real father who had arranged things at college for him."

Out of the corner of her eye, Juliet saw Lawrence nod his head in agreement.

The expression on David Whitman's face darkened. "Not long after that, David got sick, real sick. There wasn't anybody to take care of him but me. I didn't know what to do. I tried my best." The young man's voice broke off. He could not continue for several minutes. "He died one night."

Juliet felt the tears well up at the edge of her eyelids. Poor David Thoreau Jones. Poor David Whitman. Her tears were for both of them.

"I didn't know what to do next. Then an idea occurred to me. David Thoreau Jones had a real future ahead of him. He was going to college and get a first-class education. David Whitman was headed out the door of the orphanage and down the road to nowhere."

"So you switched identities," Juliet said, still shaken.

He nodded eagerly. "That very night I traded clothes, beds, books, everything."

"So it was David Whitman who died according to the officials at the orphanage."

"And it was David Thoreau Jones who lived."

"You became David Thoreau Jones."

"I became David Thoreau Jones from that moment on. I didn't see any harm in it. The scholarship to Harvard wasn't going to do poor David any good. So I took his place."

"And you bided your time," interjected Lawrence.

"Not exactly. I went on to Harvard. I polished my social skills. I found a way to make it through the classes. I tried to make the right kind of friends and the right kind of connections. Then a few years ago I read in the newspapers about a young heiress who had shocked New York by taking over her father's business concerns. His name had been Stonewall Jackson Jones—King Midas—and she was Miss Juliet Jones. That was when I started to make my plans."

"You were very clever, David," she said. "The best lawyers, bankers, and accountants in the city found your credentials to be legitimate."

"They were legitimate. David Thoreau Jones *was* your long lost—if somewhat illegitimate—distant cousin."

"And you, sir, are nothing more than an opportunist," she declared hotly.

David sat back in the comfortable library chair and casually crossed his legs. "That isn't a crime, Duchess. People—both men and women—do it all the time." He gave Lawrence a pointed look. "Even those of the upper classes and the aristocracy."

Lawrence made an aggressive move toward

the younger man. Juliet put out a hand to stop him.

"I would like to know something," said the imposter. "What gave me away?"

Lawrence was the one who answered his question. "You did."

David furrowed his blond brows. "I did?"

There was no affection between the two men. There never had been. Lawrence apparently saw no reason not to be blunt. "It was the first time I saw you in Central Park with Juliet. I remember even then thinking to myself: 'I wonder what his game is.'"

David snickered. "You mean you were going on some kind of instinct about me?"

"That's exactly what I mean." Lawrence's expression bore no trace of apology. "A professional learns to trust his instincts."

"That's right. You were a soldier."

"Then there were the convenient—the too convenient, in my opinion—accidents that occurred in New York. You were the only one who could have been behind them."

"How do you figure that?"

"You were the only one who had anything to gain."

"But I explained to you that no one would gain by my death," Juliet reminded her husband. "I made all the necessary monetary and legal decisions to ensure that."

"And you were right. Except I don't believe the accidents were ever supposed to cause your death." Lawrence switched his attention from her to the young man lounging in the chair. "Were they, David?"

"Going on another one of your instincts, Deakin?"

"Process of elimination this time," he said with a feral grin. "I think you were out to impress the lady. I think you had plans of your own when it came to Juliet. Only your plans and schemes didn't quite work out the way you had hoped."

"You really are a bloody bastard," David swore at him, but he stayed put in his seat. He was too smart to go up against a man half a head taller than he was, thirty pounds heavier, and vastly more experienced in the art of fighting.

"It takes one to recognize one," said Lawrence Grenfell Wicke.

Juliet tugged on his sleeve. "You never told me what you suspected about those accidents in New York, Lawrence."

"I had no proof, my dear."

"You still don't," pointed out David.

"We don't need proof that you tried to cause the accidents. We already have proof that you are a cad and a bounder, sir," she declared.

David looked at her with eyes that were a reflection of her own. "I have my regrets, Juliet."

She bit down hard on the inside of her mouth to keep the tears at bay. She tried to be harsh with him. "It is easy to so say once you have been found out."

David Whitman appeared sincere. "Nevertheless, I will miss you."

She was not taken in by his charm now that she knew him for what he truly was. "You will miss me? Or you will miss all the things my money can buy you?"

"Both," he confessed in a rare moment of honesty.

The clock in the library struck the quarter hour. It was nearly midnight.

Juliet regally rose to her feet. "Lawrence, we must soon join our guests for the finale of the treasure hunt and the midnight buffet that is to follow."

"Yes, my dear."

She turned to David Whitman. "You will be packed and on the first boat bound for Australia. I will make arrangements for a quarterly allowance as long as you stay away from England, away from my husband, and away from my family. You will not claim to be my cousin or any relation to me. You must, nonetheless, conduct yourself like a gentleman at all times. The minute you step out of line, I will cut you off without a penny. Do you understand?"

"I do."

"She is more generous than I would be, Whitman," growled Lawrence.

"David, your arm. You are to escort me upstairs to the Grand Ballroom."

"I am?"

"What has transpired here in this room tonight is to remain between the three of us. No one else need ever know."

"She is one hell of a lot more generous than I would be," declared Lawrence.

Juliet glanced over her shoulder at her husband. "If I were you, my dear, I would gather up the Deakin Diamonds. I would not leave a king's ransom lying about the house."

27

THERE was no substitute for sex.

Lawrence reached this momentous conclusion as he sat in his favorite chair, his boots propped up on the matching footstool. He was presumably reading the *Times*. Instead, he found that his eyes and his attention kept wandering to his wife.

Juliet was sitting at the library table, fountain pen in hand, writing in a red leather book. Embossed in gold leaf on the spine was the year 1878.

In was midafternoon, between luncheon and tea, three days after the famous weekend treasure hunt. The last guests—indeed, his own brother and sister-in-law—had left only this morning. To his immense relief.

He wanted Juliet to himself.

Lawrence had discovered that he was a selfish creature when it came to his wife. The country house party preparations and the emotional strain of the past few weeks had left Juliet quite exhausted.

But tonight he would slip into her bed and do far more than gather his wife into his arms and hold her while she fell asleep. Tonight he would make love to her again and again to his heart's content.

It was odd, decided the Duke of Deakin, that the more a man had a woman the more he wanted her. His appetite for the lady had not slackened during the months since their marriage; it had increased. Hell, he would make love to Juliet every day of the week if he had his way.

"Once every fifty years is quite enough," Juliet announced out loud.

"Once every fifty years?" Lawrence repeated, hoping and praying that their minds for once were *not* on the same track.

Juliet glanced up at him. "I think once every fifty years is often enough to throw a gala weekend house party like the one we have just had."

"I couldn't agree more," he stated emphatically.

She shook her head, dislodging a wisp of silky blond hair. "I know this will not come as a surprise to you, Lawrence, since I mentioned it soon after we met. But Society, in general, is not my cup of tea."

"I believe, my dear Juliet, you said that you found going out in Society taxing."

She gave him a polite look. "You have a good memory, my dear husband."

"I believe you also said that there was more to life than eating, drinking, and making merry," he added.

"You have a very good memory, husband."

He went on as if she had not spoken. "That you had more on your mind than another tiresome social season of afternoon teas, dinner parties, and fancy dress balls, watching a chukker or two of polo from your carriage, the latest Paris fashions or empty-headed, broad-shouldered dancing partners."

"You have an excellent memory, sir."

His black eyes glittered. He grinned. It was a decidedly wicked and devilish grin. "And, of course, you pronounced that there was more to life than balls."

"You have too good a memory, and *that* was a double entendre," she pointed out, not altogether able to do so with disapproval. "You are naughty."

"I certainly hope so," he murmured under his breath, thinking of what he intended to show his lady wife once they had retired to their chambers for the night.

"Still, I feel it must be done for posterity," Juliet said with a sigh.

He was under the impression that was how one insured there was a posterity. They were obviously talking at cross-purposes again.

"What must be done for posterity, my dear?" he inquired, putting his newspaper down. Why pretend any longer that he had the slightest interest in the news when he had more important business on his mind?

"The recording of this weekend's events. The list of guests who attended, who stayed in which room, and who slept in which bed, what was served for luncheon and tea and dinner, the planned activities, the clues for the treasure hunt, the prizes, the table favors. . . ."

"I see."

"Perhaps one day, many years hence, another Duchess of Deakin will pick up this volume, read through its pages and marvel at the party we gave."

"Just as you did with my grandmother's."

"I somehow feel as if I know Alicia Anne, at least a little, after having read her social diaries. They are a fascinating glimpse into your family history, as well as a social commentary on the early decades of this century. I particularly found those relating to the Regency—"

Lawrence cleared his throat. "Quite."

She laughed. "I know you do not want to hear me prattle on about it any longer, but it was thanks to Alicia Anne, in part, that we recovered the Deakin Diamonds."

"That is true. I have you and my grandmother to thank. But especially you, my dear." He waited a moment and then added: "I am sorry about David, you know."

"You were right to undertake an investigation, Lawrence," she said with complete approval. "Ignorance is not bliss, as I have discovered the hard way."

He realized he had that certain smile on his face.

"Lawrence—"

"Sorry, my dear." He put his newspaper aside and rose to his feet. He sauntered over to the library table and perched on the edge nearest to where she was writing. He wasn't exactly sneaking up on his wife. Rather, it was a gradual maneuver to gain her attention. "Euphemia certainly took David's departure in her stride."

"Aunt Effie never quite hit it off with David." Juliet sighed. "Her instincts and yours were far more reliable than my own in this case. I care not so much that David wasn't a blood relative, but that he turned out to be a liar, a scoundrel, and a sneak. I do not care at all for sneaks."

Lawrence tugged on his collar. It seemed a bit tight around his neck today. Then he picked up the nondescript rock that was used as a paperweight and tossed it back and forth several times between his hands. He finally caught it in his fist.

Juliet watched him. "Did you know that a man's heart is the same size as his clenched fist?"

Lawrence stared down at his hand. "Truly? Wherever did you learn something like that?"

Juliet laughed and gazed about the huge library with its thousands upon thousands of books. "From a book."

"Aren't you finished with your scribbling yet?" he inquired impatiently.

She put her pen down and closed the red leather volume. "Yes, I am finished scribbling for now."

"I would like to speak to you, madam."

She gazed up at him with those incredible blue eyes of her. "You have my full attention, sir."

He had already lost his train of thought. "I have never been a glib man."

"I find you most glib," said Juliet.

"I think of myself as a man of actions, rather than words," he went on.

"I find you erudite, as well."

"What I am trying to say—"

"Yes—?" she prompted.

"I heard you mention something one afternoon when you were having tea with Nanny and Euphemia."

She screwed up her face and tapped her bottom lip with her fingertip. "I frequently take tea with Nanny and Aunt Effie. You are going to have to be more specific, sir."

He blew out his breath. If only she would just come out and say the words. It would give him the courage he needed.

Lawrence gave an airy gesture with his hand and made a small production of recalling exactly which afternoon it might have been. "I think it was some weeks ago."

"Some weeks ago."

"You were discussing a number of topics, as I recollect."

"A number of topics."

"I only came into the sitting room at the last."

"And—"

"Nanny was thanking you for everything you had done for so many people."

"Ah, now I remember. I said that there was no need for thanks because I loved Grantley."

His face brightened. "Yes, that was the conversation."

Juliet stood and turned her head. She gazed out the window at the vast expanse of green lawn that stretched out before the house, and the natural park and blue lake in the distance. "And I do love Grantley. I love everything about it: the house, the gardens, the people, its history, even all those somber faces hanging in the Long Gallery."

Lawrence slammed his fist down on the table in frustration, forgetting that he still had the damned rock in his hand. He swore loudly.

"I meant no offense to your ancestors by the remark, sir."

"I took no offense, madam. My hand slipped and I knocked it against this blasted old ugly rock."

Juliet reached out and plucked the stone from his grasp. "I do not think it is so ugly anymore. Perhaps I am getting used to it. Or perhaps"—she gave him a pointed look—"I am getting used to dealing with a diamond in the rough."

This wasn't working, Lawrence decided. He was going to have to take a more direct approach. "Madam, you may recall that one night I told you the story about the Black Heart."

"It was a bedtime story, if I correctly recall the occasion," she said coyly.

"It was." He had a sneaking suspicion that this was one of those merry dances his wife was so adept at leading him on when it suited her fancy.

"Once upon a time—" she began, fussing with the bodice of her dress. She looked up at him with wide, innocent eyes. "Well, wasn't that how it started?"

Lawrence reluctantly tore his gaze from her bosom. "Yes, that was how it started." It was his preoccupation, his utter and complete fascination—nay, his obsession—with her breasts that had started this whole affair back in New York. "Once upon a time there was a black-haired Duke of Deakin."

"There was a young, handsome, black-haired duke of the realm named Deakin," she expounded as she playfully rolled the ugly stone from one hand to the other. "He was a mighty warrior. He was without equal in battle. He had the strength of ten ordinary men."

"I do believe you know the story better than I do, Juliet."

"I love fairy tales," she confessed. "Indeed, sometimes I even believe in fairy tales."

"May I skip the part where the duke storms his enemy's castle and takes the fair maiden captive?"

She sniffed. "If you must."

He picked up in the middle of the tale. "The duke took the lady as his wife. But because he did not woo her before he wed and bed her, she would not grant him the gift of her love."

"Love is a gift that must be given willingly. We can't *make* someone love us. They either do or they don't."

He frowned. "Who said that?"

"You did."

"I did?"

She nodded her fair head. "To the unfortunate Countess of Deerhurst."

"Well, it is true." He scowled. "Now I have lost my place in the story."

"The duke showered his lady wife with many expensive gifts; gifts that included the priceless black diamonds which are now known as the Deakin Diamonds. The largest of these was called the Black Heart because it was the size of a man's"—Juliet stopped in midsentence and stared down at the ugly stone she was holding in her hand. "Lawrence—"

It was her tone of voice that captured his immediate and undivided attention. "Yes, Juliet."

"Where did this rock come from?"

He frowned and pointed toward the window. "From outside, I presume."

"When?"

"When? How should I know when?"

"Has it always been here?"

"Here? Where? Do you mean on this table?" He shrugged his shoulders. "It has been here or there or wherever for as long as I can remember. But what does it signify? I am in the midst of a most important conversation."

"I apologize. Please go on."

Yet Lawrence noticed that she continued to stare at the ridiculously ugly rock. "As I was saying, madam . . ."

Her head came up. "Yes, sir."

"The duke had a hard lesson to learn." He spotted the brief, yet telling smile on her face. "Not *that* kind of hard lesson." He was getting frustrated. "You make it most difficult to tell a simple story."

"I do not know why you are repeating a story that we have both heard, anyway."

"I am repeating the story to you, madam, because I am trying to find a way to tell you I have a gift for you."

Her face lit up. "You do. What is it? Where is it?" She began to look about under the table, behind a chair, beneath a stack of papers.

Lawrence reached for her hands and clasped them in his. "The gift I have for you, Juliet, is right here."

With that, he placed her palms over his heart. The strong, rhythmic beat of his life force was unmistakable even through his shirt.

He watched her face. He saw the moment it dawned on her. He saw the first tear as it appeared on her eyelash, as it lingered there for an instant and then rolled down her cheek and onto her breast.

Her voice was full. "Lawrence—?"

"Just as that long ago Duke of Deakin, I am giving my heart to you, my lady wife. I will do whatever is necessary to win your love. When I stood in this very room and Helena's pistol was pointed at your heart, I realized I do not want to live without you. Indeed, I cannot live without you. I will do whatever you want, whatever you ask, if only one day you will say the words to me."

"The words?"

"You said them to Nanny and Aunt Effie, and

that is not the same. I want to hear them. I need to hear them."

"What words?"

"I love you."

"I love you."

His eyes widened. His voice was low and husky. "Would you please repeat that, madam?"

Juliet went up on her tiptoes, intertwined her fingers around his neck and put her lips to his mouth. "I love you, Lawrence. I love only you. I will always love you," she vowed.

He was stunned. Then he put his head back and crowed. "And I love you, Juliet. I love you. I love you. I love you." He could not stop saying it once he started.

"I accept, by the way."

"Accept what, madam?"

"The gift of your heart. And you must have mine in return."

"I will take very good care of it," he promised. "I will treat it as my most precious possession."

"As will I."

Lawrence bent over and kissed her. Juliet kissed him back. He kissed her again, longer, deeper, more passionately. She eagerly opened her mouth beneath his and touched her tongue to his.

His hands skimmed her body and captured the swell of her breasts. He could feel her nipples tightening, hardening with each caress, with each flick of his fingertips.

They paused to catch their breath and his

wife boldly reached down and caressed him through the front of his trousers. He was as hard as a rock.

"Sir," she commented, her eyes sparkling, "I have always said that you are a very hard man to love."

He laughed. "Madam, you know what they say."

"What?"

"The best gifts come in *large* packages." He placed his hand over hers. "Surely, it is time to unwrap a lovely gift or two."

"Here?"

"Here."

"Now?"

"Now."

"But it is the middle of the afternoon."

"Then it is not too early and not too late," he reasoned.

Her head flew around. "The windows? Someone may see us."

"We will pull the drapes."

She was joining in the spirit of the occasion as Lawrence had known she would. "The door, Your Grace. Someone may walk in on us."

"The door has a lock, Your Grace. I will insert the key and turn it."

"You are a very clever man," she murmured as he reluctantly left her to pull the drapes and deal with the door.

"Let me see," he murmured playfully as he sauntered across the library toward his awaiting wife. "Where was I?"

"Have you forgotten?"

"Perhaps you could refresh my memory for me."

"You are always misplacing things, Lawrence."

"I am," he muttered, his attention going to the hooks on the front of her dress and then to the lovely swell of her breasts and her luscious pink nipples as he set her free. He leaned over and took her between his lips and drew her into his mouth.

"Ah, I see you remembered, after all," she remarked, somewhat breathlessly. "I can only hope you have not misplaced any other family jewels."

Their eyes fell simultaneously on the ugly stone on the library table as books and papers were shoved aside to make room for more important pursuits.

"You don't think—?" Juliet said, gazing at the large stone the size of a man's heart.

"Whatever it is, it can wait. It is just one more rock," he muttered, his mind on other matters. "All I want to think about is you, my love. All that I treasure is right here in my arms."

He lifted her up, pushed aside her skirts and began the task of dealing with her silk stockings.

Juliet ran her hands along his muscled shoulders. "My, what big shoulders, you have, sir."

"Thank you, madam." Her petticoat went flying across the back of a chair.

She traced a line down his bare arms. "What

big arms, you have, sir." Her lacy French drawers followed.

She gazed down at him as he broke free of
the constraints of his trousers. "My, what a big
'gift,' you have, sir."

"And," Lawrence said laughing happily, "it is
all for you, madam wife."

Epilogue

THE Black Heart weighed over 380 carats unfaceted. It was never cut or polished, but remained a diamond in the rough.

To mark the happy and joyous occasion of their first son's birth, the Black Heart was donated to the British Museum by the eighth Duke and Duchess of Deakin.

It remains there to this day.

Author's Notes

THE floor plan described during Mrs. Astor's annual ball was actually that of the Vanderbilt mansion of 1 West 57th Street, completed in 1882 and demolished, unfortunately, in 1927.

Eleanor of Toledo and Her Son by Agnolo Bronzino hangs in the Uffizi Gallery, Florence.

One of the largest black diamonds ever cut is believed to be the Black Rembrandt, a 42.27 carat stone that took three years to polish. It is valued at more than one half million dollars.

Lily

A LOVE STORY
by Cindy Bonner

Lily DeLony is the spirited but proper daughter of a hardworking, God-fearing father. She has no reason to doubt the rules of virtue and righteousness she has been brought up with—that is until she meets Marion "Shot" Beatty, the youngest of the infamous Beatty brothers who were the terror of McDade, Texas, in 1883. What happens when Lily and Marion defy all odds to come together makes for the most captivating and suspenseful novel of love that you will ever read—and for one of the most endearing heroines that you will never forget.

"The reader will cheer for Lily to the final page. A believable, engrossing tale of love and violence."
—*Abilene Reporter News*

"Absolutely spellbinding—a classic tale of true love against all odds—as supple and strong as a well-worked piece of leather." —*Booklist*

from ONYX